AMERICA's GREATEST SATIRIST
KURT VONNEGUT IS . . .

"UNIQUE . . . one of the writers who map our landscapes for us, who give names to the places we know best."
　　—DORIS LESSING,
　　　The New York Times Book Review

"OUR FINEST BLACK-HUMORIST.
. . . We laugh in self-defense."
　　—*The Atlantic Monthly*

"AN UNIMITATIVE AND INIMITABLE SOCIAL SATIRIST."
　　—*Harper's Magazine*

"A MEDICINE MAN, CONJURING UP FANTASIES TO WARN THE WORLD."
　　—*The Charlotte Observer*

"VONNEGUT IS GEORGE ORWELL, DR. CALIGARI, AND FLASH GORDON COMPOUNDED IN ONE WRITER . . . A ZANY BUT MORAL MAD SCIENTIST."
　　—*Time*

"A CAUSE FOR CELEBRATION."
　　—*Chicago Sun-Times*

"A LAUGHING PROPHET OF DOOM."
　　—*The New York Times*

BY KURT VONNEGUT

GALÁPAGOS

KURT VONNEGUT

DIAL PRESS TRADE PAPERBACKS

2009 Dial Press Trade Paperback Edition

Copyright © 1985 by Kurt Vonnegut
Cover illustration by Kurt Vonnegut. Copyright © 2002
Kurt Vonnegut/Origami Express, LLC. www.vonnegut.com

Published in the United States by Dial Press Trade Paperbacks,
an imprint of The Random House Publishing Group, a division of
Random House, Inc., New York.

DIAL PRESS and DIAL PRESS TRADE PAPERBACKS are registered trademarks of
Random House, Inc., and the colophon is a trademark of Random House, Inc.

Originally published in hardcover in the United States by Delacorte Press/Seymour
Lawrence, an imprint of The Random House Publishing Group, a division of
Random House, Inc., in 1985.

ISBN 978-0-385-33387-0

Printed in the United States of America

www.dialpress.com

29 28 27 26 25 24 23 22 21

Book design by Nancy Field

The Kurt Vonnegut, Jr. Trust came into existence after
the death of Kurt Vonnegut, Jr., and is committed to
the continued protection of his works.

In memory of Hillis L. Howie,
(1903–1982) amateur naturalist—
A good man who
took me and my best friend Ben Hitz
and some other boys
out to the American Wild West
from Indianapolis, Indiana,
in the summer of 1938.

Mr. Howie introduced us to real Indians
and had us sleep out of doors every night
and bury our dung,
and he taught us how to ride horses,
and he told us the names of many plants
    and animals,
and what they needed to do
in order to stay alive
and reproduce themselves.

One night Mr. Howie scared us half to death
on purpose,
screaming like a wildcat near our camp.
A real wildcat screamed back.

In spite of everything, I still believe people are really good at heart.

—ANNE FRANK (1929–1944)

BOOK ONE

THE THING WAS

1

THE THING WAS:

One million years ago, back in 1986 A.D., Guayaquil was the chief seaport of the little South American democracy of Ecuador, whose capital was Quito, high in the Andes Mountains. Guayaquil was two degrees south of the equator, the imaginary bellyband of the planet after which the country itself was named. It was always very hot there, and humid, too, for the city was built in the doldrums—on a springy marsh through which the mingled waters of several rivers draining the mountains flowed.

This seaport was several kilometers from the open sea. Rafts of vegetable matter often clogged the soupy waters, engulfing pilings and anchor lines.

• • •

Human beings had much bigger brains back then than they do today, and so they could be beguiled by mysteries. One such mystery in 1986 was how so many creatures which could not swim great distances had reached the Galápagos Islands, an archipelago of volcanic peaks due west of Guayaquil—separated from the mainland by one thousand kilometers of very deep water, very cold water fresh from the Antarctic. When human beings discovered those islands, there were already geckos and iguanas and rice rats and lava lizards and spiders and ants and beetles and grasshoppers and mites and ticks in residence, not to mention enormous land tortoises.

What form of transportation had they used?

Many people were able to satisfy their big brains with this answer: They came on natural rafts.

• • •

Other people argued that such rafts became waterlogged and rotted to pieces so quickly that nobody had ever seen one out of sight of land, and that the current between the islands and the mainland would carry any such rustic vessel northward rather than westward.

Or they asserted that all those landlubberly creatures had walked dry-shod across a natural bridge or had swum short distances between stepping-stones, and that one such formation or another had since disappeared beneath the waves. But scientists using their big brains and cunning instruments had by 1986 made maps of the ocean floor. There wasn't a trace, they said, of an intervening land mass of any kind.

• • •

Other people back in that era of big brains and fancy thinking asserted that the islands had once been part of the mainland, and had been split off by some stupendous catastrophe.

But the islands didn't look as though they had been split off from anything. They were clearly young volcanoes, which had been vomited up right where they were. Many of them were such newborns out there that they could be expected to blow again at any time. Back in 1986, they hadn't even sprouted much coral yet, and so were without blue lagoons and white beaches, amenities many human beings used to regard as foretastes of an ideal afterlife.

A million years later, they do possess white beaches and blue lagoons. But when this story begins, they were still ugly humps and domes and cones and spires of lava, brittle and abrasive, whose cracks and pits and bowls and valleys brimmed over not with rich topsoil or sweet water, but with the finest, driest volcanic ash.

• • •

Another theory back then was that God Almighty had created all those creatures where the explorers found them, so they had had no need for transportation.

• • •

Another theory was that they had been shooed ashore there two by two—down the gangplank of Noah's ark.

If there really was a Noah's ark, and there may have been—I might entitle my story "A Second Noah's Ark."

2

THERE WAS NO MYSTERY a million years ago as to
how a thirty-five-year-old American male named James
Wait, who could not swim a stroke, intended to get from
the South American continent to the Galápagos Islands.
He certainly wasn't going to squat on a natural raft of
vegetable matter and hope for the best. He had just
bought a ticket at his hotel in downtown Guayaquil for a
two-week cruise on what was to be the maiden voyage of
a new passenger ship called the *Bahía de Darwin,* Spanish
for "Darwin Bay." This first Galápagos trip for the ship,
which flew the Ecuadorian flag, had been publicized and
advertised all over the world during the past year as "the
Nature Cruise of the Century."

Wait was traveling alone. He was prematurely bald
and he was pudgy, and his color was bad, like the crust on
a pie in a cheap cafeteria, and he was bespectacled, so that
he might plausibly claim to be in his fifties, in case he saw
some advantage in making such a claim. He wished to
seem harmless and shy.

He was the only customer now in the cocktail

lounge of the Hotel El Dorado, on the broad Calle Diez de Agosto, where he had taken a room. And the bartender, a twenty-year-old descendant of proud Inca noblemen, named Jesús Ortiz, got the feeling that this drab and friendless man, who claimed to be a Canadian, had had his spirit broken by some terrible injustice or tragedy. Wait wanted everybody who saw him to feel that way.

Jesús Ortiz, who is one of the nicest people in this story of mine, pitied rather than scorned this lonesome tourist. He found it sad, as Wait had hoped he would, that Wait had just spent a lot of money in the hotel boutique—on a straw hat and rope sandals and yellow shorts and a blue-and-white-and-purple cotton shirt, which he was wearing now. Wait had had considerable dignity, Ortiz thought, when he had arrived from the airport in a business suit. But now, at great expense, he had turned himself into a clown, a caricature of a North American tourist in the tropics.

The price tag was still stapled to the hem of Wait's crackling new shirt, and Ortiz, very politely and in good English, told him so.

"Oh?" said Wait. He knew the tag was there, and he wanted it to remain there. But he went through a charade of self-mocking embarrassment, and seemed about to pluck off the tag. But then, as though overwhelmed by some sorrow he was trying to flee from, he appeared to forget all about it.

• • •

Wait was a fisherman, and the price tag was his bait, a way of encouraging strangers to speak to him, to say in one way or another what Ortiz had said: "Excuse me, Señor, but I can't help noticing—"

Wait was registered at the hotel under the name on his bogus Canadian passport, which was Willard Flemming. He was a supremely successful swindler.

Ortiz himself was in no danger from him, but an unescorted woman who looked as though she had a little money, and who was without a husband and past childbearing, surely would have been. Wait had so far courted and married seventeen such persons—and then cleaned out their jewelry boxes and safe-deposit boxes and bank accounts, and disappeared.

He was so successful at what he did that he had become a millionaire, with interest-bearing savings accounts under various aliases in banks all over North America, and he had never been arrested for anything. For all he knew, nobody was even trying to catch him. As far as the police were concerned, he reasoned, he was one of seventeen faithless husbands, each with a different name, instead of a single habitual criminal whose real name was James Wait.

• • •

It is hard to believe nowadays that people could ever have been as brilliantly duplicitous as James Wait—until I remind myself that just about every adult human being back then had a brain weighing about three kilograms!

There was no end to the evil schemes that a thought machine that oversized couldn't imagine and execute.

So I raise this question, although there is nobody around to answer it: Can it be doubted that three-kilogram brains were once nearly fatal defects in the evolution of the human race?

A second query: What source was there back then, save for our overelaborate nervous circuitry, for the evils we were seeing or hearing about simply everywhere?

My answer: There was no other source. This was a very innocent planet, except for those great big brains.

3

THE HOTEL EL DORADO was a brand-new, five-story tourist accommodation—built of unadorned cement block. It had the proportions and mood of a glass-front bookcase, high and wide and shallow. Each bedroom had a floor-to-ceiling wall of glass looking westward—toward the waterfront for deep-draft vessels dredged in the delta three kilometers away.

In the past, that waterfront had teemed with commerce, and ships from all over the planet had delivered meat and grain and vegetables and fruit and vehicles and clothing and machinery and household appliances, and so on, and carried away, in fair exchange, Ecuadorian coffee and cocoa and sugar and petroleum and gold, and Indian arts and crafts, including "Panama" hats, which had always come from Ecuador and not from Panama.

But there were only two ships out there now, as James Wait sat in the bar, nursing a rum and Coca-Cola. He was not a drinker, actually, since he lived by his wits, and could not afford to have the delicate switches of the big computer in his skull short-circuited by alcohol. His drink was a theatrical prop—like the price tag on his ridiculous shirt.

He was in no position to judge whether the state of affairs at the waterfront was normal or not. Until two days before, he had never even heard of Guayaquil, and this was the first time in his life he had ever been below the equator. As far as he was concerned, the El Dorado was no different from all the other characterless hostelries he had used as hideouts in the past—in Moose Jaw, Saskatchewan, in San Ignacio, Mexico, in Watervliet, New York, and on and on.

He had picked the name of the city where he was now from an arrivals-and-departures board at Kennedy International Airport in New York City. He had just pauperized and deserted his seventeenth wife—a seventy-year-old widow in Skokie, Illinois, right outside Chicago. Guayaquil sounded to him like the last place she would ever think of looking for him.

This woman was so ugly and stupid, she probably never should have been born. And yet Wait was the second person to have married her.

And he wasn't going to stay at the El Dorado very long, either, since he had bought a ticket for "the Nature Cruise of the Century" from the travel agent who had a desk in the lobby. It was late in the afternoon now, and hotter than the hinges of hell outside. There was no breeze outside, but he did not care, since he was inside, and the hotel was air conditioned, and he would soon be away from there anyway. His ship, the *Bahía de Darwin,* was scheduled to sail at high noon on the very next day, which was Friday, November 28, 1986—a million years ago.

•   •   •

The bay for which Wait's means of transportation was named fanned south from the Galápagos Island of Genovesa. Wait had never heard of the Galápagos Islands before. He expected them to be like Hawaii, where he had once honeymooned, or Guam, where he had once hidden out—with broad white beaches and blue lagoons and swaying palms and nut-brown native girls.

The travel agent had given him a brochure which described the cruise, but Wait hadn't looked inside it yet. It was supine on the bar in front of him. The brochure was truthful about how forbidding most of the islands were, and warned prospective passengers, as the hotel travel agent had not warned Wait, that they had better be in reasonably good physical condition and have sturdy boots and rough clothing, since they would often have to wade ashore and scramble up rock faces like amphibious infantry.

•   •   •

Darwin Bay was named in honor of the great English scientist Charles Darwin, who had visited Genovesa and several of its neighbors for five weeks back in 1835— when he was a mere stripling of twenty-six, nine years younger than Wait. Darwin was then the unpaid naturalist aboard Her Majesty's Ship *Beagle,* on a mapping expedition that would take him completely around the world and would last five years.

In the cruise brochure, which was intended to delight nature-lovers rather than pleasure-seekers, Darwin's own description of a typical Galápagos Island was reproduced, and was taken from his first book, *The Voyage of the Beagle:*

"Nothing could be less inviting than the first appearance. A broken field of black basaltic lava, thrown into the most rugged waves, and crossed by great fissures, is everywhere covered by stunted, sun-burnt brushwood, which shows little signs of life. The dry and parched surface, being heated by the noon-day sun, gave to the air a close and sultry feeling, like that from a stove: we fancied even that the bushes smelt unpleasantly."

Darwin continued: "The entire surface . . . seems to have been permeated, like a sieve, by the subterranean vapours: here and there the lava, whilst soft, had been blown into great bubbles; and in other parts, the tops of caverns similarly formed have fallen in, leaving circular parts with steep sides." He was vividly reminded, he wrote, ". . . . of those parts of Staffordshire, where the great iron foundries are most numerous."

• • •

There was a portrait of Darwin behind the bar at the El Dorado, framed in shelves and bottles—an enlarged reproduction of a steel engraving, depicting him not as a youth in the islands, but as a portly family man back home in England, with a beard as lush as a Christmas wreath. That same portrait was on the bosom of T-shirts for sale in the boutique, and Wait had bought two of those. That was what Darwin looked like when he was finally persuaded by friends and relatives to set down on paper his notions of how life forms everywhere, including himself and his friends and relatives, and even his Queen, had come to be as they were in the nineteenth century. He thereupon penned the most broadly influential scientific volume produced during the entire era of great big brains. It did more to stabilize people's volatile opinions of how to identify success or failure than any other tome. Imagine that! And the name of his book summed up its pitiless contents: *On the Origin of Species by Means of Natural Selection, or the Preservation of Favoured Races in the Struggle for Life.*

• • •

Wait had never read that book, nor did the name Darwin mean anything to him, although he had successfully passed himself off as an educated man from time to time. He was considering claiming, during "the Nature Cruise of the Century," to be a mechanical engineer from Moose Jaw, Saskatchewan, whose wife had recently died of cancer.

Actually, his formal education had stopped after two years of instruction in automobile repair and maintenance at the vocational high school in his native city of Midland City, Ohio. He was then living in the fifth of a series of foster homes, essentially an orphan, since he was the product of an incestuous relationship between a father and a daughter who had run away from town, forever and together, soon after he was born.

When he himself was old enough to run away, he hitchhiked to the island of Manhattan. A pimp there befriended him and taught him how to be a successful homosexual prostitute, to leave price tags on his clothes, to really enjoy lovers whenever possible, and so on. Wait was once quite beautiful.

When his beauty began to fade, he became an instructor in ballroom dancing at a dance studio. He was a natural dancer, and he had been told back in Midland City that his parents had been very good dancers, too. His sense of rhythm was probably inherited. And it was at the dance studio that he met and courted and married the first of his seventeen wives so far.

• • •

All through his childhood, Wait was severely punished by foster parents for nothing and everything. It was expected by them that, because of his inbred parentage, he would become a moral monster.

So here that monster was now—in the Hotel El Dorado, happy and rich and well, as far as he knew, and keen for the next test of his survival skills.

• • •

Like James Wait, incidentally, I, too, was once a teenage runaway.

4

THE ANGLO-SAXON CHARLES DARWIN, underspoken and gentlemanly, impersonal and asexual and blankly observant in his writings, was a hero in teeming, passionate, polyglot Guayaquil because he was the inspiration for a tourist boom. If it weren't for Darwin, there would not have been a Hotel El Dorado or a *Bahía de Darwin* to accommodate James Wait. There would have been no boutique to clothe him so comically.

If Charles Darwin had not declared the Galápagos Islands marvelously instructive, Guayaquil would have been just one more hot and filthy seaport, and the islands would have been worth no more to Ecuador than the slag heaps of Staffordshire.

Darwin did not change the islands, but only people's opinion of them. That was how important mere opinions used to be back in the era of great big brains.

Mere opinions, in fact, were as likely to govern people's actions as hard evidence, and were subject to sudden reversals as hard evidence could never be. So the Galápagos Islands could be hell in one moment and heaven in the next, and Julius Caesar could be a statesman in one moment and a butcher in the next, and Ecuadorian paper money could be traded for food, shelter, and clothing in one moment and line the bottom of a birdcage in the next, and the universe could be created by God Almighty in one moment and by a big explosion in the next—and on and on.

Thanks to their decreased brainpower, people aren't diverted from the main business of life by the hobgoblins of opinions anymore.

• • •

White people discovered the Galápagos Islands in 1535 when a Spanish ship came upon them after being blown off course by a storm. Nobody was living there, nor were remains of any human settlement ever found there.

This unlucky ship wished nothing more than to carry the Bishop of Panama to Peru, never losing sight of the South American coast. There was this storm, which rudely hustled it westward, ever westward, where prevailing human opinion insisted there was only sea and more sea.

But when the storm lifted, the Spaniards found that they had delivered their bishop into a sailor's nightmare where the bits of land were mockeries, without safe anchorage or shade or sweet water or dangling fruit, or human beings of any kind. They were becalmed, and running out of water and food. The ocean was like a mirror. They put a longboat over the side, and towed their vessel and their spiritual leader out of there.

They did not claim the islands for Spain, any more than they would have claimed hell for Spain. And for three full centuries after revised human opinion allowed the archipelago to appear on maps, no other nation wished to own it. But then in 1832, one of the smallest and poorest countries on the planet, which was Ecuador, asked the peoples of the world to share this opinion with them: that the islands were part of Ecuador.

No one objected. At the time, it seemed a harmless and even comical opinion. It was as though Ecuador, in a spasm of imperialistic dementia, had annexed to its territory a passing cloud of asteroids.

But then young Charles Darwin, only three years later, began to persuade others that the often freakish plants and animals which had found ways to survive on the islands made them extremely valuable, if only people would look at them as he did—from a scientific point of view.

Only one English word adequately describes his transformation of the islands from worthless to priceless: *magical*.

• • •

Yes, and by the time of James Wait's arrival in Guayaquil so many persons with an interest in natural history had come there, on their way to the islands to see what

Darwin had seen, to feel what Darwin had felt, that three cruise ships had their home port there, the newest of which was the *Bahía de Darwin*. There were several modern tourist hotels, the newest of which was the El Dorado, and there were souvenir shops and boutiques and restaurants for tourists all up and down the Calle Diez de Agosto.

The thing was, though: When James Wait got there, a worldwide financial crisis, a sudden revision of human opinions as to the value of money and stocks and bonds and mortgages and so on, bits of paper, had ruined the tourist business not only in Ecuador but practically everywhere. So that the El Dorado was the only hotel still open in Guayaquil, and the *Bahía de Darwin* was the only cruise ship still prepared to sail.

The El Dorado was staying open only as an assembly point for persons with tickets for "the Nature Cruise of the Century," since it was owned by the same Ecuadorian company which owned the ship. But now, less than twenty-four hours before the cruise was to begin, there were only six guests, including James Wait, in the two-hundred-bed hotel. And the other five guests were:

*Zenji Hiroguchi, twenty-nine, a Japanese computer genius;

Hisako Hiroguchi, twenty-six, his very pregnant wife, who was a teacher of ikebana, the Japanese art of flower arranging;

*Andrew MacIntosh, fifty-five, an American financier and adventurer of great inherited wealth, a widower;

Selena MacIntosh, eighteen, his congenitally blind daughter;

And Mary Hepburn, fifty-one, an American widow from Ilium, New York, whom practically nobody in the hotel had seen because she had stayed in her room on the fifth floor, and had taken all her meals up there, since arriving all alone the night before.

The two with stars by their names would be dead before the sun went down. This convention of starring certain names will continue throughout my story, incidentally, alerting readers to the fact that some characters will shortly face the ultimate Darwinian test of strength and wiliness.

• • •

I was there, too, but perfectly invisible.

5

THE *BAHÍA DE DARWIN* was also doomed, but not yet ready for a star by her name. It would be five more sundowns before her engines quit forever, and ten more years before she sank to the ocean floor. She was not only the newest and largest and fastest and most luxurious cruise ship based in Guayaquil. She was the only one designed specifically for the Galápagos tourist trade, whose destiny, from the moment her keel was laid, was understood to be a steady churning out to the islands and back again, out to the islands and back again.

She was built in Malmö, Sweden, where I myself worked on her. It was said by the skeleton crew of Swedes and Ecuadorians who delivered her from Malmö to Guayaquil that a storm she passed through in the North Atlantic would be the last rough water or cold weather she would ever know.

She was a floating restaurant and lecture hall and nightclub and hotel for one hundred paying guests. She had radar and sonar, and an electronic navigator which gave continuously her position on the face of the earth, to the nearest hundred meters. She was so thoroughly automated that a person all alone on the bridge, with no one in the engine room or on deck, could start her up, hoist her anchor, put her in gear, and drive her off like a family automobile. She had eighty-five flush toilets and twelve bidets, and telephones in the staterooms and on the bridge which, via satellite, could reach other telephones anywhere.

She had television, so people could keep up with the news of the day.

Her owners, a pair of old German brothers in Quito, boasted that their ship would never be out of touch with the rest of the world for an instant. Little did they know.

• • •

She was seventy meters long.

The ship on which Charles Darwin was the unpaid naturalist, the *Beagle,* was only twenty-eight meters long.

When the *Bahía de Darwin* was launched in Malmö, eleven hundred metric tons of saltwater had to find someplace else to go. I was dead by then.

When the *Beagle* was launched in Falmouth, England, only two hundred and fifteen metric tons of saltwater had to find someplace else to go.

The *Bahía de Darwin* was a metal motor ship.

The *Beagle* was a sailboat made out of trees, and carried ten cannons for repelling pirates and savages.

• • •

The two older cruise ships with which the *Bahía de Darwin* was meant to compete had gone out of business before the struggle could begin. Both had been booked to capacity for many months to come, but then, because of the financial crisis, they had been swamped with cancellations. They were anchored in backwaters of the marshland now, out of sight of the city, and far from any road or habitation. Their owners had stripped them of their electronic gear and other valuables—in anticipation of a prolonged period of lawlessness.

Ecuador, after all, like the Galápagos Islands, was mostly lava and ash, and so could not begin to feed its nine million people. It was bankrupt, and so could no longer buy food from countries with plenty of topsoil, so the seaport of Guayaquil was idle, and the people were beginning to starve to death.

Business was business.

• • •

Neighboring Peru and Colombia were bankrupt, too. The only ship at the Guayaquil waterfront other than the *Bahía de Darwin* was a rusty Colombian freighter, the *San Mateo,* stranded there for want of the means to buy food or fuel. She was anchored offshore, and had been there so long that an enormous raft of vegetable matter had built up around her anchor line. A baby elephant might have reached the Galápagos Islands on a raft that size.

Mexico and Chile and Brazil and Argentina were likewise bankrupt—and Indonesia and the Philippines and Pakistan and India and Thailand and Italy and Ireland and Belgium and Turkey. Whole nations were suddenly in the same situation as the *San Mateo,* unable to buy with their paper money and coins, or their written promises to pay later, even the barest essentials. Persons with anything life sustaining to sell, fellow citizens as well as foreigners, were refusing to exchange their goods for money. They were suddenly saying to people with nothing but paper representations of wealth, "Wake up, you idiots! Whatever made you think paper was so valuable?"

• • •

There was still plenty of food and fuel and so on for all the human beings on the planet, as numerous as they had become, but millions upon millions of them were starting to starve to death now. The healthiest of them could go without food for only about forty days, and then death would come.

And this famine was as purely a product of oversize brains as Beethoven's Ninth Symphony.

It was all in people's heads. People had simply changed their opinions of paper wealth, but, for all practical purposes, the planet might as well have been knocked out of orbit by a meteor the size of Luxembourg.

6

THIS FINANCIAL CRISIS, which could never happen today, was simply the latest in a series of murderous twentieth century catastrophes which had originated entirely in human brains. From the violence people were doing to themselves and each other, and to all other living things, for that matter, a visitor from another planet might have assumed that the environment had gone haywire, and that the people were in such a frenzy because Nature was about to kill them all.

But the planet a million years ago was as moist and nourishing as it is today—and unique, in that respect, in the entire Milky Way. All that had changed was people's opinion of the place.

To the credit of humanity as it used to be: More and more people were saying that their brains were irresponsible, unreliable, hideously dangerous, wholly unrealistic— were simply no damn good.

In the microcosm of the Hotel El Dorado, for example, the widow Mary Hepburn, who had been taking all her meals in her room, was cursing her own brain sotto voce for the advice it was giving her, which was to commit suicide.

"You are my enemy," she whispered. "Why would I want to carry such a terrible enemy inside of me?" She had been a biology teacher in the public high school in Ilium, New York, now defunct, for a quarter of a century, and so was familiar with the very odd tale of the evolution of a then-extinct creature named by human beings the "Irish elk." "Given a choice between a brain like you and the antlers of an Irish elk," she told her own central nervous system, "I'd take the antlers of the Irish elk."

These animals used to have antlers the size of ballroom chandeliers. They were fascinating examples, she used to tell her students, of how tolerant nature could be of clearly ridiculous mistakes in evolution. Irish elk survived for two and a half million years, in spite of the fact that their antlers were too unwieldy for fighting or self-defense, and kept them from seeking food in thick forests and heavy brush.

・　・　・

Mary had also taught that the human brain was the most admirable survival device yet produced by evolution. But now her own big brain was urging her to take the polyethylene garment bag from around a red evening dress in her closet there in Guayaquil, and to wrap it around her head, thus depriving her cells of oxygen.

・　・　・

26

Before that, her wonderful brain had entrusted a thief at the airport with a suitcase containing all her toilet articles and clothes which would have been suitable for the hotel. That had been her carry-on luggage on a flight from Quito to Guayaquil. At least she still had the contents of the suitcase she had checked through rather than carried, which included the evening dress in the closet, which was for parties on the *Bahía de Darwin*. She was also still in possession of a wet suit and flippers and mask for diving, two bathing suits, a pair of rugged hiking boots, and a set of war surplus United States Marine Corps combat fatigues for trips ashore, which she was wearing now. As for the pants suit she had worn on the flight from Quito: Her big brain had persuaded her to send it to the hotel laundry, to believe the sad-eyed hotel manager when he said she could surely have it back by morning, in time for breakfast. But, much to the embarrassment of the manager, that, too, had disappeared.

But the worst thing her brain had done to her, other than recommending suicide, was to insist that she come to Guayaquil despite all the news about the planetary financial crisis, despite the near certainty that "the Nature Cruise of the Century," booked to capacity only a month before, would be called off for want of passengers.

Her colossal thinking machine could be so petty, too. It would not let her go downstairs in her combat fatigues on the grounds that everybody, even though there was practically nobody in the hotel, would find her comical in such a costume. Her brain told her: "They'll laugh at you behind your back, and think you're crazy and pitiful, and your life is over anyway. You've lost your husband and your teaching job, and you don't have any children or anything else to live for, so just put yourself out of your misery with the garment bag. What could be easier? What could be more painless? What could make more sense?

• • •

To give her brain its due: It wasn't entirely its fault that 1986 really had been a perfectly awful year so far. The year had started out so promisingly, too, with Mary's husband, Roy, in seemingly perfect health and secure in his job as a millwright at GEFFCo, the principal industry in Ilium, and with the Kiwanis giving her a banquet and a plaque celebrating her twenty-five years of distinguished teaching, and the students naming her the most popular teacher for the twelfth year in a row.

At the start of 1986, she said, "Oh, Roy—we have so much to be thankful for: we're so lucky compared to most people. I could cry for happiness."

And he said, putting his arms around her, "Well now, you just go ahead and cry." She was fifty-one and he was fifty-nine, and they were great lovers of the out-of-doors, hiking and skiing and mountain-climbing and canoeing and running and bicycling and swimming, so they both had lean and youthful bodies. They did not smoke or drink, and they ate mostly fresh fruits and vegetables, with a little fish from time to time.

They had also handled their money well, giving their savings, in financial terms, the same sort of sensible nourishment and exercise that they gave themselves.

The tale of fiscal wisdom which Mary could tell about herself and Roy, of course, would be a thrill to James Wait.

• • •

And, yes, Wait, that eviscerator of widows, was speculating about Mary Hepburn as he sat in the bar of the El Dorado, although he had not met her yet, nor learned for certain how well fixed she was. He had seen her name on the hotel register, and had asked the young manager about her.

Wait liked what little the manager was able to tell him. This shy and lonesome schoolteacher upstairs, although younger than any of the wives he had ruined so far, sounded to him like his natural prey. He would stalk her at leisure during "the Nature Cruise of the Century."

• • •

If I may insert a personal note at this point: When I was alive, I often received advice from my own big brain which, in terms of my own survival, or the survival of the human race, for that matter, can be charitably described as questionable. Example: It had me join the United States Marines and go fight in Vietnam.

Thanks a lot, big brain.

7

THE NATIONAL CURRENCIES of all six guests at the El Dorado, the four Americans, one claiming to be a Canadian, and the two Japanese, were still as good as gold everywhere on the planet. Again: The value of their money was imaginary. Like the nature of the universe itself, the desirability of their American dollars and yen was all in people's heads.

And if Wait, who did not even know that there was a financial crisis going on, had carried out his masquerade as a Canadian to the extent of bringing Canadian dollars into Ecuador, he would not have been as well received as he was. Although Canada had not gone bankrupt, people's imaginations in more and more places, including Canada itself, were making them unhappy about trading anything really useful for Canadian dollars anymore.

A similar decay in imagined value was happening to the British pound and the French and Swiss francs and the West German mark. The Ecuadorian sucre, meanwhile, named in honor of Antonio José de Sucre (1795–1830), a national hero, had come to be worth less than a banana peel.

• • •

Up in her room, Mary Hepburn was wondering if she had a brain tumor, and that was why her brain was giving her the worst possible advice all the time. It was a natural thing for her to suspect, since it was a brain tumor which had killed her husband Roy only three months before. It hadn't been enough for the tumor to kill him, either. It had to addle his memory and destroy his judgment first.

She had to wonder, too, when his tumor had begun to do that to him—whether it wasn't the tumor which had made him sign them up for "the Nature Cruise of the Century" in the promising January of that ultimately horrible year.

• • •

Here was how she found out he had signed them up for the cruise: She came home from work one afternoon, expecting Roy still to be at GEFFCo. He got off work an hour later than she did. But there Roy was, already, home, and it turned out that he had quit at noon. This was a man who adored the work he did with machinery, and who had never taken off so much as an hour from his job during his twenty-nine years with GEFFCo—not for sickness, since he was never sick, not for anything.

She asked him if he was sick, and he said that he had never felt better in his life. He was proud of himself in what seemed to Mary the manner of an adolescent who was tired of being thought a good boy all the time. This was a man whose words were few and well-chosen, never silly or immature. But now he said incredibly, and with an inane expression to match, as though she were his disapproving mother: "I played hookey."

It had to have been the tumor that said that, Mary now thought in Guayaquil. And the tumor couldn't have picked a worse day for carefree truancy, for there had been an ice storm the night before, and then wind-driven sleet all day. But Roy had gone up and down Clinton Street, the main street of Ilium, stopping in store after store and telling the salespeople that he was playing hookey.

So Mary tried to be happy about that, to say and mean that it was time he loosened up and had some fun— although they had always had a lot of fun on weekends and during vacations, and at work, as far as that went. But a miasma overlay this unexpected escapade. And Roy himself, during their early supper, seemed puzzled by the afternoon. So that was that. He didn't think he would do it again, and they could forget the incident, except maybe to laugh about it now and then.

But then, right before bedtime, while they were staring at the glowing embers in the fieldstone fireplace which Roy had built with his own two horny hands, Roy said, "There's more."

"There's more of what?" said Mary.

"About this afternoon," he said. "One of the places I went was the travel agency." There was only one such establishment in Ilium, and not doing well.

"So?" she said.

"I signed us up for something," he said. It was as though he were remembering a dream. "It's all paid for. It's all taken care of. It's done. In November, you and I are flying to Ecuador, and we are going to take 'the Nature Cruise of the Century.' "

• • •

Roy and Mary Hepburn were the very first persons to respond to the advertising and publicity program for the maiden voyage of the *Bahía de Darwin,* which ship was nothing but a keel and a pile of blueprints in Malmö, Sweden, at the time. The Ilium travel agent had just received a poster announcing the cruise. He was just Scotch-taping it to his wall when Roy Hepburn walked in.

• • •

If I may interject a personal note: I myself had been working as a welder in Malmö for about a year, but the *Bahía de Darwin* had not yet materialized sufficiently so as to require my services. I would literally lose my head to that steel maiden only when springtime came. Question: Who hasn't lost his or her head in the springtime?

• • •

But to continue:

The travel poster in Ilium depicted a very strange bird standing on the edge of a volcanic island, looking out

33

at a beautiful white motor ship churning by. This bird was black and appeared to be the size of a large duck, but it had a neck as long and supple as a snake. The queerest thing about it, though, was that it seemed to have no wings, which was almost the truth. This sort of bird was endemic to the Galápagos Islands, meaning that it was found there and nowhere else on the planet. Its wings were tiny and folded flat against its body, in order that it might swim as fast and deep as a fish could. This was a much better way to catch fish than, as so many fish-eating birds were required to do, to wait for fish to come to the surface and then crash down on them with beaks agape. This very successful bird was called by human beings a "flightless cormorant." It could go where the fish were. It didn't have to wait for fish to make a fatal error.

Somewhere along the line of evolution, the ancestors of such a bird must have begun to doubt the value of their wings, just as, in 1986, human beings were beginning to question seriously the desirability of big brains.

If Darwin was right about the Law of Natural Selection, cormorants with small wings, just shoving off from shore like fishing boats, must have caught more fish than the greatest of their aviators. So they mated with each other, and those children of theirs who had the smallest wings became evern better fisherpeople, and so on.

• • •

Now the very same sort of thing has happened to people, but not with respect to their wings, of course, since they never had wings—but with respect to their hands and brains instead. And people don't have to wait any more for fish to nibble on baited hooks or blunder into nets or whatever. A person who wants a fish nowadays just goes after one like a shark in the deep blue sea.

It's so easy now.

8

Even back in January, there were any number of reasons Roy Hepburn should not have signed up for that cruise. It wasn't evident then that a world economic crisis was coming, and that the people of Ecuador would be starving when the ship was supposed to sail. But there was the matter of Mary's job. She did not yet know that she was about to be laid off, to be forced into early retirement, so she could not see how she, in good conscience, could take off three weeks in late November and early December, right in the middle of a semester.

Also, although she had never been there, she had grown very bored with the Galápagos Archipelago. There was such a wealth of films and slides and books and articles about the islands, which she had used over and over in her courses, that she could not imagine any surprise that might await her there. Little did she know.

She and Roy hadn't been out of the United States during their entire marriage. If they were going to kick up their heels and take a really glamorous trip, she thought, she would much rather go to Africa, where the wildlife was so much more thrilling, and the survival schemes were so much more dangerous. When all was said and done, the creatures of the Galápagos Islands were a pretty listless bunch, when compared with rhinos and hippos and lions and elephants and giraffes and so on.

The prospect of the voyage, in fact, made her confess to a close friend, "All of a sudden I have this feeling that I never want to see another blue-footed booby as long as I live!"

Little did she know.

• • •

Mary muted her misgivings about the trip, though, when talking to Roy, confident that he would perceive on his own that he had suffered a mild brain malfunction. But by March, Roy was out of his job, and Mary knew she was going to be let go in June. The timing of the cruise, anyway, became practical. And the cruise loomed huge in Roy's increasingly erratic imagination as ". . . the only good thing we've got to look forward to."

• • •

Here was what had happened to their jobs: GEFFCo had furloughed almost its entire work force, blue-collar and white-collar alike, in order to modernize the Ilium operation. A Japanese company, Matsumoto, was doing the job. Matsumoto was also automating the *Bahía de Darwin*. This was the same company which employed ★Zenji Hiroguchi, the young computer genius who would be staying with his wife at the Hotel El Dorado the same time that Mary was there.

When the Matsumoto Corporation got through installing computers and robots, only twelve human beings would be able to run everything. So people young enough to have children, or at least ambitious dreams for the future, left town in droves. It was, as Mary Hepburn would say on her eighty-first birthday, two weeks before a great white shark ate her, ". . . as though the Pied Piper had passed through town." Suddenly, there were almost no children to educate, and the city was bankrupt for want of taxpayers. So Ilium High School would graduate its last class in June.

• • •

In April Roy was diagnosed as having an inoperable brain tumor. "The Nature Cruise of the Century" thereupon became what he was staying alive for. "I can hang on that long at least, Mary. November—that's not far away, is it?"

"No," she said.

"I can hang on that long."

"You could have years, Roy," she said.

"Just let me take that cruise," he said. "Let me see penguins on the equator," he said. "That'll be good enough for me."

• • •

While Roy was mistaken about more and more things, he was right about there being penguins on the

Galápagos Islands. They were skinny things underneath their headwaiters' costumes. They had to be. If they had been swaddled in fat like their relatives on the ice floes to the south, half a world away, they would have roasted to death when they came ashore on the lava to lay their eggs and tend their young.

Like those of the flightless cormorants, their ancestors, too, had abandoned the glamor of aviation—electing to catch more fish instead.

• • •

About that mystifying enthusiasm a million years ago for turning over as many human activities as possible to machinery: What could that have been but yet another acknowledgment by people that their brains were no damn good?

9

WHILE ROY HEPBURN was dying, and while the whole city of Ilium was dying, for that matter, and while both the man and the city were being killed by growths inimical to a healthy and happy humanity, Roy's big brain persuaded him that he had been a sailor at the United States atomic bomb tests at Bikini Atoll, equatorial like Guayaquil, in 1946. He was going to sue his own government for millions, he said, because the radiation he had absorbed there had first prevented his and Mary's having children, and now it had caused his brain cancer.

Roy had served a hitch in the Navy, but otherwise his case against the United States of America was a weak one, since he was born in 1932, and his country's lawyers would have no trouble proving that. That would make him fourteen years old at the time of his supposed exposure.

That anachronism did not prevent his having vivid memories of the terrible things his government had made him do to so-called lower animals. As he told it, he worked virtually unassisted, first driving stakes into the ground all over the atoll, and then tying different sorts of animals to the stakes. "I guess they chose me," he said, "because animals have always trusted me."

This much was true: Animals all trusted Roy. While he had no formal education past high school, except for the apprentice program at GEFFCo, and while Mary had a master's degree in zoology from Indiana University, Roy was much better at actually relating to animals than Mary was. He could talk to birds in their own languages, for example, something she could never have done, since her ancestors were notoriously tone deaf on both sides of her family. There was no dog or farm animal, not even a guard dog at GEFFCo or a sow with piglets, so vicious that Roy couldn't, within five minutes or less, turn it into a friend of his.

So Roy's tears were understandable when he remembered tying animals to all those stakes. Such a cruel experiment had been performed on animals, of course, on sheep and pigs and cattle and horses and monkeys and ducks and chickens and geese, but surely not on a zoo such as Roy described. To hear him tell it, he had tethered peacocks and snow leopards and gorillas and crocodiles and albatrosses to the stakes. In his big brain, Bikini became the exact reverse of Noah's ark. Two of every sort of animal had been brought there in order to be atom-bombed.

• • •

The craziest detail in his story, which did not seem at all crazy to him, of course, was this one: "Donald was there." Donald was a golden retriever male who was roaming the neighborhood there in Ilium at that very moment, probably, maybe right outside the Hepburns' house, and was only four years old.

"It was all very hard," Roy would say, "but the hardest part was tying Donald to one of those stakes. I kept putting it off until I couldn't put it off any longer. Tying Donald to a stake was the last thing I had to do. He let me do it, and after I did it he licked my hand and wagged that tail of his. And I said to him, and I'm not ashamed to say I cried: 'So long, old pal. You're going to a different world now. It's sure to be a better one, since no other world could be as bad as this one is.' "

• • •

While Roy began putting on such performances, Mary was still teaching every weekday, still assuring the few students she had left that they should thank God for their great big brains. "Would you rather have the neck of a giraffe or the camouflage of a chameleon or the hide of a rhinoceros or the antlers of an Irish elk?" she would ask, and so on.

She was still spouting the same old malarkey.

Yes, and then she would go home to Roy, and his demonstrations of how misleading a brain could be. He was never hospitalized, except briefly for tests. And he was docile. He wasn't to drive a car anymore, but he understood that, and did not seem to resent it when Mary hid the keys to his Jeep station wagon. He even said that maybe they should sell it, since it didn't look like they were going to do much camping anymore. So Mary didn't have to hire a nurse to watch over Roy while she worked. Retired people in the neighborhood were glad to pick up a few dollars, keeping him company and making sure he didn't hurt himself in some way.

He was certainly no trouble to them. He watched a lot of television and enjoyed playing for hours, never leaving the yard, with Donald, the golden retriever who had died, supposedly, on Bikini Atoll.

• • •

As Mary delivered what was to be her last lecture about the Galápagos Islands, though, she would be stopped in mid-sentence for five seconds by a doubt which, if expressed in words, might have come out something like this: "Maybe I'm just a crazy lady who has wandered off the street and into this classroom and started explaining the mysteries of life to these young people. And they believe me, although I am utterly mistaken about simply everything."

She had to wonder, too, about all the supposedly great teachers of the past, who, although their brains were healthy, had turned out to be as wrong as Roy about what was really going on.

10

How many Galápagos Islands were there a million years ago? There were thirteen big ones, seventeen small ones, and three hundred and eighteen tiny ones, some nothing more than rocks rising only a meter or two above the surface of the ocean.

There are now fourteen big ones, seven small ones, and three hundred and twenty-six tiny ones. Quite a lot of volcanic activity still goes on. I make a joke: The gods are still angry.

And the northernmost of the islands, so all alone, so far from the rest, is still Santa Rosalia.

• • •

Yes, and a million years ago, on August 3, 1986, a man named *Roy Hepburn was on his deathbed in his right little, tight little home in Ilium, New York. There at the very end, what he lamented most was that he and his wife Mary had never had children. He could not urge his wife to try to have children by someone else after he was gone, since she had ceased to ovulate.

"We Hepburns are extinct as the dodoes now," he

said, and he rambled on with the names of many other creatures which had become fruitless, leafless twigs on the tree of evolution. "The Irish elk," he said. "The ivory-billed woodpecker," he said. *"Tyrannosaurus rex,"* he said, and on and on. Right up to the end, though, his dry sense of humor would pop up unexpectedly. He made two jocular additions to the lugubrious roll call, both of which were indeed without progeny. "Smallpox," he said, and then, "George Washington."

• • •

Right to the end, he believed with all his heart that his own government had done him in with radiation. He said to Mary, and to the doctor and the nurse who were there because the end could surely come at any moment now: "If only it had been just God Almighty who was mad at me!"

Mary took that to be his curtain line. He certainly looked dead after that.

But then, after ten seconds, his blue lips moved again. Mary leaned close to hear his words. She would be glad for the rest of her life that she had not missed them.

"I'll tell you what the human soul is, Mary," he whispered, his eyes closed. "Animals don't have one. It's the part of you that knows when your brain isn't working right. I always knew, Mary. There wasn't anything I could do about it, but I always knew."

And then he scared the wits out of Mary and everybody in the room by sitting up straight, his eyes open wide and fiery. "Get the Bible!" he commanded, in a voice which could be heard throughout the house.

This was the only time anything to do with formal religion was mentioned during the whole of his illness. He and Mary were no churchgoers; or prayers in even dire circumstances, but they did have a Bible somewhere. Mary wasn't quite sure where.

"Get the Bible!" he said again. "Woman, get the Bible!" He had never called her "woman" before.

So Mary went to look for it. She found it in the spare bedroom, along with Darwin's *The Voyage of the Beagle* and *A Tale of Two Cities,* by Charles Dickens.

*Roy sat up, and he called Mary "woman" again. "Woman—" he commanded, "put your hand on the Bible and repeat after me: 'I, Mary Hepburn, hereby make two solemn promises to my beloved husband on his deathbed.' "

So she said that. She expected, and in fact hoped, that the two promises would be so bizarre, perhaps having to do with suing the government, that there would be no possibility of her keeping either one. But she was not to be so lucky.

The first promise was that she do her best to get married again as soon as possible, and not waste time in moping and feeling sorry for herself.

The second was that she go to Guayaquil in November and take "the Nature Cruise of the Century" for both of them.

"My spirit will be with you every inch of the way," he said. And he died.

• • •

So here she was in Guayaquil, suspecting that she had a brain tumor herself. Her brain had her in the closet now, removing the garment bag from the red evening dress, which she called her "Jackie dress." She had given it that nickname because one of her fellow passengers was supposed to be Jacqueline Kennedy Onassis, and Mary wanted to look nice for her.

But there in the closet, Mary knew that the widow Onassis surely wasn't going to be crazy enough to come to Guayaquil—not with soldiers patrolling the streets and on rooftops, and digging foxholes and machine-gun pits in the parks.

While slipping the bag off the dress, she dislodged the dress from its hanger, and it fell to the floor. It made a red puddle there.

She did not pick it up, since she believed that she had no more use for earthly things. But she was not yet ready for a star before her name. She would in fact live for thirty more years. She would, moreover, employ certain vital materials on the planet in such a way as to make her, without question, the most important experimenter in the history of the human race.

11

If MARY HEPBURN had been in a mood to eavesdrop instead of kill herself, she might have put an ear to the back of her closet and heard susurruses next door. She had no idea who her neighbors were on either side, since there hadn't been any other guests when she arrived the night before, and she hadn't been out of her room since then.

But the makers of the susurruses were *Zenji Hiroguchi, the computer genius, and his pregnant wife Hisako, the teacher of ikebana, the Japanese art of flower arranging.

Her neighbors on the other side were Selena MacIntosh, the blind, teenage daughter of *Andrew MacIntosh, and Kazakh, her seeing-eye dog, also a female. Mary had heard no barking, because Kazakh never barked.

Kazakh never barked or played with other dogs or investigated interesting smells or noises or chased animals which had been the natural prey of her ancestors because, when she was a puppy, big-brained human beings had showed her hate and withheld food whenever she did any of those things. They let her know from the first that that was the kind of planet she was on: that natural canine activities were against the law—all of them.

They removed her sex organs so that she would never be distracted by sexual urgencies. And I was about to say that the cast of my story would soon boil down to just one male and a lot of females, including a female dog. But Kazakh wasn't really a female anymore, thanks to surgery. Like Mary Hepburn, she was out of the evolutionary game. She wasn't going to leave her genes to anyone.

• • •

Beyond Selena and Kazakh's room, with an open connecting door, lay the quarters of Selena's lusty father, the financier and adventurer *Andrew MacIntosh. He was a widower. He and the widow Mary Hepburn might have got along quite nicely, since they were such ardent outdoors people. But they would never meet. As I have already said, *Andrew MacIntosh and *Zenji Hiroguchi would be dead before the sun went down.

James Wait, incidentally, had been given a room all alone on the second floor as far as possible from the other guests. His big brain was congratulating him on seeming harmless and ordinary, but it was wrong about that. The hotel manager had spotted Wait as a crook of some kind.

• • •

This hotel manager, whose name was *Siegfried von Kleist, was a lugubrious, middle-aged member of the old and generally prosperous German community in Ecuador.

His two paternal uncles in Quito owned the hotel and the *Bahía de Darwin,* too, and they had put him in charge of the hotel for only two weeks, a period drawing to a close now, to oversee the reception of the passengers for "the Nature Cruise of the Century." He was generally an idler, having inherited considerable money, but had been shamed by his uncles into, so to speak, "pulling his own weight" in this particular family enterprise.

He was unmarried and had never reproduced, and so was insignificant from an evolutionary point of view. He might also have been considered as a marriage possibility for Mary Hepburn. But he, too, was doomed. *Siegfried von Kleist would survive the sunset, but three hours after that he would be drowned by a tidal wave.

It was now four o'clock in the afternoon. This native Ecuadorian Hun, with his watery blue eyes and drooping moustache, actually looked as though he expected to die that evening, but he could no more foretell the future than I could. Both of us felt that afternoon that the planet was wobbling on its axis, and that anything could happen next.

*Zenji Hiroguchi and *Andrew MacIntosh, incidentally, would die of gunshot wounds.

• • •

*Siegfried von Kleist is not important to my story, but his only sibling, his brother Adolf, three years his senior and also a bachelor, surely is. Adolf von Kleist, the Captain of the *Bahía de Darwin,* would in fact become the ancestor of every human being on the face of the earth today.

With the help of Mary Hepburn, he would become a latter-day Adam, so to speak. The biology teacher from Ilium, however, since she had ceased ovulating, would not, could not, become his Eve. So she had to be more like a god instead.

And this supremely important brother of the insignificant hotel manager was at that moment arriving at Guayaquil International Airport on a nearly empty transport plane from New York City, where he had been doing publicity for "the Nature Cruise of the Century."

• • •

If Mary had listened in on the Hiroguchis through her closet wall, she wouldn't have understood what was troubling them, since their susurruses were in Japanese, the only language in which they were fluent. *Zenji knew a little English and Russian. Hisako knew a little Chinese. Neither one knew any Spanish or Quechuan or German or Portuguese, the commonest languages in Ecuador.

They, too, it turned out, were bitter about what their supposedly wonderful brains had done to them. They felt especially foolish about having allowed themselves to be delivered into such a nightmare, since *Zenji was widely regarded as being one of the smartest men in the world. And it was his fault, not hers, that they had in effect become prisoners of the dynamic *Andrew MacIntosh.

Here is how that happened: ★MacIntosh had visited Japan with his blind daughter and her dog about a year before, and had met ★Zenji, and had seen the wonderful work he was doing as a salaried employee for Matsumoto. Technologically speaking, ★Zenji, although only twenty-nine, had become a grandfather. He had earlier sired a pocket computer capable of translating many spoken languages instantaneously, and he had named it "Gokubi." And then, at the time of the MacIntoshes' visit to Japan, ★Zenji had come up with a pilot model for a new generation of simultaneous voice translators, and he had named it "Mandarax."

So ★Andrew MacIntosh, whose investment banking firm raised money for businesses and itself by the sale of stocks and bonds, took young ★Zenji aside and told him that he was an idiot to be on salary, that ★MacIntosh could help him form a corporation of his own which would make him almost instantly a billionaire in dollars or a trillionaire in yen.

So ★Zenji said that he would like time to think about it.

This exploratory conversation took place in a Tokyo sushi restaurant. Sushi was raw fish wrapped around cold rice, a popular dish a million years ago. Little did anybody dream back then that everybody would be eating practically nothing but raw fish in the sweet by-and-by.

The florid, boisterous American entrepreneur and the reserved, relatively doll-like Japanese inventor communicated through Gokubi, since neither spoke the other's language at all well. There were then thousands upon thousands of Gokubis in use all over the world. The two men could not use Mandarax, since the only working model of Mandarax was under heavy guard in *Zenji's office back at Matsumoto. So *Zenji's big brain began to play with the idea of becoming as rich as the richest man in his country, who was the Emperor of Japan.

A few months later, in the following January, the same January during which Mary and Roy Hepburn thought they had so much to be grateful for, *Zenji got a letter from *MacIntosh asking him a full ten months in advance to be his guest on his estate outside of Mérida, Yucatán, in Mexico, and then on the maiden voyage of an Ecuadorian luxury ship called the *Bahía de Darwin,* in whose financing he had had a hand.

*MacIntosh had said in the letter in English, which had to be translated for *Zenji: *Let us take this opportunity to get to really know each other.*

• • •

What he meant to get from *Zenji, probably in Yucatán, or surely during "the Nature Cruise of the Century," was *Zenji's signature on an agreement to head a new corporation, whose stock *MacIntosh would merchandise.

Like James Wait, *MacIntosh was a fisherman of sorts. He hoped to catch investors, using for bait not a price tag on his shirt but a Japanese computer genius.

And now it appears to me that the tale I have to tell,

spanning a million years, doesn't change all that much from beginning to end. In the beginning, as in the end, I find myself speaking of human beings, regardless of their brain size, as fisherfolk.

• • •

So it was November now, and the Hiroguchis were in Guayaquil. On the advice of *MacIntosh, *Zenji had lied to his employers about where he was going. He had led them to believe that he was exhausted by the creation of Mandarax, and that he and Hisako wished to have two months all by themselves, far from any reminders of work, and incommunicado. He put his piece of misinformation into their big brains: he had chartered schooner with crew, whose name he did not wish to reveal, sailing from a Mexican port whose name he did not wish to reveal, for a cruise through the islands of the Caribbean.

And, although the passenger list for "the Nature Cruise of the Century" had been widely publicized, *Zenji's employers never learned that their most productive employee and his wife were also expected to be aboard. Like James Wait, they were traveling under false identities.

And, again like James Wait, they had evanesced!

Anybody looking for them would not be able to find them anywhere. Any big-brained search for them wouldn't even start on the correct continent.

12

THERE IN THEIR HOTEL ROOM next to Mary Hepburn's, the Hiroguchis were susurruing away about *Andrew MacIntosh's being an actual maniac. This was an exaggeration. *MacIntosh was surely wild and greedy and inconsiderate, but not insane. Most of what his big brain believed to be going on was actually going on. When he flew Selena and Kazakh and the Hiroguchis from Mérida to Guayaquil in his private Learjet, with himself at the controls, he had known that the city would be under martial law, or something close to it, and that the stores would all be closed, and that there would be increasingly hungry people milling around, and that the *Bahía de Darwin* would not sail as scheduled, probably, and so on.

The communications facilities in his Yucatecan mansion had kept him absolutely up to date on what was going on in Ecuador or anyplace else he might have reason to care about. At the same time he had kept the Hiroguchis, but not his blind daughter, in the dark, so to speak, about what was likely awaiting them.

His true purpose in coming to Guayaquil, which, again, he had revealed to his daughter but not to the

Hiroguchis, was to buy as many Ecuadorian assets as possible at rock-bottom prices, including, perhaps, even the El Dorado and the *Bahía de Darwin*—and gold mines and oil fields, and on and on. He was moreover going to bond ★Zenji Hiroguchi to himself forever by sharing these business opportunities with him, to lend him money so that he, too, could become a major property owner in Ecuador.

• • •

★MacIntosh had told the Hiroguchis to stay in their room at the El Dorado—because he would soon be bringing wonderful news for them. He had been on the telephone all afternoon, calling Ecuadorian financiers and banks, and the news he expected to bring was about all the properties he and the Hiroguchis could call their own in a day or two.

And then he was going to say: "And to hell with 'the Nature Cruise of the Century'!"

• • •

The Hiroguchis could no longer conceive of any good news for themselves which could be delivered by ★Andrew MacIntosh. They honestly believed him to be a madman, which misconception, ironically, had been impressed upon them by ★Zenji's own creation, which was Mandarax. There were now ten such instruments in the world, nine back in Tokyo, and one which ★Zenji had brought along for the cruise. Mandarax, unlike Gokubi, was not only a translator, but also could diagnose with respectable accuracy one thousand of the most common diseases which attacked *Homo sapiens,* including twelve varieties of nervous breakdown.

What Mandarax did in the medical field was simplicity itself, actually. Mandarax was programed to do what real doctors did, which was to ask a series of questions, each answer suggesting the next question, such as: "How is your appetite?" and then, "Do your bowels move regularly?" and, perhaps, "What did the stool look like?" and so on.

In Yucatán, the Hiroguchis had followed such a daisy chain of questions and answers, describing for Mandarax the behavior of *Andrew MacIntosh. Mandarax had at last displayed these words in Japanese on the screen, which was about the size of a playing card: *Pathological personality.*

• • •

Unfortunately for the Hiroguchis, but not for Mandarax, which couldn't feel anything or care about anything, the computer was not programed to explain that this was a rather mild affliction compared to most, and that those who had it were rarely hospitalized, that they were, in fact, among the happiest people on the planet— and that their behavior merely caused pain to those around them, and almost never to themselves. A real doctor might have gone on to say that millions of people walking the streets every day fell into a gray area, where it was difficult to say with any degree of certainty whether or not their personalities were pathological.

But the Hiroguchis were ignorant of medical matters, and so responded to the diagnosis as though it were a dread disease. So, one way or another, they wanted to get away from *Andrew MacIntosh, and then all the way back to Tokyo. But they remained dependent on him, as much as they wished they weren't. They had learned from the mournful-looking hotel manager, speaking to him through Mandarax, that all commercial flights out of Guayaquil had been canceled, and that none of the companies with planes for charter seemed to be answering their phones.

So that left the petrified Hiroguchis with only two possible ways of egress from Guayaquil: either on *MacIntosh's Learjet, or aboard the *Bahía de Darwin,* if, as was becoming harder and harder to believe, it would really sail next day.

13

*Zenji Hiroguchi begat Gokubi one million and five years ago, and then, one million years ago, this young genius begat Mandarax. Yes, and at the time of his begetting of Mandarax, his wife was about to give birth to his first human child.

There had been concern about the genes the mother, Hisako, might have passed on to her fetus, since her own mother had been exposed to radiation when the United States of America dropped an atomic bomb on Hiroshima, Japan. So a sample of Hisako's amniotic fluid was tested back in Tokyo for clues that the child might be abnormal. That fluid, incidentally, would be identical in salinity with that of the ocean into which the *Bahía de Darwin* would disappear.

The tests declared the fetus normal.

They also gave away the secret of its sex. It would come into the world as a little girl, yet another female in this tale.

• • •

The tests were incapable of detecting minor defects in the fetus, such as that it might be as tone deaf as Mary Hepburn, which it wasn't—or that it might be covered with a fine, silky pelt like a fur seal's, which would actually turn out to be the case.

The only human being *Zenji Hiroguchi would ever beget was a darling but furry daughter he would never see.

She would be born on Santa Rosalia, at the northernmost extremity of the Galápagos Islands. Her name would be Akiko.

• • •

When Akiko became an adult on Santa Rosalia, she would be very much like her mother on the inside, but in a different sort of skin. The evolutionary sequence from Gokubi to Mandarax, by contrast, was a radical improvement in the contents of a package, but with few perceptible changes in the wrapper. Akiko was protected from sunburn, and from the chilly water when she swam, and the abrasiveness of lava when she chose to sit or lie down—whereas her mother's bare skin was wholly defenseless against these ordinary hazards of island life. But Gokubi and Mandarax, as different as they were inside, inhabited nearly identical shells of high-impact black plastic, twelve centimeters high, eight wide, and two thick.

Any fool could tell Akiko from Hisako, but only an expert could tell Gokubi from Mandarax.

• • •

Gokubi and Mandarax both had pressure-sensitive buttons on their backs, set flush with their cases, by means of which a person might communicate with whatever it was that had been put inside. On the face of each was an identical screen on which images could be caused to appear, and which also functioned as a solar cell, charging tiny batteries which, again, were exactly the same in Gokubi and Mandarax.

Each had a microphone the size of a pinhead at the upper right-hand corner of its screen. It was by means of this that Gokubi or Mandarax heard spoken language, and then, in accordance with instructions from its buttons, translated them into words on its screen.

An operator of either instrument had to be as quick and graceful with his hands as a magician, if a bilingual conversation was to flow at all naturally. If I were an English-speaking person talking to a Portuguese, say, I would have to hold the instrument somewhere near the mouth of the Portuguese, but with the screen close enough to my eyes for me to read the written translation into English of what he was saying. And then I would have to flip it over quickly, so that the instrument could hear me, and so he could read from the screen what I was saying.

No person living today has hands clever enough or a brain big enough to operate a Gokubi or a Mandarax. Nobody can thread a needle, either—or play the piano, or pick his or her nose, as the case may be.

• • •

Gokubi could translate among only ten languages. Mandarax could translate among a thousand. Gokubi had to be told what language it was hearing. Mandarax could identify every one of the thousand languages after hearing only a few words, and begin to translate those words into the operator's language without being told.

Both were highly accurate clocks and perpetual calendars. The clock of *Zenji Hiroguchi's Mandarax lost only eighty-two seconds between the time he checked into the Hotel El Dorado and, thirty-one years later, when Mary Hepburn and the instrument were eaten by a great white shark.

Gokubi would have kept track of time just as accurately, but in all other respects Mandarax left its father far behind. Not only could Mandarax traffic in one hundred times more languages than its progenitor and correctly diagnose more diseases than the majority of physicians of that time. It could also name on command important events which happened in any given year. If you punched out on its back *1802,* for example, the year of Charles Darwin's birth, Mandarax would tell you that Alexandre Dumas and Victor Hugo were also born then, and that Beethoven completed his Second Symphony, and that France suppressed a Negro rebellion in Santo Domingo, and that Gottfried Treveranus coined the term *biology,* and that the Health and Morals of Apprentices Act became law in Britain, and on and on. That was also the year in which Napoleon became President of the Italian Republic.

Mandarax knew the rules, too, for two hundred games, and could recite the basic principles laid down by masters for fifty different arts and crafts. It could moreover recall on command any one of twenty thousand popular quotations from literature. So that, if you punched out on its back the word *Sunset,* for example, these lofty sentiments would appear on its screen:

> *Sunset and evening star,*
> *And one clear call for me!*
> *And may there be no moaning of the bar,*
> *When I put out to sea.*
>
> —ALFRED, LORD TENNYSON
> (1809–1892)

• • •

*Zenji Hiroguchi's Mandarax was about to be marooned for thirty-one years on Santa Rosalia, along with his pregnant wife and Mary Hepburn and the blind Selena MacIntosh and Captain Adolf von Kleist, and six other people, all females. But under those particular circumstances, Mandarax wasn't really much help.

The uselessness of all its knowledge would so anger the Captain that he threatened to throw it into the ocean. On the last day of his life, when he was eighty-six and Mary was eighty-one, he would actually carry out that threat. As the new Adam, it might be said, his final act was to cast the Apple of Knowledge into the deep blue sea.

• • •

63

Under the circumstances peculiar to Santa Rosalia, the medical advice of Mandarax was bound to sound like mockery. When Hisako Hiroguchi entered a deep depression which was to last until her death, to last for nearly twenty years, Mandarax recommended new hobbies, new friends, a change of scene and perhaps profession, and lithium. When the kidneys of Selena MacIntosh began to fail when she was only thirty-eight, Mandarax suggested that a compatible donor for a transplant be located as soon as possible. Hisako's furry daughter Akiko, when Akiko was six, came down with pneumonia, apparently caught from a fur seal who was her best friend, and Mandarax recommended antibiotics. Hisako and the blind Selena were then living together and raising Akiko together, almost like husband and wife.

And when Mandarax was asked to come up with quotations from world literature which could be used in a celebration of some event on the slag heap of Santa Rosalia, the instrument almost always came up with clunkers. Here were its thoughts when Akiko gave birth, at the age of twenty-four, to her own furry daughter and the first member of the second generation of human beings to be born on the island:

> *If I were hanged on the highest hill,*
> *Mother o' mine, O mother o' mine!*
> *I know whose love would follow me still,*
> *Mother o' mine, O mother o' mine!*
> —RUDYARD KIPLING (1865–1936)

and

In the dark womb where I began
My mother's life made me a man.
Through all the months of human birth
Her beauty fed my common earth.
I cannot see, nor breathe, nor stir,
But through the death of some of her.

—JOHN MASEFIELD (1878–1967)

and

Lord, who ordainest for mankind
Benignant toils and tender cares!
We thank Thee for the ties that bind
The mother to the child she bears.

—WILLIAM CULLEN BRYANT
(1794–1878)

and

Honor thy father and thy mother; that thy days may
be long upon the land which the Lord thy God giveth
thee.

—THE BIBLE

The father of Akikō's daughter was the oldest of the Captain's children, Kamikaze, only thirteen years old.

14

THERE WOULD BE MANY BIRTHS but no formal marriages to celebrate during the first forty-one years of the colony on Santa Rosalia, from which all humanity is now descended. There were surely pairings off from the very first. Hisako and Selena paired off for the rest of their lives. The Captain and Mary Hepburn paired off for the first ten years—until she did something which he considered absolutely unforgivable, which was to make unauthorized use of his sperm. And the six other females, while living together as a family, also formed pairs within an already very intimate sisterhood.

When the first Santa Rosalia marriage was performed by Kamikaze and Akiko in the year 2027, all of the original colonists had long since vanished into the sinuous blue tunnel which leads into the Afterlife, and Mandarax was studded with barnacles on the floor of the South Pacific. If Mandarax were still around, it would have had mostly unpleasant things to say about matrimony, such as:

Marriage: a community consisting of a master,
a mistress, and two slaves, making in all, two.
—AMBROSE BIERCE (1842–?)

and

Marriage from love, like vinegar from wine—
A sad, sour, sober beverage—by time
Is sharpen'd from its high celestial flavour,
Down to a very homely household savour.
—LORD BYRON (1788–1824)

and so on.

The last human marriage in the Galápagos Islands, and thus the last one on Earth, was performed on Fernandina Island in the year 23,011. Nobody today has any idea what a marriage is. I have to say that Mandarax's cynicism about the institution back in its heyday was largely justified. My own parents made each other miserable by getting married, and Mary Hepburn, when she was an old lady on Santa Rosalia, once told the furry Akiko that she and Roy had been, quite possibly, the only happily married couple in all of Ilium.

What made marriage so difficult back then was yet again that instigator of so many other sorts of heartbreak: the oversize brain. That cumbersome computer could hold so many contradictory opinions on so many different subjects all at once, and switch from one opinion or subject to another one so quickly, that a discussion between a husband and wife under stress could end up like a fight between blindfolded people wearing roller skates.

The Hiroguchis, for example, whose susurrations Mary had heard through the back of her closet, were then changing their opinions of themselves and each other, and of love and sex and work and the world and so on, with lightning speed.

In one second, Hisako would think that her husband was very stupid, and that she was going to have to rescue herself and her female fetus. But then in the next second she would think that he was as brilliant as everybody said he was, and that she could just stop worrying, that he would get them out of this mess very easily and soon.

In one second ★Zenji was inwardly cursing her for her helplessness, for being such a dead weight, and in the next he was vowing in his head to die, if necessary, for this goddess and her unborn daughter.

Of what possible use was such emotional volatility, not to say craziness, in the heads of animals who were supposed to stay together long enough, at least, to raise a human child, which took about fourteen years or so?

• • •

★Zenji found himself saying in the midst of a silence, "Something else is bothering you." He meant that something more personal than the general mess they were in was burning her up, and had been burning her up for quite some time.

"No," she said. That was another thing about those

big brains: They found it easy to do what Mandarax could never do, which was lie and lie.

"Something's been bothering you for the past week," he said. "Why don't you just spit it out? Tell me what it is."

"Nothing," she said. Who would want to spend fourteen years with a computer like that, when you could never be sure whether it was telling the truth or not?

They were conversing in Japanese, and not in the idiomatic American English of a million years ago, which I have employed throughout this story. *Zenji, incidentally, was toying nervously with Mandarax, passing it from one hand to the other, and had unintentionally set it so that it was translating anything either one of them said into Navaho.

• • •

"Well—if you must know—" said Hisako at last, "back in Yucatán I was playing with Mandarax one afternoon on the *Omoo*," which was *MacIntosh's one-hundred-dred-meter yacht. "You were diving for sunken treasure." This was something *MacIntosh actually had *Zenji doing, although *Zenji could scarcely swim: scuba-diving down forty meters to a Spanish galleon, and bringing up broken dishes and cannonballs. *MacIntosh also had his blind daughter Selena diving, her right wrist attached to his right ankle by a three-meter nylon cord.

"I accidentally found out something Mandarax could do which you somehow forgot to tell me Mandarax could do," Hisako went on. "Do you want to guess what it was?"

"No, I do not," he said. It was his turn to lie.

"Mandarax," she said, "turns out to be a very good teacher of the art of flower arranging." That was what she had been so proud of being, of course. But her self-respect had been severely crippled by the discovery that a little black box could not only teach what she taught, but could do so in a thousand different tongues.

"I was going to tell you. I meant to tell you," he said. This was another lie, and her learning that Mandarax knew ikebana was as improbable as her guessing the combination to a bank vault. She had been very reluctant to learn how to work Mandarax, and would remain so until she died.

But, by golly if she hadn't fiddled with the buttons there on the *Omoo* until, suddenly, Mandarax was telling her that the most beautiful flower arrangements had one, two, or at the most three, elements. In arrangements of three elements, said Mandarax, all three might be the same, or two of the three might be the same, but all three should never be different. Mandarax told her the ideal ratios between the altitudes of the elements in arrangements of more than one element, and between the elements and the diameters and altitudes of their vases or bowls—or sometimes baskets.

Ikebana turned out to be as easily codified as the practice of modern medicine.

• • •

★Zenji Hiroguchi had not himself taught Mandarax ikebana or anything else it knew. He had left that to underlings. The underling who taught Mandarax ikebana had simply taken a tape recorder to Hisako's famous ikebana class, and then boiled things down.

• • •

★Zenji said to Hisako that he had had Mandarax learn ikebana as a pleasant surprise for Mrs. Onassis, to whom he intended to present the instrument on the final night of "the Nature Cruise of the Century." "I did it for her," he said, "because she is supposed to be such a lover of beauty."

This happened to be the truth, but Hisako did not believe him. That was how bad things had become back in 1986. Nobody believed anybody anymore, since there was so much lying going on.

"Oh, yes," said Hisako, "I am sure you did it for Mrs. Onassis, and to honor your wife as well. You have placed me among the immortals." She was talking about the heavy thinkers Mandarax could quote.

She turned really mean now, and wanted to diminish his accomplishments as much as he, in her opinion, had diminished her own. "I must be awfully stupid," she said, a statement Mandarax faithfully translated into written Navaho. "It has taken me an unforgivably long time to realize how much malice there is, how much contempt for others there is, in what you do."

"You, ★Doctor Hiroguchi," she went on, "think

71

that everybody but yourself is just taking up space on this planet, and we make too much noise and waste valuable natural resources and have too many children and leave garbage around. So it would be a much nicer place if the few stupid services we are able to perform for the likes of you were taken over by machinery. That wonderful Mandarax you're scratching your ear with now: what is that but an excuse for a mean-spirited egomaniac never to pay or even thank any human being with a knowledge of languages or mathematics or history or medicine or literature or ikebana or anything?"

• • •

I have already given my own opinion as to the cause for the craze back then for having machines do everything that human beings did—and I mean *everything*. I just want to add that my father, who was a science-fiction writer, once wrote a novel about a man whom everybody laughed at because he was building sports robots. He created a golf robot who could make a hole in one every time, and a basketball robot who could hit the basket every time, and a tennis robot who served an ace every time, and so on.

At first, people couldn't see any use for robots like that, and the inventor's wife walked out on him, the way Father's wife, incidentally, had walked out on him—and his children tried to put him into a nuthouse. But then he let advertisers know that his robots would also endorse automobiles or beer or razors or wristwatches or perfume or whatever. He made a fortune, according to my father, because so many sports enthusiasts wanted to be exactly like those robots.

Don't ask me why.

15

*ANDREW MACINTOSH, meanwhile, was in his blind daughter's room, waiting for the telephone to ring—to bring him the good news which he would then share with the Hiroguchis. He was fluent in Spanish, and he had been on the telephone all afternoon with his offices on the island of Manhattan and with frightened Ecuadorian financiers and officials. He was doing business in his daughter's room because he wanted her to hear what he was doing. These two were very close. Selena had never known a mother, since her mother had died while giving birth to her.

I think of Selena now, with her meaningless green eyes, as an experiment by Nature—since her blindness was inherited and she could pass it on. She was eighteen there in Guayaquil, with her best reproductive years ahead of her. She would be only twenty-eight when Mary Hepburn asked her if she would like to take part in her unauthorized experiments on Santa Rosalia with the Captain's sperm. Selena would refuse. But if she had found any advantages in blindness, she could have passed them on.

• • •

Little did young Selena know in Guayaquil, as she listened to her sociopathic father wheel and deal on the telephone, that her destiny was to pair off with Hisako Hiroguchi, two rooms away, and to raise a furry baby.

In Guayaquil she was paired off with her father, who apparently owned the planet they were on, and who could do whatever he pleased whenever he pleased, and wherever he pleased. Her big brain told her that she was going to get through life safely and amusingly inside a sort of electromagnetic bubble created by her father's indomitable personality, which would continue to protect her even after he died—even after it came to be his turn to enter the blue tunnel into the Afterlife.

• • •

Before I forget: On Santa Rosalia, Selena's blindness gave her one advantage over all the other colonists which was a great joy to her, but which, nonetheless, was not worth passing on to yet another generation:

More than anybody else on the island, Selena enjoyed the feel of little Akiko's fur.

• • •

*Andrew MacIntosh had told the top financial people in Ecuador that he was prepared to transfer instantly to any designated fiduciary in Ecuador fifty million American dollars, still as good as gold. Most of the supposed wealth held by American banks at that point had become so wholly imaginary, so weightless and impalpable, that

75

any amount of it could be transferred instantly to Ecuador, or anyplace else capable of receiving a written message by wire or radio.

*MacIntosh was waiting to hear from Quito what properties Ecuadorians would be willing to put into the names of himself, his daughter, and the Hiroguchis, also instantly, in exchange for such a sum.

It wasn't even going to be his own money. He had arranged to borrow it, whatever it was, from the Chase Manhattan Bank. They found it somewhere, whatever it was, to loan to him.

Yes, and if the deal went through, Ecuador could wire or radio pieces of the mirage to fertile countries and get real food in return.

And the people would eat up all the food, gobble, gobble, yum, yum, and it would become nothing but excrement and memories. What then for little Ecuador?

• • •

*MacIntosh's call was supposed to come at five-thirty on the dot. He had half an hour more to wait and he ordered two rare filet mignons with all the trimmings from room service. There were still plenty of good things to eat at the El Dorado, hoarded for arriving passengers for "the Nature Cruise of the Century," and especially for Mrs. Onassis. Soldiers at that moment were stringing barbed wire at a distance of one block in every direction around the hotel—to protect the food.

The same thing was happening at the waterfront. Barbed wire was being strung around the *Bahía de Darwin,* which, as everyone in Guayaquil knew, had been provisioned to serve three gourmet meals a day, no two alike, for fourteen days—to one hundred passengers. A person looking at the beautiful ship, and capable of doing a little arithmetic, might have had this thought: "I am so hungry, and my wife and children are so hungry, and my mother and father are so hungry—and there are forty-two hundred delicious meals in there."

• • •

The man who brought the two filet mignon suppers to Selena's room had made such calculations, and carried in his big brain an inventory of the good things to eat in the hotel's larder as well. He himself wasn't hungry yet, since the hotel staff was still being fed. His family, a small one by Ecuadorian standards, consisting of a pregnant wife, her mother, his father, and an orphaned nephew he was raising, were also well enough fed so far. Like all the other employees, he had been stealing food from the hotel for his family.

This was Jesús Ortiz, the young Inca bartender who had recently been serving James Wait downstairs. He had been pressed into service as a room waiter by *Siegfried von Kleist, the manager, who himself had taken over as bartender. The hotel was suddenly short-handed. The two regular room-service waiters seemed to have disappeared. That might be all right, that they had disappeared, since no large volume of room service had been expected. They might be asleep somewhere.

So Ortiz had those two steaks for his big brain to think about in the kitchen, and then in the elevator, and then in the corridor outside Selena's room. The hotel's employees were not eating and stealing food that good. They were generally proud of that. They were still saving the best for what they spoke of as "Señora Kennedy," actually Mrs. Onassis, which was their collective term for all the famous and rich and powerful people who were still supposed to be coming.

Ortiz's brain was so big that it could show him movies in his head which starred him and his dependents as millionaires. And this man, little more than a boy, was so innocent that he believed the dream could come true, since he had no bad habits and was willing to work so hard, if only he could get some hints on succeeding in life from people who were already millionaires.

He had tried, without much satisfaction, to get some advice on living well from James Wait downstairs, who, while so laughably unprepossessing, had a wallet stuffed, as Ortiz had observed respectfully, with credit cards and American twenty-dollar bills.

He thought this about the steaks, too, as he knocked on Selena's door: The people inside there deserved them, and that he would deserve them, too, once he had become a millionaire. And this was a highly intelligent and enterprising young man. Working in Guayaquil hotels since he was ten years old, he had become fluent in six languages, which was more than half as many languages as Gokubi knew, and six times as many languages as James Wait or Mary Hepburn knew, and three times as many languages as the Hiroguchis knew, and two times as many languages as the MacIntoshes knew. He was also a good cook and baker, and had taken a course in accounting and another in business law in night school.

So his inclination was to like whatever he saw and heard as Selena let him into the room. He already knew her green eyes were blind. Otherwise, he would have been fooled. She did not act or look as though she were blind. She was so beautiful. His big brain had him fall in love with her.

• • •

*Andrew MacIntosh was standing at the floor-to-ceiling window wall, looking out over the marsh and slums at the *Bahía de Darwin,* which he expected to be his, or perhaps Selena's, or perhaps the Hiroguchis', before the sun went down. The person who was going to call him at five-thirty, the head of an emergency consortium of financiers in Quito, high in the clouds, was Gottfried von Kleist, chairman of the board of the largest bank of Ecuador, an uncle of the manager of the El Dorado and the captain of the *Bahía de Darwin,* and co-owner with his elder brother Wilhelm of the ship and the hotel.

Turning to look at Ortiz, who had just come in with the filet mignons, *MacIntosh was rehearsing in his head the first thing he was going to say to Gottfried von Kleist in Spanish: "Before you tell me the rest of the good news, dear colleague, give me your word of honor that I am gazing at my own ship in the distance, from the top floor of my own hotel."

• • •

*MacIntosh was barefoot and wearing nothing but a pair of khaki shorts whose fly was unbuttoned and under which he wore no underwear, so that his penis was no more a secret than the pendulum on a grandfather clock.

• • •

Yes, and I pause to marvel now at how little interested this man was in reproduction, in being a huge success biologically—despite his exhibitionistic sexuality and his mania for claiming as his own property as many of the planet's life-support systems as possible. The most famous amassers of survival schemes back then typically had very few children. There were exceptions, of course. Those who did reproduce a lot, though, and who might be thought to want so much property for the comfort of their descendants, commonly made psychological cripples of their own children. Their heirs were more often than not zombies, easily fleeced by men and women as greedy as the person who had left them much too much of everything a human animal could ever want or need.

*Andrew MacIntosh didn't even care if he himself lived or died—as evidenced by his enthusiasms for skydiving and the racing of high-performance motor vehicles and so on.

So I have to say that human brains back then had become such copious and irresponsible generators of suggestions as to what might be done with life, that they made acting for the benefit of future generations seem one of many arbitrary games which might be played by narrow enthusiasts—like poker or polo or the bond market, or the writing of science-fiction novels.

More and more people back then, and not just *Andrew MacIntosh, had found ensuring the survival of the human race a total bore.

It was a lot more fun, so to speak, to hit and hit a tennis ball.

• • •

The seeing-eye dog Kazakh sat by the baggage rack at the foot of Selena's king-size bed. Kazakh was a female German shepherd. She was at ease, and free to be herself, since she was not at the moment wearing her harness and handle. And her small brain, cued by the smell of meat, made her look up at Ortiz with her big brown eyes most hopefully, and to wag her tail.

Dogs back then were far superior to people when it came to distinguishing between different odors. Thanks to Darwin's Law of Natural Selection, all human beings now have senses of smell as acute as Kazakh's. And they have surpassed dogs in one respect: They can smell things underwater.

Dogs still can't even swim underwater, although they have had a million years in which to learn. They goof around as much as ever. They can't even catch fish yet. And I would have to say that the whole rest of the animal world has done strikingly little to improve its survival tactics in all that time, except for humankind.

16

WHAT *ANDREW MACINTOSH now said to Jesús Ortiz was so offensive, and, in view of the hunger pangs spreading throughout Ecuador, so dangerous, that his big brain really must have been sick in some serious way—if giving a damn what happened next was a sign of mental health. The outrageous insult he was about to offer to this friendly and good-hearted waiter, moreover, was not deliberate.

This was a boxy man of medium stature, his head a box set atop a larger one, and with very thick arms and legs. He was as lusty and able an outdoorsman as Mary Hepburn's husband Roy had been, but eager to take terrifying chances, too, which Roy had never been. *MacIntosh had teeth so big and white perfect, and he gave Ortiz such a good look, Ortiz was reminded of keys on a grand piano.

*MacIntosh said to him in Spanish, "Uncover the steaks and put them both on the floor for the dog, and then get out of here."

• • •

Speaking of teeth: There have never been dentists on Santa Rosalia or any of the other human colonies in the Galápagos Islands. As would have been the case a million years ago, a typical colonist can expect to be edentate by the time he or she is thirty years old, having suffered many skull-cracking toothaches on the way. And this is more than a blow to mere vanity, surely, since teeth set in living gums are now people's only tools.

Really. Except for their teeth, people now have no tools at all.

• • •

Mary Hepburn and the Captain had good teeth when they arrived on Santa Rosalia, although they were both well over thirty, thanks to regular visits to dentists, who drilled out rot and drained abscesses and so on. But they were toothless when they died. Selena MacIntosh was so young when she died in a suicide pact with Hisako Hiroguchi that she still had a lot of her teeth, but by no means all of them. Hisako was completely toothless then.

And if I were criticizing human bodies as they were a million years ago, the kind of body I had, as though they were machines somebody intended to put on the market, I would have two main points to make—one of which I have surely made by now in my story: "The brain is much too big to be practical." The other would be: "Something is always going wrong with our teeth. They don't last anything like a lifetime, usually. What chain of events in evolution should we thank for our mouthfuls of rotting crockery?''

It would be nice to say that the Law of Natural Selection, which has done people so many favors in such a short time, had taken care of the tooth problem, too. In a way it has, but its solution has been draconian. It hasn't made teeth more durable. It has simply cut the average human life span down to about thirty years.

• • •

Now back to Guayaquil, and *Andrew MacIntosh's telling Jesús Ortiz to put the filet mignons on the floor:

"I beg your pardon, sir?" said Ortiz in English.

"Put them both in front of the dog," said *MacIntosh.

So Ortiz did that, his big brain in total confusion, revising entirely Ortiz's opinion of himself, humanity, the past and future, and the nature of the universe.

Before Ortiz had time to straighten up from serving the dog, *MacIntosh said yet again, "Get out of here."

• • •

It pains me even now, even a million years later, to write about such human misbehavior.

A million years later, I feel like apologizing for the human race. That's all I can say.

• • •

If Selena was Nature's experiment with blindness, then her father was Nature's experiment with heartlessness. Yes, and Jesús Ortiz was Nature's experiment with admiration for the rich, and I was Nature's experiment with insatiable voyeurism, and my father was Nature's experiment with cynicism, and my mother was Nature's experiment with optimism, and the Captain of the *Bahía de Darwin* was Nature's experiment with ill-founded self-confidence, and James Wait was Nature's experiment with purposeless greed, and Hisako Hiroguchi was Nature's experiment with depression, and Akiko was Nature's experiment with furriness, and on and on.

I am reminded of one of my father's novels, *The Era of Hopeful Monsters*. It was about a planet where the humanoids ignored their most serious survival problems until the last possible moment. And then, with all the forests being killed and all the lakes being poisoned by acid rain, and all the groundwater made unpotable by industrial wastes and so on, the humanoids found themselves the parents of children with wings or antlers or fins, with a hundred eyes, with no eyes, with huge brains, with no brains, and on and on. These were Nature's experiments with creatures which might, as a matter of luck, be better planetary citizens than the humanoids. Most died, or had to be shot, or whatever, but a few were really quite promising, and they intermarried and had young like themselves.

I will now call my own lifetime a million years ago "the Era of Hopeful Monsters," with most of the monsters novel in terms of personality rather than body type. And there are no such experiments, either with bodies or personalities, going on at the present time.

• • •

Big brains back then were not only capable of being cruel for the sake of cruelty. They could also feel all sorts of pain to which lower animals were entirely insensitive. No other sort of animal on earth could feel, as Jesús Ortiz felt as he descended in the elevator to the lobby, that he had been mangled by what *MacIntosh had said to him. He could not even be sure that there was enough of himself left to make living worthwhile.

And his brain was so complicated that he was seeing all sorts of pictures inside his skull which no lower animal could ever see, all as imaginary, as purely matters of human opinion, as the fifty million dollars *Andrew MacIntosh was prepared to transfer instantly from Manhattan to Ecuador when the right words came over the telephone. He saw a picture of Señora Kennedy, Jacqueline Kennedy Onassis, which was indistinguishable from pictures he had seen of the Virgin Mary. Ortiz was a Roman Catholic. Everybody in Ecuador was a Roman Catholic. The von Kleists were all Roman Catholics. Even the cannibals in the Ecuadorian rain forest, the elusive Kanka-bonos, were Roman Catholics.

This Señora Kennedy was beautiful and sad and pure and kind and all powerful. In the mind of Ortiz, though, she also presided over a host of minor deities, who were also going to take part in "the Nature Cruise of the Century," which included the six guests already at the hotel. Ortiz had expected nothing but goodness from any of them, and felt, as had most Ecuadorians until hunger

87

started to set in, that their coming to Ecuador would be a glorious moment in their nation's history, and that every conceivable luxury should be lavished on them.

But now the truth about one of these supposedly wonderful visitors, *Andrew MacIntosh, had polluted Ortiz's mental picture not only of all the other minor deities, but of Señora Kennedy herself.

So that head-and-shoulders portrait grew fangs like a vampire, and the skin dropped off the face, but the hair stayed on. It was a grinning skull now, wishing nothing but pestilence and death for little Ecuador.

• • •

It was a scary picture, and Ortiz could not make it go away. He thought that he might be able to ditch it in the heat outside, so he crossed the lobby, heedless of *Siegfried von Kleist's calls from the bar. *Von Kleist was asking him what was the matter, where was he going, and so on. Ortiz was the hotel's best employee, the most loyal and resourceful and uniformly cheerful one, and *von Kleist really needed him.

• • •

Here is why the hotel manager had no children, incidentally, although he was heterosexual and his sperm looked fine under a microscope and so on: There was a fifty-fifty chance that he was a carrier of an inherited and incurable disease of the brain, unknown in the present day, called Huntington's chorea. Back then, Huntington's chorea was one of the thousand most common diseases which Mandarax could diagnose.

It is a matter of pure, gambling-casino luck that there are no carriers of Huntington's chorea today. It was the same dumb luck which had made *Siegfried von Kleist a possible carrier back then. His father had learned that he was a carrier only in middle life, after he had reproduced twice.

And that meant, of course, that *Siegfried's taller and older and more glamorous brother, Adolf, the captain of the *Bahía de Darwin,* might also be a carrier. So *Siegfried, who was about to die without issue, and Adolf, who would eventually become the common sire of the entire human race, had both, for admirably unselfish reasons, declined to engage in biologically significant copulation a million years ago.

• • •

*Siegfried and Adolf kept it a secret that they might have this defect in their genes. That secrecy spared them personal embarrassment, surely—but it protected all their relatives, too. If it had been generally known that the brothers might transmit Huntington's chorea to their offspring, all the von Kleists would likely have found it difficult to make good marriages, even though there was no chance that they, too, were carriers.

The thing was: The disease, if they had it, had come to the brothers through their paternal grandmother, who was the second wife of their paternal grandfather, and

89

who had only one child—their father, the Ecuadorian sculptor and architect, Sebastian von Kleist.

How bad a defect was it? Well—it was certainly a lot worse than having a child all covered with fur.

In fact, of all the horrible diseases known to Mandarax, Huntington's chorea may have been the worst. It was surely the most treacherous, the nastiest, of all surprises. It usually lay in ambush, and undetectable by any known test, until the wretch who had inherited it was well into his or her adult years. The father of the brothers, for example, led an unclouded and productive life until he was fifty-four—at which time he began to dance involuntarily, and to see things which weren't there. And then he killed his wife, a fact which was hushed up. The murder was reported to the police, and so treated by them, as a household accident.

• • •

So these two brothers had been expecting to go crazy at any moment, to start dancing and hallucinating, for twenty-five years now. Each one had a fifty-fifty chance of doing that. If either one went crazy, that would be proof that he could pass on the defect to yet another generation. If either one became an old, old man without going crazy, that would be proof that he was not a carrier, nor would any of his descendants be carriers, either. It would turn out that he might have reproduced with impunity.

• • •

As things turned out, the flip of a coin, the Captain was not a carrier, but his brother was. At least poor *Siegfried wasn't going to suffer long. He started going crazy when he had only a few more hours to live—on the afternoon of Thursday, November 27, 1986. There he was, standing in back of the bar at the El Dorado, with James Wait seated before him and the portrait of Charles Darwin at his back. He had just seen his most trustworthy employee, Jesús Ortiz, go out the front door, terribly upset about something.

And then *Siegfried's big brain had him swoon into madness for a moment, and then back to sanity again.

• • •

At that early stage of the disease, the only stage the unlucky brother would know, it was still possible for his soul to recognize that his brain had become dangerous, and to help him maintain a semblance of mental health through sheer willpower. So he kept a straight face and tried to return to business as usual by putting a question to Wait.

"What do you do for a living, Mr. Flemming?" he inquired.

When *Siegfried spoke these words, they came back to him hellishly, as though he were shouting into an empty steel barrel at the top of his lungs. He had become extremely sensitive to noises.

And Wait's reply, although spoken softly, was also an ear splitter. "I used to be an engineer," said Wait, "but I lost interest in that and in everything, to tell the truth, after my wife died. I guess you'd call me a survivor now."

•   •   •

So Jesús Ortiz left the hotel after having been so hideously insulted by *Andrew MacIntosh. He intended to walk all over the neighborhood until he had calmed down some. But he soon discovered that barbed wire and soldiers had turned the area around the hotel into a cordon sanitaire. The necessity for such a barrier was also evident. Crowds of people of all ages on the other side of the wire looked at him as soulfully as had Kazakh, the seeing-eye dog, hoping against hope that he might have food for them.

He stayed within the fence, and walked around the hotel again and again. On each of three laps he passed the open doorway of the laundry room. Right inside was a gray steel box fixed to the wall. He knew what it contained: the junctions which married the hotel's telephones to the outside world. A good citizen of a million years ago might have thought of such a box, "What the telephone company hath joined together, let no man put asunder."

Yes, and such was the overt sentiment in the brain of Jesús Ortiz. He would never harm a box that important to so many people. But brains back then were so big that they could actually deceive their owners. His brain wanted him to disconnect all the telephones the first time he went past the laundry room, but it knew how opposed his soul was to bad citizenship. So, in order to keep him from becoming paralyzed, his brain kept reassuring him, in effect, "No, no—of course we would never do such a thing."

On the fourth lap, it got him into the laundry room, but also gave him a cover story for what he was doing in there. Good citizen that he was, he was searching for the green pants suit of a hotel guest, Mary Hepburn, which had apparently disappeared into some other universe the night before.

And then he opened the box and ripped apart the junctions. In a matter of seconds, a typical brain of a million years ago had turned the best citizen in Guayaquil into a ravening terrorist.

17

On THE ISLAND OF MANHATTAN, a middle-aged American publicity man contemplated the collapse of his masterpiece, which was "the Nature Cruise of the Century." He had just moved into new offices within the hollow crown of the Chrysler Building, formerly the showroom of a harp company which found itself bankrupt— like the City of Ilium and Ecuador and the Philippines and Turkey, and on and on. His name was Bobby King.

He was in the same time zone as Guayaquil, and a line drawn due south from the deep crease in his brow to just below the equator would have found a terminal in an even deeper crease in the brow of *Andrew MacIntosh in Guayaquil. *MacIntosh was trying to shout life into a dead telephone. *MacIntosh might as well have been holding a stuffed Galápagos marine iguana alongside his boxy head as he cried out ever more imperiously: "Hello! Hello!"

Bobby King had a stuffed Galápagos marine iguana on his desk; had in fact amused more than one visitor by pretending that he had mistaken it for his telephone, holding it alongside his head and saying, "Hello! Hello!"

He was in no joking mood now, though, surely. In his own way, he had done as much as Charles Darwin to make the Galápagos Islands famous—with a ten-month campaign of publicity and advertising which had persuaded millions of people all over the planet that the maiden voyage of the *Bahía de Darwin* would indeed be "the Nature Cruise of the Century." In the process, he had made celebrities of many of the islands' creatures, the flightless cormorants, the blue-footed boobies, the larcenous frigate birds, and on and on.

His clients were the Ministry of Travel of Ecuador, Ecuatoriana Airlines, and the owners of the Hotel El Dorado and the *Bahía de Darwin,* the paternal uncles of ★Siegfried and Captain Adolf von Kleist. Neither the hotel manager nor the Captain had to work for livings, incidentally. They were fabulously well to do through inheritance, but felt that they should keep busy all the same.

It now appeared certain to King, although he had not been told so yet, that his work had been for nothing, that "the Nature Cruise of the Century" would not take place.

As for the stuffed marine iguana on his desk: He had made that reptile the totemic animal for the cruise—had caused its image to be painted on either side of the *Bahía de Darwin*'s bow, and to appear as a logo in every ad and at the top of every publicity release.

In real life, the creature could be more than a meter long, and look as fearsome as a Chinese dragon. Actually, though, it was no more dangerous to life forms of any sort, with the exception of seaweed, than a liverwurst. Here is what its life is like in the present day, which is exactly what its life was like a million years ago:

It has no enemies, so it sits in one place, staring into the middle distance at nothing, wanting nothing, worried about nothing, until it is hungry. It then waddles down to the ocean and swims slowly and not all that ably until it is a few meters from shore. Then it dives like a submarine, and stuffs itself with seaweed, which is at that time indigestible. The seaweed is going to have to be cooked before it is digestible.

So the marine iguana pops to the surface, swims ashore, and sits on the lava in the sunshine again. It is using itself for a covered stewpot, getting hotter and hotter while the sunshine cooks the seaweed. It continues to stare into the middle distance at nothing, as before, but with this difference: It now spits up increasingly hot saltwater from time to time.

During the million years I have spent in these islands, the Law of Natural Selection has found no way to improve, or, for that matter, to worsen this particular survival scheme.

• • •

King knew that six persons had actually reached Guayaquil, and were in the Hotel El Dorado at that very moment, still expecting to take "the Nature Cruise of the Century." This was a minor shock to him. He had as-

sumed that those who had made their own arrangements
to get there would surely stay away, since the news from
the area was so bad.

He had the names of all six. One was entirely unknown to him; a Canadian named Willard Flemming.
That was actually James Wait, of course. King could not
imagine how this person had gotten onto the passenger
list, which, with the exception of Mary Hepburn and a
Japanese veterinarian and his wife, was supposed to be
composed of newsmakers and trend-setters of the highest
potency.

It puzzled King that Mary Hepburn was down there,
but not her husband, Roy. He hadn't heard that Roy was
dead. And he knew something about the Hepburns, even
though they were complete nobodies on a passenger list of
celebrities, because they were the very first persons to sign
up for "the Nature Cruise of the Century." That was at a
time when King had reason to doubt that any really famous person could be induced to make the trip.

When the Hepburns signed on, in fact, King had
played with the idea of turning them into mini-celebrities
somehow, with appearances on talk shows and newspaper
interviews and so on. He would never meet them, but he
did talk to Mary on the telephone, hoping against hope
that there might be something interesting about the
Hepburns, even though they held the most ordinary
sorts of jobs in a drab industrial town with the highest
unemployment rate in the country. One or the other
might have a famous ancestor or relative, or Roy might

have been a hero in some war, or they might have won a lottery, or they might have suffered a recent tragedy, or whatever.

And parts of King's conversation with Mary back in January had gone like this:

"Well—I am a distant relative of Daniel Boone," she said. "My maiden name was Boone, and I was born in Kentucky."

"That's wonderful!" said King. "You're his great-great-great-granddaughter or what?"

"I don't think it's quite that direct," she said. "It never meant much to me, so I never tried to get it straight."

"But your maiden name was Boone."

"Yes, but that's just a coincidence. My father's name was Boone, but he wasn't any relative of Daniel Boone. I'm related to Daniel Boone on my mother's side."

"If your father's name was Boone, and he was a Kentuckian, then he had to be related to Daniel Boone some way, don't you think?" said King.

"Not necessarily," she said, "because his father was a horse trainer from Hungary named Miklós Gömbös, who changed his name to Michael Boone."

On the subject of prizes or honors she or Roy might have won, Mary said that her husband certainly deserved plenty of them for all the good work he had done at GEFFCo, but that that company didn't believe in anything of that sort except for its very top executives.

"No military medals—nothing like that," he said.

"He was in the Navy," she said, "but he didn't fight."

If King had called three months later, of course, and gotten Roy on the phone, he would have received an earful about Roy's tragic exploits during the bomb tests in the Pacific.

"You have children?" said King.

"Not in the usual sense," said Mary. "But I consider every student a child of mine, and Roy is active in scouting, and he considers every member of his troop to be a son of his."

"That's a wonderful attitude," said King, "and it has been awfully nice to talk to you, and I hope you and your husband enjoy the trip."

"I'm sure we will," she said, "but I still have to get up enough nerve to tell the principal that I want three weeks off right in the middle of a semester."

"You'll have so many wonderful things to tell your students when you get back," said King, "that he'll be glad to let you go." King, incidentally, had never seen the Galápagos Islands firsthand, and never would. Like Mary Hepburn, he had certainly seen plenty of pictures of them.

"Oh—" said Mary as he was about to hang up, "you were asking about honors and prizes and medals and all that . . ."

"Yes?" said King.

"I'm just about to get a kind of prize, or what feels like a prize to me. I'm not supposed to know about it, so I probably shouldn't tell you about it."

"My lips are sealed," said King.

"I just happened to find out about it by accident," said Mary. "But this year's senior class is going to dedicate its yearbook to me. They give me a nickname in the dedication, which I just happened to see in a printshop where I was picking up some birth announcements for a friend. She had twins—a boy and a girl."

"Aha!" said King.

"Do you know the nickname those nice young people are giving me?" said Mary.

"No," said King.

" 'Mother Nature Personified,' " said Mary.

• • •

And there are no tombs in the Galápagos Islands. The ocean gets all the bodies to use as it will. But if there were a tombstone for Mary Hepburn, no other inscription would do but this one: "Mother Nature Personified." In what way was she so like Mother Nature? In the face of utter hopelessness on Santa Rosalia, she still wanted human babies to be born there. Nothing could keep her from doing all she could to keep life going on and on and on.

18

WHEN BOBBY KING heard that Mary Hepburn was one of the six unfortunate enough to have reached Guayaquil, he thought about her for the first time in months. He thought that perhaps Roy was with her, since they had sounded like such an inseparable couple, and that his name had been omitted accidentally by the Hotel El Dorado's manager, whose teletyped communications were becoming more hectic by the hour.

• • •

King knew about me, by the way, although not by name.

He knew a workman had been killed during the building of the ship.

But he no more wanted to publicize this piece of information, which might imply to the superstitious that the *Bahía de Darwin* had a ghost, than the von Kleist family wished it known that one of its members was hospitalized with Huntington's chorea, and that two more of its members had a fifty-fifty chance of being carriers of that disease.

• • •

Did the Captain ever tell Mary Hepburn during their years together on Santa Rosalia that he might be a carrier of Huntington's chorea? He revealed that terrible secret only after they had been marooned ten years, and he realized that she had been playing fast and loose with his sperm.

• • •

Of the six guests at the El Dorado, King was acquainted with only two: *Andrew MacIntosh and his blind daughter Selena—and, of course, Kazakh, Selena's dog. Anybody who knew the MacIntoshes also knew the dog, although Kazakh, thanks to surgery and training, had virtually no personality. The MacIntoshes were frequenters of several restaurants which were King's clients, and *MacIntosh, but not the dog and the daughter, had been on talk shows with some of his clients. King had watched the shows with Selena and the dog on a backstage monitor. It was his impression that the daughter had little more personality than the dog when she wasn't right next to her father. And her father was all she could talk about.

*Andrew MacIntosh certainly enjoyed his exposure on talk shows. He was a welcome guest on them because he was so outrageous. He held forth about what fun life was if you had unlimited money to spend. He pitied and scorned people who weren't rich, and so on.

Thanks to the rigors of Santa Rosalia, Selena would develop a personality very distinct from her father's before she went down the blue tunnel into the Afterlife. She would also be fluent in Japanese. In the era of big brains, life stories could end up any which way.

Look at mine.

• • •

After Roy and Mary Hepburn, the MacIntoshes and the Hiroguchis were the next people to join the passenger list for "the Nature Cruise of the Century." That was in February. The Hiroguchis were to be *MacIntosh's guests, and they would travel under false names, so that *Zenji Hiroguchi's employers would not discover that he was negotiating a business deal with *MacIntosh.

As far as King and *Siegfried von Kleist and anybody else connected with the cruise knew, the Hiroguchis were the Kenzaburos, and *Zenji was a veterinarian.

That meant that fully half of the guests at the El Dorado weren't who they were supposed to be. As a fillip to all this big-brained deceiving going on, Mary Hepburn's war-surplus combat fatigues still bore the embroidered last name of their previous owner over the left breast pocket, which was Kaplan. And when she and James Wait finally met in the cocktail lounge, he would tell her his false name and she would tell him her true name, but he would keep calling her "Mrs. Kaplan" anyway, and extol the Jewish people and so on.

And they would later be married by the Captain on the sundeck of the *Bahía de Darwin,* and as far as she knew, she had become the wife of Willard Flemming, and as far as he knew, he had become the husband of Mary Kaplan.

This sort of confusion would be impossible in the present day, since nobody has a name anymore—or a profession, or a life story to tell. All that anybody has in the way of a reputation anymore is an odor which, from birth to death, cannot be modified. People are who they are, and that is that. The Law of Natural Selection has made human beings absolutely honest in that regard. Everybody is exactly what he or she seems to be.

• • •

When *Andrew MacIntosh signed up for three staterooms on the *Bahía de Darwin*'s maiden voyage, Bobby King had reason to be mystified. *MacIntosh had a private yacht, the *Omoo,* which was nearly as large as the cruise ship, and so could have gone to the Galápagos Islands on his own—without submitting to the close contacts with strangers and the disciplines which would be imposed by "the Nature Cruise of the Century." The cruise passengers, for example, would not be able to go ashore whenever they pleased, and to behave there however they pleased. They were to be escorted and supervised at all times by guides, all of them trained by scientists at the Darwin Research Station on Santa Cruz Island, and all of them holding graduate degrees in one of the natural sciences.

So when King, making his rounds of restaurants and clubs one night, saw *MacIntosh and his daughter and her dog and two other people having a late supper in a celebrity hangout called Elaine's, he stopped by their table to say how pleased he was that they were taking the cruise. He wanted very much to hear why they were taking it— so that he might use their reasons as inducements for other newsmakers to come along.

Only after greeting the MacIntoshes did King realize who the other two people at the table were. He knew them both to speak to, and he did so now. The woman was the most admired female on the planet, Mrs. Jacqueline Bouvier Kennedy Onassis, and her escort that evening was the great dancer Rudolf Nureyev.

Nureyev, incidentally, was a former citizen of the Soviet Union, who had been granted political asylum in Great Britain. And I was still alive then, and I was a United States citizen who had been granted political asylum in Sweden.

Yes, and we both liked to dance.

• • •

At the risk of reminding *MacIntosh that he owned an oceangoing yacht, King asked him what he had found so attractive about the *Bahía de Darwin*. *MacIntosh, who was highly intelligent and well read, thereupon delivered a speech on the damage selfish and ignorant persons had done to the Galápagos Islands while going ashore unsupervised. This material was all lifted from an article in the *National Geographic* magazine, which he read from cover to cover every month. The magazine's point was that Ecuador would require a navy the size of the combined fleets of the world to keep persons from going ashore on the islands and doing as they pleased, so that the fragile habitats could be preserved only if individuals were educated to exercise self-restraint. "No good citizen of the planet," said the article, "should ever go ashore unless escorted by a well-trained guide."

• • •

When Mary Hepburn and the Captain and Hisako Hiroguchi and Selena MacIntosh and the rest of them were marooned on Santa Rosalia, they would not have a trained guide along. And, for their first few years there, they would raise perfect hell with the fragile habitat.

Just in the nick of time they realized that it was their own habitat they were wrecking—that they weren't merely visitors.

• • •

There in Elaine's Restaurant, *MacIntosh angered his spellbound audience with tales of boots crushing the camouflaged nests of iguanas, of greedy fingers stealing the eggs of boobies, and on and on. His most moving atrocity story by far, though, again lifted from the *National Geographic,* was of persons cradling fur seal pups in their arms as though they were human infants—for the sake of photographs. When the pup was returned to its mother, he said bitterly, she would no longer nurse it because its smell had been changed.

"So what happens to that darling pup, which has just had the great honor of being cuddled by a bighearted nature lover?" asked *MacIntosh. "It starves to death—all for the sake of a photograph."

So his answer to Bobby King's question was that he was setting a good example he hoped others would follow by taking "the Nature Cruise of the Century."

• • •

It is a joke to me that this man should have presented himself as an ardent conservationist, since so many of the companies he served as a director or in which he was a major stockholder were notorious damagers of the water or the soil or the atmosphere. But it wasn't a joke to *MacIntosh, who had come into this world incapable of caring much about anything. So, in order to hide this deficiency, he had become a great actor, pretending even to himself that he cared passionately about all sorts of things.

With the same degree of conviction, he had earlier given his daughter an entirely different explanation of why they were going to the islands on the *Bahía de Darwin* instead of the *Omoo*. The Hiroguchis might feel trapped on the *Omoo,* with nobody but the MacIntoshes to talk to. They might panic under such circumstances, and *Zenji might refuse to negotiate anymore, and ask to be put ashore at the nearest port so that he and his wife could fly back home.

Like so many other pathological personalities in positions of power a million years ago, he might do almost anything on impulse, feeling nothing much. The logical explanations for his actions, invented at leisure, always came afterwards.

And let that sort of behavior back in the era of the big brains be taken as a capsule history of the war I had the honor to fight in, which was the Vietnam War.

19

Like most pathological personalities, *Andrew MacIntosh never cared much whether what he said was true or not—and so he was tremendously persuasive. And he so moved the widow Onassis and Rudolf Nureyev that they asked Bobby King for more information about "the Nature Cruise of the Century," which he sent to them on the following morning by special messenger.

As luck would have it, there was going to be a documentary about the lives of blue-footed boobies on the islands shown on educational television that evening, so King enclosed notes saying that they might want to watch it. These birds would later become crucial to the survival of the little human colony on Santa Rosalia. If those birds hadn't been so stupid, so incapable of learning that human beings were dangerous, the first settlers would almost certainly have starved to death.

• • •

The high point of that program, like the high point of Mary Hepburn's lectures on the islands at Ilium High

School, was film footage of the courtship dance of the blue-footed boobies. The dance went like this:

There were these two fairly large sea birds standing around on the lava. They were about the size of flightless cormorants, and had the same long, snaky necks and fish-spear beaks. But they had not given up on aviation, and so had big, strong wings. Their legs and webbed feet were bright, rubbery blue. They caught fish by crashing down on them from the sky.

Fish! Fish! Fish!

They looked alike, although one was a male and the other was a female. They seemed to be on separate errands, and not interested in each other in the least—although there wasn't much business for either one of them to do on the lava, since they didn't eat bugs or seeds. They weren't looking for nesting materials, since it was much too early in the game for that.

The male stopped doing what he was so busy doing, which was nothing. He caught sight of the female. He looked away from her, and then back again, standing still and making no sound. They both had voices, but at no point in the dance would either make a sound.

She looked this way and that, and then her gaze met his accidentally. They were then five meters apart or more.

When Mary showed the film of the dance at the high school, she used to say at this point, as though she were speaking for the female: "What on Earth could this strange person want with me? Really! How bizarre!"

The male raised one bright blue foot. He spread it in air like a paper fan.

Mary Hepburn, again in the persona of the female, used to say, "What is that supposed to be? A Wonder of the World? Does he think that's the only blue foot in the islands?"

The male put that foot down and raised the other one, bringing himself one pace closer to the female. Then he showed her the first one again, and then the second one again, looking her straight in the eye.

Mary would say for her, "I'm getting out of here." But the female didn't get out of there. She seemed glued to the lava as the male showed her one foot and then the other one, coming closer all the time.

And then the female raised one of her blue feet, and Mary used to say, "You think you've got such beautiful feet? Take a look at this, if you want to see a beautiful foot. Yes, and I've got another one, too."

The female put down one foot and raised the other one, bringing herself one pace closer to the male.

Mary used to shut up then. There would be no more anthropomorphic jokes. It was up to the birds now to carry the show. Advancing toward each other in the same grave and stately manner, neither bird speeding up or slowing down, they were at last breast to breast and toe to toe.

At Ilium High School, the students did not expect to see the birds copulate. The film was so famous, since Mary had shown it in the auditorium in early May, as an educational celebration of springtime, for years and years, that everybody knew that they would not get to see the birds copulate.

What those birds did on camera, though, was supremely erotic all the same. Already breast-to breast and toe to toe, they made their sinuous necks as erect as flagpoles. They tilted their heads back as far as they would go. They pressed their long throats and the undersides of their jaws together. They formed a tower, the two of them—a single structure, pointed on top and resting on four blue feet.

Thus was a marriage solemnized.

There were no witnesses, no other boobies to celebrate what a nice couple they were or how well they had danced. In the film Mary Hepburn used to show at the high school, which was the same film Bobby King thought Mrs. Onassis and Rudolf Nureyev might enjoy watching on educational television, the only witnesses were the big-brained members of the camera crew.

The name of the film was *Sky-Pointing,* the same name big-brained scientists gave to the moment when the beaks of both birds were pointed in the direction exactly opposite to the pull of gravity.

And Mrs. Onassis was so moved by this film that she had her secretary call Bobby King the next morning, to inquire if it was too late to reserve two outside staterooms on the main deck of the *Bahía de Darwin* for "the Nature Cruise of the Century."

20

MARY HEPBURN used to give her students extra credit if they would write a little poem or essay about the courtship dance. Something like half of them would turn something in, and about half who did thought the dance was proof that animals worshiped God. The rest of the responses were all over the place. One student turned in a poem which Mary would remember to her dying day, and which she taught to Mandarax. The student was named Noble Claggett, and he would be killed in the war in Vietnam—but there his poem would be inside of Mandarax, along with bits by some of the greatest writers who ever lived. It went like this:

> *Of course I love you,*
> *So let's have a kid*
> *Who will say exactly*
> *What its parents did;*
> *"Of course I love you,*
> *So let's have a kid*
> *Who will say exactly*
> *What its parents did;*

> *'Of course I love you,*
> *So let's have a kid*
> *Who will say exactly*
> *What its parents did—' "*
> *Et cetera.*

> —NOBLE CLAGGETT
> (1947–1966)

Some students would ask permission to write about some other Galápagos Islands creature, and Mary, being such a good teacher, would of course answer, "Yes." And the favorite alternates were those teasers and robbers of the boobies, the great frigate birds. These James Waits of the bird world survived on fish which boobies caught, and got their nesting materials from nests which boobies built. A certain sort of student found this hilarious, and such a student was almost invariably male.

And a unique physical feature of male great frigate birds was also bound to attract the attention of immature human males concerned with erectile performances of their own sex organs. Each male great frigate bird at mating time tried to attract the attention of females by inflating a bright red balloon at the base of his throat. At mating time, a typical rookery when viewed from the air resembled an enormous party for human children, at which every child had received a red balloon. The island would in fact be paved with male great frigate birds with their heads tilted back, their qualifications as husbands inflated by their lungs to the bursting point—while, over-head, the females wheeled.

One by one the females would drop from the sky, having chosen this or that red balloon.

• • •

After Mary Hepburn showed her film about the great frigate birds, and the windowshades in the classroom were raised and the lights turned back on, some student, again almost invariably a male, was sure to ask, sometimes clinically, sometimes as a comedian, sometimes bitterly, hating and fearing women: "Do the females always try to pick the biggest ones?"

So Mary was ready with a reply as consistent, word by word, as any quotation known by Mandarax: "To answer that, we would have to interview female great frigate birds, and no one has done that yet, so far as I know. Some people have devoted their lives to studying them, though, and it is their opinion that the females are in fact choosing the red balloons which mark the best nesting sites. That makes sense in terms of survival, you see.

"And that brings us back to the really deep mystery of the blue-footed boobies' courtship dance, which seems to have absolutely no connection with the elements of booby survival, with nesting or fish. What does it have to do with, then? Dare we call it 'religion'? Or, if we lack that sort of courage, might we at least call it 'art'?

"Your comments, please."

• • •

The courtship dance of the blue-footed boobies, which Mrs. Onassis suddenly wanted to see so much in person, has not changed one iota in a million years. Neither have these birds learned to be afraid of anything. Neither have they shown the slightest inclination to give up on aviation and become submarines.

As for the meaning of the courtship dance of the blue-footed boobies: The birds are huge molecules with bright blue feet and have no choice in the matter. By their very nature, they have to dance exactly like that.

Human beings used to be molecules which could do many, many different sorts of dances, or decline to dance at all—as they pleased. My mother could do the waltz, the tango, the rumba, the Charleston, the Lindy hop, the jitterbug, the Watusi, and the twist. Father refused to do any dances, as was his privilege.

21

WHEN MRS. ONASSIS said she wanted to go on "the Nature Cruise of the Century," then everybody wanted to go, and Roy and Mary Hepburn were almost entirely forgotten, with their pitiful little cabin below the waterline. By the end of March, King was able to release a passenger list headed by Mrs. Onassis, and followed by names almost as glamorous as hers—Dr. Henry Kissinger, Mick Jagger, Paloma Picasso, William F. Buckley, Jr., and of course *Andrew MacIntosh, and Rudolf Nureyev and Walter Cronkite, and on and on. *Zenji Hiroguchi, traveling under the name Zenji Kenzaburo, was said in the release to be a world famous expert in animal diseases, so as to make him seem more or less in scale with all the other passengers.

Two names were left off the list as a matter of delicacy, so as not to raise the embarrassing question of who they were, exactly, since they were really nobody at all. They were Roy and Mary Hepburn, with their pitiful little cabin below the waterline.

But then this slightly bobtailed list became the official list. So when Ecuatoriana Airlines in May sent a telegram to everybody on the list, notifying them that there would be a special overnight flight for any of them who happened to be in New York City on the evening before the *Bahía de Darwin* was to sail, Mary Hepburn was not among those notified. Limousines would pick them up anywhere in the city, and take them to the airport. Each seat on the plane could be converted into a bed, and the tourist seats had been replaced with cabaret tables and a dance floor, where a company from the Ecuadorian Ballet Folklórico would perform characteristic dances of various Indian tribes, including the fire dance of the elusive Kanka-bonos. Gourmet meals would be served, along with wines worthy of the greatest restaurants in France. All this would be free of charge, but Roy and Mary Hepburn never heard about it.

Yes, and they never got a letter that everybody else got in June—from Dr. José Sepúlveda de la Madrid, the president of Ecuador, inviting them to a state breakfast in their honor at the Hotel El Dorado, followed by a parade in which they would ride in horse-drawn carriages decked with flowers—from the hotel to the waterfront, where they would board the ship.

Nor did Mary get a telegram King sent to everybody else on the first of November, which acknowledged that storm clouds on the economic horizon were indeed worrisome. The economy of Ecuador, however, remained sound, so that there was no reason to believe that the *Bahía de Darwin* would not sail as planned. What the letter didn't say, although King knew it, was that the passenger list had been cut approximately in half by cancellations from virtually every country represented there but Japan and the United States. So that almost everybody still intent on going would be on that special flight from New York City.

And now King's secretary came into his office to tell him that she had just heard on the radio that the State Department had just advised American citizens not to travel in Ecuador at the present time.

So that was that for what King considered the finest piece of work he had ever done. Without knowing anything about naval architecture, he had made a ship more attractive by persuading its owners not to call it, as they were about to do, the *Antonio José de Sucre,* but the *Bahía de Darwin.* He had transformed what was to have been a routine, two-week trip out to the islands and back into the nature cruise of the century. How had he worked such a miracle? By never calling it anything but "the Nature Cruise of the Century."

If, as now seemed certain to King, the *Bahía de Darwin* would not set out on "the Nature Cruise of the Century" at noon the next day, certain side effects of his campaign would endure. He had taught people a lot of natural history with his publicity releases about the wonders which Mrs. Onassis and Dr. Kissinger and Mick Jagger and so on would see. He had created two new celebrities: Robert Pépin, the chef King had declared to be "the greatest chef in France" after hiring him to run the galley for the maiden voyage, and Captain Adolf von Kleist, the captain of the *Bahía de Darwin*, who, with his big nose and air of hiding some unspeakable personal tragedy from the world, had turned out to be on television talk shows a first-rate comedian.

King had in his files a transcript of the Captain's performance on *The Tonight Show*, starring Johnny Carson. On that show, as on all the others, the Captain was dazzling in the gold-and-white uniform he was entitled to wear as an admiral in the Ecuadorian Naval Reserve. The transcript went like this:

• • •

CARSON: "Von Kleist" doesn't sound like a very South American name somehow.

CAPTAIN: It's Inca—one of the commonest Inca names, in fact, like "Smith" or "Jones" in English. You read the accounts of the Spanish explorers who destroyed the Inca Empire because it was so un-Christian—

CARSON: Yes—?

CAPTAIN: I assume you've read them.

CARSON: They're on my bedside table—along with *Ecstasy and Me,* the autobiography of Hedy Lamarr.

CAPTAIN: Then you know that one out of every three Indians they burned for heresy was named von Kleist.

CARSON: How big is the Ecuadorian navy?

CAPTAIN: Four submarines. They are always under-water. They never come up.

CARSON: Never come up?

CAPTAIN: Not for years and years.

CARSON: But they keep in touch by radio?

CAPTAIN: No. They maintain radio silence. It's their own idea. We would be glad to hear from them, but they prefer to maintain radio silence.

CARSON: Why have they stayed underwater so long?

CAPTAIN: You will have to ask them about that. Ecuador is a democracy, you know. Even those of us in the Navy have very wide latitude in what we can or cannot do.

CARSON: Some people think Hitler might still be alive—and living in South America. Do you think there's any chance of that?

CAPTAIN: I know there are persons in Ecuador who would love to have him for dinner.

CARSON: Nazi sympathizers.

CAPTAIN: I don't know about that. It's possible, I suppose.

CARSON: If they would be glad to have Hitler for dinner—

CAPTAIN: Then they must be cannibals. I was thinking of the Kanka-bonos. They are glad to have almost anybody for dinner. They are—what is the English word? It's on the tip of my tongue.

CARSON: I think I'll pass on this one.

CAPTAIN: They are—they are—the Kanka-bonos are—

CARSON: Take your time.

CAPTAIN: Aha! They are "apolitical." That's the word. Apolitical is what the Kanka-bonos are.

CARSON: But they are citizens of Ecuador?

CAPTAIN: Yes. Of course. I told you it was a democracy. One cannibal, one vote.

CARSON: There is a question which several ladies have asked me to ask you, and maybe it is too personal—

CAPTAIN: Why a man of my beauty and charm should never have tasted the joys of marriage?

CARSON: I've had some experience in these matters myself—as you may or may not know.

CAPTAIN: It would not be fair to the woman.

CARSON: Now things are getting too personal. Let's talk about blue-footed boobies. Maybe now is the time to show the film you brought.

CAPTAIN: No, no. I'm perfectly willing to discuss my failure to plight a troth. It would not be fair of me to marry a woman, since at any time I might be given command of a submarine.

CARSON: And you would have to go under, and never come up again.

CAPTAIN: That is the tradition.

• • •

King sighed massively. The passenger list was on his desktop, with about half the names crossed off—Mexicans and Argentinians and Italians and Filipinos, and so on, foolish enough to have kept their fortunes in their own national currencies. The names remaining, save for the six persons already in Guayaquil, were all in the New York City area, easily reached by telephone.

"I guess we have some telephoning to do," King said to his secretary.

She offered to do the calling. He said, "No." It was not a duty he felt free to delegate. He had persuaded all these celebrities to take part in the cruise, had wooed the most potent newsmakers among them as a lover might. Now he was going to have to give them the bad news personally, as a responsible lover should. At least he wouldn't have much trouble finding most of them. There were forty-two of them, counting mates or companions who were nonentities, but they had organized themselves into a few dinner parties, duly reported in gossip columns that day, in order to pass pleasantly the hours remaining until limousines came to cushion and muffle them away to Kennedy International Airport—for Ecuatoriana's special ten o'clock flight to Guayaquil.

And at least he wouldn't have to talk about getting back their money for them. The trip wasn't to have cost them a nickel—and they had already received free matched luggage and toiletries, and Panama hats besides.

For the sad amusement of himself and his secretary, King now played his joke with the stuffed marine iguana. He picked it up and held it alongside his head as though it were a telephone, and he said, "Mrs. Onassis? I am afraid I have some disappointing news for you. You're not going to get to see the courtship dance of the blue-footed boobies after all."

• • •

King's apologetic telephoning was a gallant formality. No one still expected to board the plane at ten that night. By ten that night, incidentally, *Andrew MacIntosh, Zenji Hiroguchi, and the Captain's brother *Siegfried would all be dead, and would all have completed their short journeys through the blue tunnel into the Afterlife.

All the people on the passenger list that King talked to had already made new plans for the coming two weeks. Many would go skiing within the safe boundaries of the United States instead. At one dinner party for six, everybody had already decided to go to a combination fat farm and tennis camp in Phoenix, Arizona.

And the last call King made before leaving his office was to a man who had become a very close friend during the past ten months, who was Dr. Teodoro Donoso, a poet and physician from Quito, who was Ecuador's ambassador to the United Nations. He had earned his medical degree at Harvard, and several other Ecuadorians King had dealt with had been educated in the United States. The Captain of the *Bahía de Darwin,* Adolf von Kleist, was a graduate of the United States Naval Academy at Annapolis. The Captain's brother *Siegfried was a graduate of the Cornell Hotel School at Ithaca, New York.

There was a lot of noise from what sounded like a wild party going on at the embassy, which Dr. Donoso suppressed by closing a door.

"What are those people celebrating?" King asked.

"It's the Ballet Folklórico," said the Ambassador, "rehearsing the fire dance of the Kanka-bonos."

"They don't know the trip's been called off?" said King.

It turned out that they did know, and that they intended to stay in the United States in order to earn dollars for their families back home by performing in nightclubs and theaters a dance Bobby King had made so famous in his publicity—the fire dance of the Kanka-bonos.

"Are there any real Kanka-bonos in the bunch?" said King.

"My guess is that there aren't any real Kanka-bonos anywhere," said the Ambassador. He had in fact written a twenty-six-line poem called "The Last Kanka-bono," about the extinction of a little tribe in the Ecuadorian rain forest. At the start of the poem, there were eleven Kanka-bonos. At the end there was just one, and he wasn't feeling well. This was an exercise in fiction, however, since the poet, like most Ecuadorians, had never seen a Kanka-bono. He had heard that the tribe was down to only fourteen members, so that their final extinction by the encroachments of civilization seemed inevitable.

Little did he know that in a matter of less than a century the blood of every human being on earth would be predominantly Kanka-bono, with a little von Kleist and Hiroguchi thrown in.

And this astonishing turn of events would be made to happen, in large part, by one of the only two absolute nobodies on the original passenger list for "the Nature Cruise of the Century." That was Mary Hepburn. The other nobody was her husband, who himself played a crucial role in shaping human destiny by booking, when facing his own extinction, that one cheap little cabin below the waterline.

22

AMBASSADOR DONOSO'S twenty-six lines of mourning for "The Last Kanka-bono" were premature, to say the least. He should have wept on paper for "The Last Mainland South American" and "The Last Mainland North American" and "The Last Mainland European" and "The Last Mainland African" and "The Last Mainland Asian" instead.

He guessed right, at any rate, as to what was going to happen to the morale of the people of Ecuador within the next hour or so, when he said to Bobby King on the telephone: "Everybody down there is just going to fall apart when they find out that Mrs. Onassis isn't coming after all."

"Things can change so much in just thirty days," said King. " 'The Nature Cruise of the Century' was supposed to be just one of many things Ecuadorians had to look forward to. Suddenly it became the only thing."

"It is as though we prepared a great crystal bowl of champagne punch," said Donoso, "and then, overnight, it turned into a rusty bucket of nitroglycerin." He said that "the Nature Cruise of the Century" had at least post-poned Ecuador's facing up to its insoluble economic problems for a week or two. The governments of Colombia to the north and Peru to the south and east had already been overthrown, and were now military dictatorships. The new leaders of Peru, in fact, in order to divert the big brains of their people from all their troubles, were just about to declare war on Ecuador.

• • •

"If Mrs. Onassis were to go there now," said Donoso, "people would receive her as though she were a rescuer, a worker of miracles. She would be expected to summon ships laden with food to Guayaquil—and to have United States bombers drop cereal and milk and fresh fruit for the children by parachute!"

Nobody nowadays, I must say, expects to be rescued from anything, once he or she is more than nine months old. That's how long human childhood lasts nowadays.

• • •

I myself was rescued from folly and carelessness until I was ten years old—until Mother walked out on Father and me. I was on my own after that. Mary Hepburn didn't become independent of her parents until she received her master's degree at the age of twenty-two. Adolf von Kleist, the Captain of the *Bahía de Darwin,* was regularly bailed out by his parents from gambling debts and charges of drunken driving and assault and resisting arrest and vandalism and so on until he was twenty-six—when his father came down with Huntington's chorea and murdered his mother. Only then did he begin to assume responsibility for mistakes he made.

Back when childhoods were often so protracted, it is unsurprising that so many people got into the lifelong habit of believing, even after their parents were gone, that somebody was always watching over them—God or a saint or a guardian angel or the stars or whatever.

People have no such illusions today. They learn very early what kind of a world this really is, and it is a rare adult indeed who hasn't seen a careless sibling or parent eaten alive by a killer whale or shark.

• • •

A million years ago, there were passionate arguments about whether it was right or wrong for people to use mechanical means to keep sperm from fertilizing ova or to dislodge fertilized ova from uteri—in order to keep the number of people from exceeding the food supply.

That problem is all taken care of nowadays, without anybody's having to do anything unnatural. Killer whales and sharks keep the human population nice and manageable, and nobody starves.

• • •

Mary Hepburn used to teach not only general biology at Ilium High School, but a course in human sexuality, too. This necessitated her describing various birth-control devices which she herself had never used, since her husband was the only lover she had ever had, and she and Roy had wanted to have babies from the very first.

She, who had failed to get pregnant despite years of profound sexual intimacies with Roy, had to admonish her students about how easy it was for a human female to get pregnant from the most fleeting, insensate, seemingly inconsequential contact with a male. And after she had been teaching a few years, most of her cautionary tales involved students she had known personally—right there at Ilium High.

Scarcely a semester passed at the high school without at least one unwanted pregnancy, and during the memorable spring semester of 1981 there were six. And, true enough, about half of these babies having babies spoke of true love for those with whom they had mated. But the other half swore, in the face of contradictory evidence which could only be described as overwhelming, that they had never, to the best of their recollection, engaged in any activity which could result in the birth of a child.

And Mary would say to a female colleague at the end of the memorable spring semester of 1981, "For some people, getting pregnant is as easy as catching cold." And there certainly was an analogy there: Colds and babies were both caused by germs which loved nothing so much as a mucous membrane.

• • •

After ten years on Santa Rosalia Island, Mary Hepburn would discover firsthand exactly how easily a teenage virgin could be made pregnant by the seed of a male who was seeking sexual release and nothing else, who did not even like her.

23

So, WITHOUT ANY IDEA that he was going to become the sire of all humankind, I got into the head of
Captain Adolf von Kleist as he rode in a taxicab from
Guayaquil International Airport to the *Bahía de Darwin*. I
did not know that humanity was about to be diminished
to a tiny point, by luck, and then, again by luck, to be
permitted to expand again. I believed that the chaos in-
volving billions of big-brained people thrashing around
every which way, and reproducing and reproducing,
would go on and on. It did not seem likely that an individual could be significant in such an unplanned uproar.

My choosing the Captain's head for a vehicle, then,
was the equivalent of putting a coin in a slot machine in
an enormous gambling casino, and hitting a jackpot right
away.

It was his uniform which attracted me as much as
anything. He was wearing the white-and-gold uniform of
a Reserve admiral. I myself had been a private, and so was
curious to know what the world looked like to a person
of very high military rank and social standing.

And I was mystified to find his big brain thinking

about meteorites. That was often my experience back then: I would get into the head of somebody in what to me was a particularly interesting situation, and discover that the person's big brain was thinking about things which had nothing to do with the problem right at hand.

Here was the thing about the Captain and meteorites: He had paid little attention to most of his instructors at the United States Naval Academy, and had graduated at the very bottom of his class. He in fact would have been expelled for cheating in an examination on celestial navigation, if his parents hadn't interceded through diplomatic channels. But he had been impressed by one lecture on the subject of meteorites. The instructor said that showers of great boulders from outer space had been quite common over the eons, and their impacts had been so terrific, possibly, as to have caused the extinction of many life forms, including the dinosaurs. He said that human beings had every reason to expect more such planet smashers at any time, and should devise apparatus for distinguishing between enemy missiles and meteorites.

Otherwise, utterly meaningless wrath from outer space could trigger World War Three.

And this apocalyptic warning so suited the wiring of the Captain's brain, even before his father came down with Huntington's chorea, that he would ever after believe that that was indeed the most likely way in which humanity would be exterminated: by meteorites.

To the Captain, it was such a much more honorable

and poetical and even beautiful way for humanity to die than World War Three would be.

• • •

When I got to know his big brain better, I understood that there was a certain logic to his thinking about meteorites while he was looking out at Guayaquil with its hungry crowds under martial law. Even without the glamor of a meteorite shower, the world appeared to be ending for the people of Guayaquil.

• • •

In a sense, too, this man had already been hit by a meteorite: by the murder of his mother by his father. And his feeling that life was a meaningless nightmare, with nobody watching or caring what was going on, was actually quite familiar to me.

That was how I felt after I shot a grandmother in Vietnam. She was as toothless and bent over as Mary Hepburn would be at the end of her life. I shot her because she had just killed my best friend and my worst enemy in my platoon with a single hand-grenade.

This episode made me sorry to be alive, made me envy stones. I would rather have been a stone at the service of the Natural Order.

• • •

The Captain went straight from the airport to his ship, without stopping off at the hotel to see his brother.

He had been drinking champagne during the long flight from New York City, and so had a splitting headache.

And when we got aboard the *Bahía de Darwin*, it was obvious to me that his functions as captain, like his functions as a Reserve admiral, were purely ceremonial. Others would be doing the navigating and engineering and maintaining crew discipline and so on while he socialized with the distinguished passengers. He knew very little about the operation of the ship, nor did he feel he needed to know much about it. His familiarity with the Galápagos Islands was likewise sketchy. He had made ceremonial visits as an admiral to the naval base on the island of Baltra and the Darwin Research Station on Santa Cruz—again as essentially a passenger on board a ship of which he was nominally the commander. But all the rest of the islands were terra incognita to him. He would have been a more instructive guide on the ski slopes of Switzerland, say, or on the carpets of the casino at Monte Carlo, or to the stables serving at Palm Beach polo fields.

But again—what did that matter? On "the Nature Cruise of the Century," there would be guides and lecturers trained at the Darwin Research Station and holding graduate degrees in the natural sciences. The Captain intended to listen to them carefully, and learn about the islands right along with the rest of the passengers.

• • •

Riding in the Captain's skull, I had hoped to find out what it was like to be a supreme commander. I found out, instead, what it was like to be a social butterfly. We were received with all possible signs of military respect when we came up the gangplank. But, once aboard, no officers or crewmen asked us for instructions about anything as they made the final preparations for the arrival of Mrs. Onassis and the rest of them.

So far as the Captain knew, the ship was still going to sail the next day. He had not been told otherwise. Since he had been back in Ecuador for only an hour, and still had a bellyful of good New York food and a champagne headache, it had yet to dawn on him what awful trouble he and his ship were in.

● ● ●

There is another human defect which the Law of Natural Selection has yet to remedy: When people of today have full bellies, they are exactly like their ancestors of a million years ago: very slow to acknowledge any awful troubles they may be in. Then is when they forget to keep a sharp lookout for sharks and whales.

This was a particularly tragic flaw a million years ago, since the people who were best informed about the state of the planet, like *Andrew MacIntosh, for example, and rich and powerful enough to slow down all the waste and destruction going on, were by definition well fed.

So everything was always just fine as far as they were concerned.

For all the computers and measuring instruments and news gatherers and evaluators and memory banks and libraries and experts on this and that at their disposal, their deaf and blind bellies remained the final judges of how urgent this or that problem, such as the destruction of North America's and Europe's forests by acid rain, say, might really be.

And here was the sort of advice a full belly gave and still gives, and which the Captain's full belly gave him when the first mate of the *Bahía de Darwin,* Hernando Cruz, told him that none of the guides had shown up or been heard from, and that a third of the crewmen had deserted so far, feeling that they had better look after their families: "Be patient. Smile. Be confident. Everything will turn out for the best somehow."

24

MARY HEPBURN had seen and appreciated the Captain's comical performance on *The Tonight Show,* and then another one on *Good Morning America.* To that extent, she felt she already knew him some before her big brain made her come to Guayaquil.

He was on *The Tonight Show* two weeks after Roy died, and he was the first person to make her laugh out loud after that sad event. There she was in the living room of her little house, with the houses on all sides of hers empty and for sale, and heard herself laugh out loud about the ridiculous Ecuadorian submarine fleet, whose tradition was to go underwater and never come up again.

She supposed then that von Kleist was a lot like Roy in loving nature and machinery. Otherwise, why would he have been chosen to be the Captain of the *Bahía de Darwin?*

Now her big brain had her say out loud to the Captain's image on the cathode-ray tube, to the considerable embarrassment of her soul, although there was no one to hear her: "Would you by any chance like to marry me?"

• • •

It would turn out that she knew at least a little bit more about machinery than he did, just from living with Roy. After Roy died, and the lawn mower wouldn't start, for example, she was able to change the spark plug and get it going—something the Captain could never have done.

And she knew a whole lot more about the islands. It was Mary who correctly identified the island on which they would be marooned. The Captain, grasping for shreds of self-respect and authority after his big brain had made such a mess of things, declared the island to be Rábida, which it surely wasn't and which, in any case, he had never seen.

And what allowed Mary to recognize Santa Rosalia were the dominant sorts of finches there. These drab little birds, incidentally, so uninteresting to most tourists and to Mary's students, had been as exciting to young Charles Darwin as the great land tortoises or the boobies or marine iguanas, or any other creatures there. The thing was: The finches looked very much alike, but they were in fact divided into thirteen species, each species with its own peculiar diet and method for getting food.

None had close relatives on the mainland of South America or anywhere. Their ancestors might, too, have arrived on Noah's ark or a natural raft, since it was wholly out of character for a finch to set out on a flight of a thousand kilometers over open ocean.

There were no woodpeckers on the islands, but there was a finch which ate what woodpeckers would have eaten. It couldn't peck wood, and so it took a twig or a spine from a cactus in its blunt little beak, and used that to dig insects out of their hiding places.

Another sort of finch was a bloodsucker, surviving by pecking at the long neck of an unheeding booby until it had raised little beads of blood. Then it sipped that perfect diet to its heart's content. This bird was called by human beings: *Geospiza difficilis.*

The principal nesting place of these queer finches, their Garden of Eden, was the Island of Santa Rosalia. She would probably never have heard of that island, so removed from the rest of the archipelago, and so rarely visited by anyone, if it weren't for its swarms of *Geospiza difficilis.* And she surely wouldn't have lectured so much about it if the bloodsuckers hadn't been the only finches she could make her students give much of a damn about.

Great teacher that she was, she would go along with her students by describing the birds as ". . . ideal pets for Count Dracula." This entirely fictitious count, she knew, was a far more significant person to most of her students than George Washington, for instance, who was merely the founder of their country.

They were better informed about Dracula, too, so that Mary could expand her joke admitting that he might not enjoy *Geospiza difficilis* as a pet after all, since he, whom she then called *"Homo transylvaniensis,"* slept all through the daytime, whereas *Geospiza difficilis* slept all through the night. "So perhaps," she would decide with mock sadness, "the best pet for Count Dracula remains a member of the family Desmodontidae—which is a scientific way of saying: 'vampire bat.' "

• • •

And then she would top that joke by saying, "If you should find yourself on Santa Rosalia, and you have killed a specimen of *Geospiza difficilis,* what must you do to make sure that it stays dead forever?" Her answer was this: "You must bury it at a crossroads, of course, with a little stake driven through its heart."

• • •

What was so thought provoking about all sorts of Galápagos finches to young Charles Darwin, though, was that they were behaving as best they could like a wide variety of much more specialized birds on the continents. He was still prepared to believe, if it turned out to make sense, that God Almighty had created all the creatures just as Darwin found them on his trip around the world. But his big brain had to wonder why the Creator in the case of the Galápagos Islands would have given every conceivable job for a small land bird to an often ill-adapted finch? What would have prevented the Creator, if he thought the islands should have a woodpecker-type bird, from creating a real woodpecker? If he thought a vampire was a good idea, why didn't he give the job to a vampire bat instead of a finch, for heaven's sakes? A vampire finch?

• • •

And Mary used to state the same intellectual problem to her students, concluding: "Your comments, please."

• • •

When she went ashore for the first time on the black peak where the *Bahía de Darwin* had been run aground, Mary stumbled. She broke her fall in such a way as to abrade the knuckles on her right hand. It wasn't a painful event. She made the most cursory examination of her injuries. There were these scratches from which beads of blood arose.

But then a finch, utterly fearless, lit on her finger. She was unsurprised, since she had heard many stories of finches landing on people's heads and hands and drinking cups or whatever. So she resolved to enjoy this welcome to the islands, and held her hand still, and spoke sweetly to the bird. "And which of the thirteen sorts of finch are you?" she said.

As though it understood her question, the bird now showed her what sort it was by sipping up the red beads on her knuckles.

So she took another look around at the island, never imagining that she was going to spend the rest of her life there, providing thousands of meals for vampire finches. She said to the Captain, for whom she had lost all respect, "You say this is Rábida Island?"

"Yes," he said. "I'm quite sure of it."

"Well, I hate to tell you this after all you've been through, but you're wrong again," she said. "This has to be Santa Rosalia."

"How can you be so sure?" he said.

And she said, "This little bird just told me so."

25

On the island of Manhattan, Bobby King turned out the light in his office atop the Chrysler Building, said good-night to his secretary, and went home. He will not appear in this tale again. Nothing more he did from that moment on until, many busy years later, he entered the blue tunnel into the Afterlife, would have the slightest bearing on the future of the human race.

In Guayaquil at the same moment that Bobby King reached home, ★Zenji Hiroguchi was leaving his room at the Hotel El Dorado, angry with his pregnant wife. She had said unforgivable things about his motives in creating Gokubi and then Mandarax. He pressed the button for the elevator, and snapped his fingers and breathed very shallowly.

And then out into the corridor came the person he least wanted to see, the cause of all his troubles as far as he was concerned, who was ★Andrew MacIntosh.

"Oh—there you are," said ★MacIntosh. "I was just going to tell you that there is some sort of trouble with the telephones. As soon as they're fixed, I will have very good news for you."

*Zenji, whose genes live on today, was so jangled by his wife and now by *MacIntosh that he could not speak. So he punched out this message on the keys of Mandarax in Japanese, and had Mandarax display the words to *MacIntosh on its little screen: *I do not wish to talk now. I am very upset. Please leave me alone.*

Like Bobby King, incidentally, *MacIntosh would have no further influence on the future of the human race. If his daughter had agreed ten years later to be artificially inseminated on Santa Rosalia, it might have been a very different story. I think it's safe to say that he would have liked very much to participate in Mary Hepburn's experiments with the Captain's sperm. If Selena had been more venturesome, everybody today might then have been descended as he was, from the stout-hearted Scottish warriors who had repelled invading Roman legions so long ago. What a missed opportunity! As Mandarax would have it:

> *For of all sad words of tongue or pen,*
> *The saddest are these: "It might have been!"*
> —JOHN GREENLEAF WHITTIER (1807–1892)

"What can I do to help?" said *MacIntosh. "I'll do anything to help. Just name it."

*Zenji found that he couldn't even shake his head. The best he could do was to close his eyes tight. And then the elevator arrived, and *Zenji thought the top of his

head would blow off when *MacIntosh got into it with
him.

"Look—" said *MacIntosh on the way down, "I'm
your friend. You can tell me anything. If I'm what's bothering you, you can tell me to take a flying fuck at a rolling
doughnut, and I'll be the first to sympathize. I make mistakes. I'm human."

When they got down to the lobby, *Zenji's big
brain gave him the impractical, almost infantile advice that
he should somehow run away from *MacIntosh—that he
could beat this athletic American in a footrace.

So right out the front door of the hotel he went, and
onto the cordoned-off section of the Calle Diez de
Agosto, with *MacIntosh right beside him.

The two of them were across the lobby and out into
the sunset so quickly that the unlucky von Kleist brother,
*Siegfried, behind the bar in the cocktail lounge, couldn't
even shout a warning to them in time. Too late, he cried,
"Please! Please! I wouldn't go out there, if I were you!"
And then he ran after them.

• • •

Many events which would have repercussions a million years later were taking place in a small space on the
planet in a very short time. While the unlucky von Kleist
brother was running after *MacIntosh and *Hiroguchi,
the lucky one was taking a shower in his cabin just aft of
the bridge of the *Bahía de Darwin.* He wasn't doing anything particularly important to the future of humankind,

other than surviving, other than staying alive, but his first mate, whose name was Hernando Cruz, was about to take a radically influential action.

Cruz was outside on the sun deck, gazing, as it happened, at the only other ship in sight, the Colombian freighter *San Mateo,* long anchored in the estuary. Cruz was a stocky, bald man about the Captain's age, who had made fifty cruises out to the islands and back on other ships. He had been part of the skeleton crew which brought the *Bahía de Darwin* from Malmö. He had supervised her outfitting in Guayaquil, while the nominal captain had made a publicity tour of the United States. This man had stocked his big brain with a perfect understanding of every part of the ship, from the mighty diesels below to the ice-maker behind the bar in the main saloon. He moreover knew the personal strengths and weaknesses of every crewman, and had earned his respect.

This was the real captain, who would really run the ship while Adolf von Kleist, potching around in the shower now and singing, would charm the passengers at mealtimes, and dance with each and every one of the ladies at night.

Cruz was least concerned with what he happened to be looking at, the *San Mateo* and the great raft of vegetable matter which had accumulated around her anchor line. That rusty little ship had become such a permanent fixture that it might as well have been a lifeless rock out there. But now he saw that a small tanker had come alongside the *San Mateo,* and was nursing it as a whale might have nursed a calf. It was excreting diesel fuel through a flexible tube. That would be mother's milk to the engine of the *San Mateo*.

What had happened was that the *San Mateo*'s owners had received a large number of United States dollars in exchange for Colombian cocaine, and smuggled those dollars into Ecuador, where they were traded not only for diesel fuel, but for the most precious commodity of all, which was food, which was fuel for human beings. So there was still a certain amount of international commerce going on.

Cruz could not divine the details of the corruption which had made the fueling and provisioning of the *San Mateo* possible, but he surely meditated on corruption in general, to wit: Anybody who had liquid wealth, whether he deserved it or not, could have anything he wanted. The captain in the shower was such a person, as Cruz was not. The painstakingly accumulated lifetime savings of Cruz, all in sucres, had turned to trash.

He envied the elation the *San Mateo*'s crewmen were feeling, now that they were going home. Since rising at dawn, Cruz himself had been thinking seriously about going home. He had a pregnant wife and eleven children in a nice house out by the airport, and they were scared. They certainly needed him, and yet, until now, abandoning a ship to which he was duty bound, no matter for what reason, had seemed to him a form of suicide, an obliteration of all that was admirable in his character and reputation.

But now he decided to walk off the *Bahía de Darwin* anyway. He patted the rail around the sun deck, and he said this softly in Spanish: "Good luck, my Swedish princess. I shall dream of you."

His case was very much like that of Jesús Ortiz, who had disconnected the El Dorado's telephones. His big brain had concealed from his soul until the last possible moment its conclusion that it was now time for him to act antisocially.

• • •

That left Adolf von Kleist completely in charge, although he did not know shit from Shinola about navigation, the Galápagos Islands, or the operation and maintenance of a ship that size.

The combination of the Captain's incompetence and the decision of Hernando Cruz to go to the aid of his own flesh and blood, although the stuff of low comedy at the time, has turned out to be of incalculable value to present-day humankind. So much for comedy. So much for supposedly serious stuff.

• • •

If "the Nature Cruise of the Century" had come off as planned, the division of duties between the Captain and his first mate would have been typical of the management of so many organizations a million years ago, with the nominal leader specializing in sociable balderdash, and with the supposed second-in-command burdened with the responsibility of understanding how things really worked, and what was really going on.

The best-run nations commonly had such symbiotic pairings at the top. And when I think about the suicidal mistakes nations used to make in olden times, I see that those polities were trying to get along with just an Adolf von Kleist at the top, without an Hernando Cruz. Too late, the surviving inhabitants of such a nation would crawl from ruins of their own creation and realize that, throughout all their self-imposed agony, there had been absolutely nobody at the top who had understood how things really worked, what it was all about, what was really going on.

26

THE LUCKY VON KLEIST BROTHER, the common sire
of everybody alive today, was tall and thin, and had a beak
like an eagle's. He had a great head of curly hair which
had once been golden, which now was white. He had
been put in command of the *Bahía de Darwin,* with the
understanding that his first mate would do all the serious
thinking, for the same reason *Siegfried had been put in
charge of the hotel: His uncles in Quito had wanted a
close relative to watch over their famous guests and valuable property.

The Captain and his brother had beautiful homes in
the chilly mists above Quito, which they would never see
again. They had also inherited considerable wealth from
their murdered mother and both sets of grandparents. Almost none of it was in worthless sucres. Almost all of it
was managed by the Chase Manhattan Bank in New York
City, which had caused it to be represented by U.S. dollars and Japanese yen.

Dancing there in the shower stall, the Captain did
not think he had much to worry about, as troubled as

things seemed to be in Guayaquil. No matter what happened, Hernando Cruz would know what to do.

His big brain came up with what he thought might be a good idea to pass on to Cruz after he had dried himself off. If it looked like crewmen were about to desert, he thought, Cruz could remind them that the *Bahía de Darwin* was technically a ship of war, which meant that deserters would be subject to strict punishment under regulations of the Navy.

This was bad law, but he was right that the ship on paper was a part of the Ecuadorian Navy. The Captain himself, in his role as admiral, had welcomed her to that fighting force when she arrived from Malmö during the summer. Her decks had yet to be carpeted, and the bare steel was dotted here and there with plugged holes which could accept the mounts for machine guns and rocket launchers and racks of depth charges and so on, should war ever come.

She would then become an armored troop carrier, with, as the Captain had said on *The Tonight Show*, ". . . ten bottles of Dom Pérignon and one bidet for every hundred enlisted men."

• • •

The Captain had some other ideas in the shower, but they had all come from Hernando Cruz. For instance: If the cruise was canceled, which seemed almost a certainty, then Cruz and a few men would anchor the ship out on the marsh somewhere, away from looters. Cruz could think of no reason for the Captain to come along on a trip like that.

If all hell broke loose, and there seemed no safe place for the ship anywhere near the city, then Cruz planned to take her out to the naval base on the Galápagos Island of Baltra. Again, Cruz hadn't been able to think of a reason for the Captain to come along.

Or, if the celebrities from New York City were still, incredibly, going to arrive the next morning, then it would be vital that the Captain be aboard to greet and reassure them. While waiting for them, Cruz would anchor the *Bahía de Darwin* offshore, like the Colombian freighter *San Mateo*. He would bring the ship back to the wharf only when the celebrities were right there, ready to board. He would get them out into the safety of the open ocean as quickly as possible, and then, depending on the news, he might actually take them on the promised tour of the islands.

More likely, though: He would deliver them to some safer port than Guayaquil, but surely no port in Peru or Chile or Colombia, which was to say the entire west coast of South America. The citizens in all those countries were at least as desperate as those of Ecuador.

Panama was a possibility.

If necessary, Hernando Cruz intended to take the celebrities all the way to San Diego. There was certainly more than enough food and fuel and water on the ship for a trip that long. And the celebrities could telephone their friends and relatives en route, telling them that, no matter how bad the news from the rest of the world might be, they were living high on the hog as usual.

• • •

One emergency plan the Captain didn't consider there in the shower was that he himself take full charge of the ship, with only Mary Hepburn to help him—and that he run it aground on Santa Rosalia, which would become the cradle of all humankind.

• • •

Here is a quotation well known to Mandarax:

A little neglect may breed great mischief . . . for want of a nail the shoe was lost; for want of a shoe the horse was lost; for want of a horse the rider was lost.
—BENJAMIN FRANKLIN (1706–1790)

Yes, and a little neglect can breed good news just as easily. For want of Hernando Cruz aboard the *Bahía de Darwin,* humanity was saved. Cruz would never have run the ship aground on Santa Rosalia.

And now he was driving away from the waterfront in his Cadillac El Dorado, its trunk packed solid with delicacies intended for "the Nature Cruise of the Century." He had stolen all that food for his family at dawn that day, long before the troops and the hungry mob arrived.

His vehicle, which he had bought with graft from the outfitting and provisioning of the *Bahía de Darwin,* had the same name as the hotel—the same name as the legendary city of great riches and opportunity which his Spanish ancestors had sought but never found. His ancestors used to torture Indians—to make them tell where El Dorado was.

It is hard to imagine anybody's torturing anybody nowadays. How could you even capture somebody you wanted to torture with just your flippers and your mouth? How could you even stage a manhunt, now that people can swim so fast and stay underwater for so long? The person you were after would not only look pretty much like everybody else, but could also be hiding out at any depth practically anywhere.

●   ●   ●

Hernando Cruz had done his bit for humanity.

The Peruvian Air Force would soon do its bit, as well, but not until six o'clock that evening, after ★Andrew MacIntosh and ★Zenji Hiroguchi were dead—at which time Peru would declare war on Ecuador. Peru had been bankrupt for fourteen days longer than Ecuador, so that hunger was that much more advanced there. Ground soldiers were going home, and taking their weapons with them. Only the small Peruvian Air Force was still reliable, and the military junta was keeping it that way by giving its members the best of whatever food was still around.

One thing which made the Air Force such a high morale unit was that its equipment, bought on credit and delivered before the bankruptcy, was so up to date. It had eight new French fighter-bombers and each of these planes, moreover, was equipped with an American air-to-ground missile with a Japanese brain which could home in on radar signals, or on heat from an engine, depending on instructions from the pilot. The pilot was in turn being instructed by computers on the ground and in his cockpit. The warhead of each missile carried a new Israeli explosive which was capable of creating one fifth as much devastation as the atomic bomb the United States dropped on the mother of Hisako Hiroguchi during World War Two.

This new explosive was regarded as a great boon to big-brained military scientists. As long as they killed people with conventional rather than nuclear weapons, they were praised as humanitarian statesmen. As long as they did not use nuclear weapons, it appeared, nobody was going to give the right name to all the killing that had been going on since the end of the Second World War, which was surely "World War Three."

• • •

The Peruvian junta gave this as its official reason for going to war: that the Galápagos Islands were rightfully Peru's, and that Peru was going to get them back again.

• • •

Nobody today is nearly smart enough to make the sorts of weapons even the poorest nations had a million years ago. Yes, and they were being used all the time. During my entire lifetime, there wasn't a day when, somewhere on the planet, there weren't at least three wars going on.

And the Law of Natural Selection was powerless to respond to such new technologies. No female of any species, unless, maybe, she was a rhinoceros, could expect to give birth to a baby who was fireproof, bombproof, or bulletproof.

The best that the Law of Natural Selection could come up with in my time was somebody who wasn't afraid of anything, even though there was so much to fear. I knew a few people like that in Vietnam—to the extent that such people were knowable. And such a person was *Andrew MacIntosh.

27

SELENA MACINTOSH would never know for certain that her father was dead until she was reunited with him at the far end of the blue tunnel into the Afterlife. All she could be sure of was that he had departed her room at the El Dorado, and exchanged some words with *Zenji Hiroguchi out in the corridor. Then the two went down together in the elevator. After that, she would never again receive news about either one of them.

Here is the story on her blindness, by the way: She had retinitis pigmentosa, caused by a defective gene inherited on the female side. She had got it from her mother, who could see perfectly well, and who had concealed from her husband the certainty that this was a gene she carried.

This was another disease with which Mandarax was familiar, since it was one of the top one thousand serious diseases of *Homo sapiens*. Mandarax, when asked about it by Mary on Santa Rosalia, would pronounce Selena's case a severe one, since she was blind at birth. It was more usual for retinitis pigmentosa, said Mandarax, son of Gokubi, to let its hosts and hostesses see the world clearly for as long as thirty years sometimes. Mandarax confirmed, too, what Selena herself had told Mary: that if she had a baby, there was a fifty-fifty chance that it would be blind. And if that baby was a female, whether it went blind or not, and that baby grew up and reproduced, there would be a fifty-fifty chance that its child would be blind.

• • •

It is amazing that two such relatively rare hereditary defects, retinitis pigmentosa and Huntington's chorea, should have been causes for worry to the first human settlers of Santa Rosalia, since the settlers numbered only ten.

As I have already said, the Captain luckily turned out not to be a carrier. Selena was surely a carrier. If she had reproduced, though, I think humankind would still be free of retinitis pigmentosa now—thanks to the Law of Natural Selection, and sharks and killer whales.

• • •

Here is how her father and *Zenji Hiroguchi died, incidentally, while she and her dog Kazakh listened to the noise of the crowd outside: They were shot in their heads from behind, so they never knew what hit them. And the soldier who shot them is another person who should be credited with having done a little something whose effects are still visible after a million years. I am not talking about the shootings. I am talking about his breaking into the back door of a shuttered souvenir shop which faced the El Dorado.

If he had not burglarized that shop, there would almost certainly be no human beings on the face of the earth today. I mean it. Everybody alive today should thank God that this soldier was insane.

His name was Private Geraldo Delgado, and he had deserted his unit, taking his first-aid kit and canteen and trenchknife, automatic assault rifle and two grenades and several clips of ammunition and so on with him. He was only eighteen years old, and was a paranoid schizophrenic. He should never have been issued live ammunition.

His big brain was telling him all sorts of things that were not true—that he was the greatest dancer in the world, that he was the son of Frank Sinatra, that people envious of his dancing ability were attempting to destroy his brains with little radios, and on and on.

Delgado, facing starvation like so many other people in Guayaquil, thought his big problem was enemies with little radios. And when he broke in through the back door of what was plainly a defunct souvenir shop, it wasn't a souvenir shop to him. To him it was the headquarters of the Ecuadorian Ballet Folklórico, and he was now going to get his chance to prove that he really was the greatest dancer in the world.

• • •

There are still plenty of hallucinators today, people who respond passionately to all sorts of things which aren't really going on. This could be a legacy from the Kanka-bonos. But people like that can't get hold of weapons now, and they're easy to swim away from. Even if they found a grenade or a machine gun or a knife or whatever left over from olden times, how could they ever make use of it with just their flippers and their mouths?

• • •

When I was a child in Cohoes, my mother took me to see the circus in Albany one time, although we could not afford it and Father did not approve of circuses. And there were trained seals and sea lions there who could balance balls on their noses and blow horns and clap their flippers on cue and so on.

But they could never have loaded and cocked a machine gun, or pulled the pin on a hand grenade and thrown it any distance with any accuracy.

• • •

As to how a person as crazy as Delgado got into the army in the first place: He looked all right and he acted all right when he talked to the recruiting officer, just as I did when I enlisted in the United States Marines. And Delgado was taken in during the previous summer, about the time Roy Hepburn died, for short-term service specifically associated with "the Nature Cruise of the Century." His unit was to be a spit-and-polish drill team which was to strut its stuff before Mrs. Onassis and the rest of them.

They were going to have assault rifles and steel helmets and all that, but surely not live ammunition.

And Delgado was a wonderful marcher and polisher of brass buttons and shiner of shoes. But then Ecuador was convulsed by this economic crisis, and live ammunition was passed out to the soldiery.

He was a harrowing example of quick evolution, but then so was any soldier. When I was through with Marine boot camp, and I was sent to Vietnam and issued live ammunition, I bore almost no resemblance to the feckless animal I had been in civilian life. And I did worse things than Delgado.

• • •

Now, then: The store that Delgado broke into was in a block of locked business establishments facing the El Dorado. The soldiers who had strung barbed wire around the hotel considered the stores as part of their barrier. So that when Delgado broke open the back door of one, and then unlocked its front door just a hair and peeked out, he had made a hole in the barrier, through which somebody else might pass. This breach was his contribution to the future of humankind, since very important people would pass through it in a very short while, and reach the hotel.

• • •

When Delgado looked out through the crack in the door, he saw two of his enemies. One of them was flourishing a little radio which could scramble his brains—or so he thought. This wasn't a radio. It was Mandarax, and the two supposed enemies were *Zenji Hiroguchi and *Andrew MacIntosh. They were walking briskly along the inside of the barricade, as they were entitled to do, since they were guests at the hotel.

*Hiroguchi was still boiling mad, and *MacIntosh was joshing him about taking life too seriously. They went right past the store where Delgado was lurking. So Delgado stepped out through the front door and shot them both in what he believed to be self-defense.

So I don't have to put stars in front of the names of Zenji Hiroguchi and Andrew MacIntosh anymore. I only did that to remind readers that they were the two of the six guests at the El Dorado who would be dead before the sun went down.

They were dead now, and the sun was going down on a world where so many people believed, a million years ago, that only the fit survived.

• • •

Delgado, the survivor, disappeared into the store again, and headed for the back door, where he expected to find more enemies to outsurvive.

But there were only six little brown beggar children out there—all girls. When this horrifying military freak leapt out at the little girls with all his killing equipment, they were too hungry and too resigned to death to run away. They opened their mouths instead—and rolled their brown eyes, and patted their stomachs, and pointed down their gullets to show how hungry they were.

Children all over the world were doing that back then, and not just in that one back alley in Ecuador.

So Delgado just kept going, and he was never caught and punished or hospitalized or whatever. He was just one more soldier in a city teeming with soldiers, and nobody had gotten a good look at his face, which, in the shadow of his steel helmet, wasn't all that different from anybody else's face anyway. And, like the great survivor he was, he would rape a woman the next day and become the father of one of the last ten million children or so to be born on the South American mainland.

• • •

After he was gone, the six little girls went into the shop, seeking food or anything which might be traded for food. These were orphans from the Ecuadorian rain forest across the mountains to the east—from far, far away. Their parents had all been killed by insecticides sprayed from the air, and a bush pilot had brought them to Guaya-quil, where they had become children of the streets.

These children were predominantly Indian, but had Negro ancestors as well—African slaves who had escaped into the rain forest long ago.

These were Kanka-bonos. They would grow to womanhood on Santa Rosalia, where, along with Hisako Hiroguchi, they would become the mothers of all modern humankind.

• • •

Before they could get to Santa Rosalia, though, they would first have to reach the hotel. And the soldiers and the barricades would surely have stopped them from getting there, if Private Geraldo Delgado had not opened up that pathway through the store.

28

THESE CHILDREN would become six Eves to Captain
von Kleist's Adam on Santa Rosalia, and they wouldn't
have been in Guayaquil if it weren't for a young Ecuadorian bush pilot named Eduardo Ximénez. During the previous summer, on the day after Roy Hepburn was buried,
in fact, Ximénez was flying his own four-passenger amphibious plane over the rain forest, near the headwaters of
the Tiputini River, which flowed to the Atlantic rather
than the Pacific Ocean. He had just delivered a French
anthropologist and his survival equipment to a point
downstream, on the border of Peru, where the French-
man planned to begin a search for the elusive Kanka-
bonos.

Ximénez was headed next for Guayaquil, five hundred kilometers away and across two high and rugged
mountain barriers. In Guayaquil, he was to pick up two
Argentinian millionaire sportsmen, and take them to the
landing field on the Galápagos island of Baltra, where
they had chartered a deep-sea fishing boat and crew. They
would not be going after just any sort of fish, either.

They hoped to hook great white sharks, the same creatures who, thirty-one years later, would swallow Mary Hepburn and Captain von Kleist and Mandarax.

• • •

Ximénez saw from the air these letters trampled in the mud of the riverbank: SOS. He landed on the water and then made his plane waddle ashore like a duck.

He was greeted by an eighty-year-old Roman Catholic priest from Ireland named Father Bernard Fitzgerald, who had lived with the Kanka-bonos for half a century. With him were the six little girls, the last of the Kanka-bonos. He and they had trampled the letters in the riverbank.

Father Fitzgerald, incidentally, had a great-grandfather in common with John F. Kennedy, the first husband of Mrs. Onassis and the thirty-fifth president of the United States. If he had mated with an Indian, which he never did, everybody now alive might claim to be an Irish blue blood—not that anybody today claims to be much of anything.

After only about nine months of life, people even forget who their mothers were.

• • •

The girls had been at choir practice with Father Fitzgerald when everybody else in the tribe got sprayed. Some of the victims were still dying, so the old priest was going to stay with them. He wanted Ximénez, though, to take the girls someplace where somebody could look after them.

So in only five hours those girls were flown from the Stone Age to the Electronics Age, from the freshwater swamps of the jungle to the brackish marshes of Guayaquil. They spoke only Kanka-bono, which only a few dying relatives in the jungle and, as things would turn out, one dirty old white man in Guayaquil could understand.

Ximénez was from Quito, and had no place of his own where he could put up the girls in Guayaquil. He himself hired a room at the Hotel El Dorado, the same room which would later be occupied by Selena MacIntosh and her dog. On the advice of police he took the girls to an orphanage next door to the cathedral downtown, where nuns gladly accepted responsibility for them. There was still plenty of food for everyone.

Ximénez then went to the hotel, and he told the story to the bartender there, who was Jesús Ortiz, the same man who would later disconnect all the telephones from the outside world.

• • •

So Ximénez was one aviator who had quite a lot to do with the future of humanity. And another one was an American named Paul W. Tibbets. It was Tibbets who had dropped an atomic bomb on Hisako Hiroguchi's mother during World War Two. People would probably be as furry as they are today, even if Tibbets hadn't dropped the bomb. But they certainly got furrier faster because of him.

•   •   •

The orphanage put out a call for anybody who could speak Kanka-bono, to serve as an interpreter. An old drunk and petty thief appeared, a purebred white man who, amazingly, was a grandfather of the lightest of the girls. When a youngster, he had gone prospecting for valuable minerals in the rain forest, and had lived with the Kanka-bonos for three years. He had welcomed Father Fitzgerald to the tribe when the priest first arrived from Ireland.

His name was Domingo Quezeda, and he was from excellent stock. His father had been head of the Philosophy Department of the Central University in Quito. If they were so inclined, then, people today might claim to be descended from a long line of aristocratic Spanish intellectuals.

•   •   •

When I was a little boy in Cohoes, and could detect nothing in the life of our little family about which I could be proud, my mother told me that I had the blood of French noblemen flowing in my veins. I would probably be living in a chateau on a vast estate over there, she said, if it hadn't been for the French Revolution. That was on her side of the family. I was also somehow related through her, she went on, to Carter Braxton, one of the signers of the Declaration of Independence. I should hold my head up high, she said, because of the blood flowing in my veins.

I thought that was pretty good. So then I disturbed my father at his typewriter, and asked him what my heritage was from his side of the family. I didn't know then what sperm was, and so wouldn't understand his answer for several years. "My boy," he said, "you are descended from a long line of determined, resourceful, microscopic tadpoles—champions every one."

• • •

Old Quezeda, stinking like a battlefield, told the girls that they could trust only him, which was easy enough for them to believe, since he was the grandfather of one and the only person who would converse with them. They had to believe everything he said. They were without the means to be skeptical, since their new environment had nothing in common with the rain forest. They had many truths they were prepared to defend stubbornly and proudly, but none of them applied to anything they had so far seen in Guayaquil, except for one, a classically fatal belief in urban areas a million years ago: Relatives would never want to hurt them. Quezeda in fact wished to expose them to terrible dangers as thieves and beggars, and, as soon as was remotely possible, as prostitutes. He would do this in order to feed his big brain's thirst for self-esteem and alcohol. He was at last going to be a man of wealth and importance.

He took the girls on walks around the city, showing them, as far as the nuns at the orphanage were aware, the parks and the cathedral and the museums and so on. He was in fact teaching them what was hateful about tourists, and where to find them and how to fool them, and where they were most likely to keep their valuables. And they played the game of spotting policemen before policemen spotted them, and memorizing good hiding places in the downtown area, should any enemy try to catch them.

• • •

It was "just pretend" for the girls' first week in the city. But then Grandfather Domingo Quezeda and the girls, as far as the nuns and the police were concerned, vanished entirely. That vile old ancestor of all humanity had moved the girls into an empty shed by the water-front—a shed, as it happened, belonging to one of the two older cruise ships with which the *Bahía de Darwin* was meant to compete. The shed was empty because tourism had declined to the point where the old ship was out of business.

At least the girls had each other. And during their early years on Santa Rosalia, until Mary Hepburn made them the gift of babies, that was what they were most grateful for: At least they had each other—and their own language and their own religious beliefs and jokes and songs and so on.

And that was what they would leave to their children on Santa Rosalia when they entered, one by one, the blue tunnel into the Afterlife: the comforts of at least having each other, and the Kanka-bono language, and the Kanka-bono religion, and the Kanka-bono jokes and songs.

• • •

During their bad old days in Guayaquil, old Quezeda offered his stinking body for their experimentation as he taught them, as little as they were, the fundamental skills and attitudes of prostitutes.

They were certainly in need of rescue, long before the economic crisis. Yes, and one dusty window of the shed which was their gruesome schoolhouse framed the stern of the *Bahía de Darwin* right outside. Little did they know that that beautiful white ship would soon be their Noah's ark.

• • •

The girls finally ran away from the old man. They began to live in the streets, still begging and stealing. But, for reasons they could not understand, tourists became harder and harder to find, and, at last, there didn't seem to be anything to eat anywhere. They were truly hungry now, as they approached simply anyone, opening their mouths wide and rolling their eyes and pointing down their little throats to show how long it had been since they had eaten.

And late one afternoon, they were attracted by the sounds of the crowd around the El Dorado. They found that the back door of a shuttered shop was open, and out came Geraldo Delgado, who had just shot Andrew Mac-Intosh and Zenji Hiroguchi. So they went into the shop and out of the front door. They were inside the barrier set up by the soldiers, so there was nobody to stop them from entering the El Dorado, where they would throw themselves on the mercy of James Wait in the cocktail lounge.

29

MARY HEPBURN was meanwhile murdering herself up in her room, lying on her bed with the polyethylene sheath of her "Jackie dress" wrapped around her head. The sheath was now all steamed up inside, and she hallucinated that she was a great land tortoise lying on its back in the hot and humid hold of a sailing ship of long ago. She pawed the air in perfect futility, just as a land tortoise on its back would have done.

As she had often told her students, sailing ships bound out across the Pacific used to stop off in the Galápagos Islands to capture defenseless tortoises, who could live on their backs without food or water for months. They were so slow and tame and huge and plentiful. Sailors would capsize them without fear of being bitten or clawed. Then they would drag them down to waiting longboats on the shore, using the animals' own useless suits of armor for sleds.

They would store them on their backs in the dark, paying no further attention to them until it was time for them to be eaten. The beauty of the tortoises to the sailors was that they were fresh meat which did not have to be refrigerated or eaten right away.

• • •

Every school year back in Ilium, Mary could count on some student's being outraged that human beings should have treated such trusting creatures so cruelly. This gave her the opportunity to say that the natural order had dealt harshly with such tortoises long before there was such an animal as man.

There used to be millions of them, lumbering over every temperate land mass of any size, she would say.

But then some tiny animals evolved into rodents. These easily found and ate the eggs of the tortoises—all of the eggs.

So, very quickly, that was that for the tortoises everywhere, except for those on a few islands which remained rodent free.

• • •

It was prophetic that Mary should imagine herself to be a land tortoise as she suffocated, since something very much like what had happened to most of the land tortoises so long ago was then beginning to happen to most of humankind.

Some new creature, invisible to the naked eye, was eating up all the eggs in human ovaries, starting at the annual Book Fair at Frankfurt, Germany. Women at the fair were experiencing a slight fever, which came and went in a day or two, and sometimes blurry vision. After that, they would be just like Mary Hepburn: They couldn't have babies anymore. Nor would any way be discovered for stopping this disease. It would spread practically everywhere.

The near extinction of mighty land tortoises by little rodents was certainly a David-and-Goliath story. Now here was another one.

• • •

Yes, and Mary came close enough to death to see the blue tunnel into the Afterlife. At that point, she rebelled against her big brain, which had brought her that far. She unwrapped the garment bag from her head, and, instead of dying, she went downstairs, where she found James Wait feeding peanuts and olives and maraschino cherries and cocktail onions from behind the bar to the six Kankabono girls.

This tableau of clumsy charity would remain imprinted in her brain for the rest of her life. She would believe ever after that he was an unselfish, compassionate, lovable human being. He was about to suffer a fatal heart attack, so nothing would ever happen to revise her high opinion of this loathsome man.

On top of everything else, this man was a murderer.

His murder had gone like this:

He was a homosexual prostitute on the island of Manhattan, and a bloated plutocrat picked him up in a bar, asking him if he realized that the price tag was still on the hem of his lovely new blue velour shirt. This man had royal blood in his veins! This was Prince Richard of Croatia-Slavonia, a direct descendant of James the First of England and Emperor Frederick the Third of Germany and Emperor Franz Joseph of Austria and King Louis the Fifteenth of France. He ran an antique shop on upper Madison Avenue, and he wasn't homosexual. He wanted young Wait to strangle him with a silken sash from his dressing gown, and then to loosen the sash after having brought him as close as possible to death.

Prince Richard had a wife and two children, who were on a skiing vacation in Switzerland, and his wife was young enough to be ovulating still, so young Wait may have prevented yet another carrier of those noble genes from being born.

There was this, too: If Prince Richard hadn't been murdered, he and his wife might have been invited by Bobby King to take part in "the Nature Cruise of the Century."

• • •

His widow would become a very successful designer of neckties, calling herself "Princess Charlotte," although she was a commoner, the daughter of a Staten Island roofer, and not entitled to that rank, or the use of his coat of arms. That crest nonetheless appeared on every tie she designed.

The late Andrew MacIntosh owned several Princess Charlotte ties.

• • •

Wait spread-eagled this porky, chinless blue-blood face up on a four-poster bed which the Prince said had belonged to Eleonore of Palatinate-Neuburg, the mother of King Joseph the First of Hungary. Wait tied him to the thick posts with nylon ropes already cut to length. These had been stored in a secret drawer under the flounce at the foot of the bed. This was an old drawer, and had one time concealed secrets of the sex life of Eleonore of Palatinate-Neuburg.

"Tie me nice and tight, so I can't get away," Prince Richard told young Wait, "but don't cut off the circulation. I would hate to get gangrene."

His big brain had had him doing this at least once a month for the past three years: hiring strangers to tie him up and strangle him just a little bit. What a survival scheme!

• • •

Prince Richard of Croatia-Slavonia, possibly with the ghosts of his progenitors looking on, instructed young James Wait to strangle him to the point where he lost consciousness. Then Wait, whom he knew only as "Jimmy," was to count slowly to twenty in this manner: "One thousand and one, one thousand and two . . ." and so on.

178

Possibly with King James and Emperor Frederick and Emperor Franz Joseph and King Louis looking on, the Prince, one of several claimants to the throne of Yugoslavia, warned "Jimmy" not to touch any part of his body or clothing, save for the sash around his neck. He would experience orgasm, but "Jimmy" was not to attempt to enhance that event with his mouth or hands. "I am not a homosexual," he said, "and I've hired you as a sort of valet—not as a prostitute.

"This may be hard for you to believe, Jimmy," he went on, "if you lead the kind of life I think you lead, but this is a spiritual experience for me, so keep it spiritual. Otherwise: no hundred-dollar tip. Do I make myself clear? I am an unusual man."

• • •

He didn't tell Wait about it, but his big brain put on quite a movie for him while he was unconscious. It showed him one end of a writhing piece of blue tubing, about five meters in diameter, big enough to drive a truck through, and lit up inside like the funnel of a tornado. It did not roar like a tornado, however. Instead, unearthly music, as though from a glass harmonica, came from the far end, which appeared to be about fifty meters away. Depending on how the tube twisted, Prince Richard could catch glimpses of the opening in the far end, a golden dot and hints of greenery.

This, of course, was the tunnel into the Afterlife.

• • •

So Wait put a small rubber ball into the mouth of this would-be liberator of the Yugoslavs, as he had been told to do, and sealed the mouth with a precut piece of adhesive tape which had been stuck to a bedpost.

Then he strangled the Prince, cutting off the blood supply to his big brain and the air supply to his lungs. Instead of counting slowly to twenty after the Prince lost consciousness and had his orgasm and saw the writhing tube, he counted slowly to three hundred instead. That was five minutes.

It was Wait's big brain's idea. It wasn't anything he himself had particularly wanted to do.

• • •

If he had ever been brought to trial for the murder, or the manslaughter, or whatever the government chose to call his crime, he would probably have pleaded temporary insanity. He would have claimed that his big brain simply wasn't working right at the time. There wasn't a person alive a million years ago who didn't know what that was like.

Apologies for momentary brain failures were the staple of everybody's conversations: "Whoops," "Excuse me," "I hope you're not hurt," "I can't believe I did that," "It happened so fast I didn't have time to think," "I have insurance against this kind of a thing," and "How can I ever forgive myself?" and "I didn't know it was loaded," and on and on.

• • •

There were beads and dollops of human sperm on the Prince's crested satin sheets, full of royal tadpoles racing each other to nowhere, as young Wait let himself out of the triple apartment on Sutton Place. He hadn't stolen anything, and he hadn't left any fingerprints. The doorman of the building, who had seen him coming and going, was able to tell the police very little about his appearance, save that he was young and white and slender, and wore a blue velour shirt from which the price tag had not been removed.

And there was something prophetic, too, in those millions of royal tadpoles on a satin sheet, with no place meaningful to go. The whole world, as far as human sperm was concerned, with the exception of the Galápagos Islands, was about to become like that satin sheet.

Dare I add this: "In the nick of time"?

30

I **WILL NOW PUT A STAR** in front of the name of
★James Wait, indicating that, after ★Siegfried von Kleist,
he will be the next to die. ★Siegfried would go into the
blue tunnel first, in about an hour and a half, and ★Wait
would follow in about fourteen hours, having first married Mary Hepburn on the sun deck of the *Bahía de Darwin* when it was well at sea.

• • •

Quoth Mandarax so long ago:

> *All is well that ends well.*
> —JOHN HEYWOOD (1497?–1580?)

This was surely the case with the life of ★James Wait.
He had come into this world as a child of the devil, supposedly, and beatings had begun almost immediately. But
here he was so close to the end now, astonished by the joy
of feeding the Kanka-bono girls. They were so grateful,
and helping them was such an easy thing to do, since the

182

bar was stocked with snacks and garnishes and condiments. The opportunity to be charitable had simply never presented itself before, but here it was now, and he was loving it. To these children, Wait was life itself.

And then the widow Hepburn appeared, as he had been hoping she would all afternoon. Nor did he have to win her trust. She liked him immediately because he was feeding the children, and she said to him, because she had seen so many hungry children on her way to the hotel from Guayaquil International Airport the previous afternoon: "Oh, good for you! Good for you!" She assumed then, and would never believe differently, that this man had seen the children outside, and had invited them in so he could feed them.

"Why can't I be like you?" Mary went on. "Here I've been upstairs, doing nothing but feel sorry for myself, when I should have been down here like you—sharing whatever we have with all those poor children out there. You make me so ashamed—but my brains just haven't been working right lately. Sometimes I could just kill my brains."

She spoke to the children in English, a language they would never understand. "Does that taste good?" she said, and "Where are your mommies and daddies?" and that sort of thing.

The little girls would never learn English, since Kanka-bono would from the first be the language of the majority on Santa Rosalia. In a century and a half, it would be the language of the majority of humankind.

Forty-two years after that, Kanka-bono would be the only language of humankind.

• • •

There was no urgency about Mary's getting the girls better things to eat. A diet of peanuts and oranges, of which there were plenty behind the bar, was ideal. The girls spit out whatever wasn't good for them—the cherries and the green olives and the little onions. They needed no help with eating.

So Mary and *Wait were free to simply watch and chat, and get to know each other.

*Wait said that he thought people were put on earth to help each other, and that was why he was feeding the children. He said that children were the future of the world, and so the planet's greatest natural resource.

"Permit me to introduce myself," he said. "I am Willard Flemming of Moose Jaw, Saskatchewan."

Mary said who and what she was, an ex-teacher and a widow.

He said how much he admired teachers, and how important they had been to him when he was young. "If it hadn't been for my teachers in high school," he said, "I never would have gone to MIT. I probably wouldn't have gone to college at all—probably would have been an automobile mechanic like my father."

"So what did you become?" she said.

"Less than nothing, since my wife died of cancer," he said.

"Oh!" she said. "I'm so sorry!"

"Well—it's not your fault, is it," he said.

"No," she said.

"Before that," he said, "I was a windmill engineer. I had this crazy idea that there was all this clean, free energy around. Does that sound crazy to you?"

"It's a beautiful idea," she said. "It was something my husband and I talked about."

"The power and light companies hated me," he said, "and the oil barons and the coal barons and the atomic energy trust."

"I should think they would!" she said.

"They can stop worrying about me now," he said. "I closed up shop after my wife died, and I've been roaming the world ever since. I don't even know what I'm looking for. I very much doubt if there's anything worth finding. I'm just sure of one thing: I can never love again."

"You have so much to give the world!" she said.

"If I ever did love again," he said, "it wouldn't be with the sort of silly, pretty little ball of fluff so many men seem to want today. I couldn't stand it."

"I wouldn't think so," she said.

"I've been spoiled," he said.

"I expect you deserved it," she said.

"And I ask myself, 'What good is money now?' " he said. "I'm sure your husband was as good a husband as my wife was a wife—"

"He really was a very good man," she said, "a perfectly wonderful man."

"So you're certainly asking the same question: 'What good is money to a person all alone?' " he said. "Suppose you have a million dollars . . ."

"Oh, Lord!" she said. "I don't have anything like that."

"All right—a hundred thousand, then . . ."

"That's a little more like it," she said.

"It's just trash now, right?" he said. "What happiness can it buy?"

"A certain amount of creature comfort, anyway," she said.

"You've got a nice house, I imagine," he said.

"Quite nice," she said.

"And a car, or maybe two or three cars, and all that," he said.

"One car," she said.

"A Mercedes, I'll bet," he said.

"A Jeep," she said.

"And you've probably got stocks and bonds, just like I do," he said.

"Roy's company had a stock bonus plan," she said.

"Oh, sure," he said. "And an insurance plan, and a retirement plan—and all the rest of the middle-class dream of security."

"We both worked," she said. "We both contributed."

"I wouldn't have a wife who didn't work," he said. "My wife worked for the phone company. After she died, the death benefits, after they were all added up, turned out to be quite a bit. But they just wanted to make me cry. They were just more reminders of how empty my life had become. And her little jewel box, with all the rings and pins and necklaces I'd given her over the years, and no children to pass it on to."

"We didn't have children, either," she said.

"It seems we have a lot in common," he said. "So who will you leave your jewelry to?"

"Oh—there isn't much," she said. "I guess the only valuable piece is a string of pearls Roy's mother left me. It has a diamond clasp. There are so few times I wear jewelry, I'd almost forgotten those pearls until this very moment."

"I certainly hope they're insured," he said.

31

How people used to talk and talk back then! Everybody was going, "Blah-blah-blah," all day long. Some of them would even do it in their sleep. My father used to blather in his sleep a lot—especially after Mother walked out on us. I would be sleeping on the couch, and it would be in the middle of the night, and there wouldn't be anybody else in the house but us—and I would hear him going, "Blah-blah-blah," in the bedroom. He would be quiet for a little while, and then he would go, "Blah-blah-blah," again.

And sometimes when I was in the Marines, or later in Sweden, somebody would wake me up to tell me to stop talking in my sleep. I would have no recollection of what I might have said. I would have to ask what I had been talking about, and it was always news to me. What could most of that blah-blah-blahing have been, both night and day, but the spilling of useless, uncalled-for signals from our preposterously huge and active brains?

There was no shutting them down! Whether we had anything for them to do or not, they ran all the time! And were they ever loud! Oh, God, were they ever loud.

When I was still alive, there were these portable radios and tape-players some young people carried with them wherever they went in cities in the United States, playing music at a volume capable of drowning out a thunderstorm. These were called "ghetto blasters." It wasn't enough, a million years ago, that we already had ghetto blasters inside our heads!

• • •

Even at this late date, I am still full of rage at a natural order which would have permitted the evolution of something as distracting and irrelevant and disruptive as those great big brains of a million years ago. If they had told the truth, then I could see some point in everybody's having one. But these things lied all the time! Look at how *James Wait was lying to Mary Hepburn!

And now *Siegfried von Kleist returned to the cocktail lounge, having witnessed the shooting of Zenji Hiroguchi and Andrew MacIntosh. If his big brain had been a truth machine, he might have given Mary and *Wait information to which they were surely entitled, and which might have been very useful to them, in case they wished to survive: that he was in the first stages of a mental crack-up, that two hotel guests had just been shot, that the crowd outside couldn't be held back much longer, that the hotel was out of touch with the rest of the world, and so on.

But no. He maintained a placid exterior. He did not wish his remaining four guests to panic. As a result, they would never find out what became of Zenji Hiroguchi and Andrew MacIntosh. For that matter, they would never hear the news, which would be announced in about an hour, that Peru had declared war on Ecuador, and neither would the Captain. When Peruvian rockets hit targets in the Guayaquil area, they would believe the Captain when he said what his big brain honestly believed to be the truth, not that it felt any compunction to tell the truth: that they were being showered by meteorites.

And, as long as there was anybody on Santa Rosalia curious as to why his or her ancestors had come there—and that sort of curiosity would finally peter out only after about three thousand years—that was the story: They were driven off the mainland by a shower of meteorites.

Quoth Mandarax:

> *Happy is the nation without a history.*
> —CESARE BONESANA, MARCHESE DI BECCARIA
> (1738—1794)

So, in a perfectly calm tone of voice, *Siegfried, the Captain's brother, asked *Wait to go upstairs, and to ask Selena MacIntosh and Hisako Hiroguchi to come down, and to help them with their luggage. "Be careful not to alarm them," he said. "Let them know that everything is perfectly all right. Just to be safe, I am going to take you all out to the airport." Guayaquil International Airport, incidentally, would be the first target to be devastated by Peruvian rocketry.

He handed Mandarax to *Wait, so that *Wait would be able to communicate with Hisako. He had recovered the instrument from beside the body of Zenji. Both bodies had been moved out of sight—into the burglarized souvenir shop. *Siegfried himself had covered them with souvenir bedspreads, which bore the same portrait of Charles Darwin which hung behind the bar.

• • •

So *Siegfried von Kleist shepherded Mary Hepburn and Hisako Hiroguchi and *James Wait and Selena MacIntosh and *Kazakh out to a gaily decorated bus parked in front of the hotel. This bus was to have carried musicians and dancers out to the airport—to regale the celebrities from New York. The six Kanka-bono girls came right along with them, and I have put a star in front of the dog's name because she would soon be killed and eaten by those children. It was no time to be a dog.

Selena wanted to know where her father was, and Hisako wanted to know where her husband was. *Siegfried said that they had gone ahead to the airport. His plan was to somehow get them on a plane, whether a commercial flight or a charter flight or a military flight, which would get them safely out of Ecuador. The truth about Andrew MacIntosh and Zenji Hiroguchi would be the last thing they heard from him before the plane took off—at which time they might still survive, no matter how frenzied with grief they became.

As a sop to Mary, he agreed to take the six girls

along. He could make no sense of their language, even with the help of Mandarax. The best Mandarax could do was to identify one word in twenty, maybe, as being closely related to Quechuan, the lingua franca of the Inca Empire. Here and there Mandarax thought it might have heard a little Arabic, too, the lingua franca of the African slave trade so long ago.

Now, there is a big-brain idea I haven't heard much about lately: human slavery. How could you ever hold somebody in bondage with nothing but your flippers and your mouth?

32

Just as everybody got nicely settled in the bus in front of the El Dorado, the news came over several radios in the crowd that "the Nature Cruise of the Century" had been canceled. That meant to the crowd, and to the soldiers, too, who were just civilians in soldier suits, that the food in the hotel now belonged to everyone. Take it from somebody who has been around for a million years: When you get right down to it, food is practically the whole story every time.

Quoth Mandarax:

> *First comes fodder, then comes morality.*
> —BERTOLT BRECHT (1898–1956)

So there was a rush for the hotel's entrances which momentarily engulfed the bus, although the bus and the people in it were of no interest to the food rioters. They banged on the sides of the bus, however, and yelled— agonized by the realization that others were already inside the hotel, and that there would be no food left for them.

It was certainly very frightening to be on the bus. It might be turned over. It might be set on fire. Rocks might be thrown, making shrapnel of window glass. The place for survivors to be was on the floor in the aisle. Hisako Hiroguchi performed her first intimate act with blind Selena, instructing her with her hands and murmured Japanese to kneel in the aisle with her head down. Then Hisako knelt beside her and *Kazakh, and put her arm across her back.

How tenderly Hisako and Selena would care for each other during the coming years! What a beautiful and sweet-natured child they would rear! How I admired them!

• • •

Yes, and *James Wait found himself posing yet again as a protector of children. He was sheltering with his own body the terrified Kanka-bono girls in the aisle. He had meant only to save himself, if he could, but Mary Hepburn had grabbed both his hands and pulled him toward her so that they formed a living fort. If there was to be flying glass, it would bite into them and not into the little girls.

Quoth Mandarax:

> Greater love hath no man than this, that a man lay down his life for his friends.
> —ST. JOHN (4 B.C.?–30?)

It was while ★Wait was in this position that his heart began to fibrillate—which is to say that its fibers began to twitch in an uncoordinated manner, so that the march of the blood in his circulatory system was no longer orderly. Here heredity was operating again. He had no way of knowing this, but ★Wait's father and mother, who were also father and daughter, were both then dead of heart attacks which had struck when they were in their early forties.

It was a lucky thing for humanity that ★Wait did not live long enough to take part in the Santa Rosalia mating games. Then again, it might not have made all that much difference if people today had inherited his time-bomb heart, since nobody would have lived long enough for the bomb to go off anyway. Anybody ★Wait's age today would be a regular Methuselah.

● ● ●

Down at the waterfront, meanwhile, another mob, another fibrillating organ in the social system of Ecuador, was stripping the *Bahía de Darwin* not only of its food, but of its television sets and telephones and radar and sonar and radios and light bulbs and compasses and toilet paper and carpeting and soap and pots and pans and charts and mattresses and outboard motors and inflatable landing craft, and on and on. These survivors would even try to steal the winch which lowered or raised the anchors, but succeeded only in damaging it beyond repair.

At least they left the lifeboats—but bereft of their emergency food supplies.

And Captain von Kleist, in fear of his life, had been driven up into the crow's nest, clad only in his underwear.

• • •

The crowd at the El Dorado swept past the bus like a tidal wave—leaving it high and dry, so to speak. It was free to go where it pleased. There was nobody much around, except for a few people lying down here and there, injured or killed in the rush.

So *Siegfried von Kleist, heroically suppressing the spasms and ignoring the hallucinations symptomatic of Huntington's chorea, took his place in the driver's seat. He thought it best that his ten passengers stay in the aisle where they were—invisible from the outside, and calming one another with body heat.

He started the engine, and saw that he had a full tank of gasoline. He turned on the air conditioning. He announced in English, the only language he had in common with any of his passengers, that it would be very cool inside in a minute or two. This was a promise he could keep.

It was twilight outside now, so he turned on his parking lights.

• • •

It was at about that time that Peru declared war on Ecuador. Two of Peru's fighter bombers were then over

Ecuadorian territories, one with its rocket tuned to the radar signals coming from Guayaquil International Airport, and the other with its rocket tuned to radar signals coming from the naval base on the Galápagos Island of Baltra, lair of a sail training ship, six Coast Guard ships, two oceangoing tugs, a patrol submarine, a dry dock, and, high and dry in the dry dock, a destroyer. The destroyer was the largest ship in the Ecuadorian Navy, save for one—the *Bahía de Darwin*.

Quoth Mandarax:

> *It was the best of times, it was the worst of times, it was the age of wisdom, it was the age of foolishness, it was the epoch of belief, it was the epoch of incredulity, it was the season of Light, it was the season of Darkness, it was the spring of hope, it was the winter of despair, we had everything before us, we had nothing before us, we were all going direct to Heaven, we were all going direct the other way.*
>
> —CHARLES DICKENS (1812–1870)

33

I SOMETIMES SPECULATE as to what humanity might have become if the first settlers on Santa Rosalia had been the original passenger list and crew for "the Nature Cruise of the Century"—Captain von Kleist, surely, and Hisako Hiroguchi and Selena MacIntosh and Mary Hepburn, and, instead of the Kanka-bono girls, the sailors and officers and Jacqueline Onassis and Dr. Henry Kissinger and Rudolf Nureyev and Mick Jagger and Paloma Picasso and Walter Cronkite and Bobby King and Robert Pépin, "the greatest chef in France," and, of course, Andrew MacIntosh and Zenji Hiroguchi, and on and on.

The island could have supported that many individuals—just barely. There would have been some struggles, some fights, I guess—some killings, even, if food or water ran short. And I suppose some of them would have imagined that Nature or something was very pleased if they emerged victorious. But their survival wouldn't have amounted to a hill of beans, as far as evolution was concerned, if they didn't reproduce, and most of the women on the passenger list were past child-bearing age, and so not worth fighting for.

During the first thirteen years on Santa Rosalia, before Akiko reached puberty, in fact, the only fertile women would have been Selena, who was blind, and Hisako Hiroguchi, who had already given birth to a baby all covered with fur, and three others who were normal. And probably all of them would have been impregnated by victors, even against their will. But in the long run, I don't think it would have made much difference which males did the impregnating, Mick Jagger or Dr. Henry Kissinger or the Captain or the cabin boy. Humanity would still be pretty much what it is today.

In the long run, the survivors would still have been not the most ferocious strugglers but the most efficient fisherfolk. That's how things work in the islands here.

• • •

There were live Maine lobsters who also came within a hair of having their survival skills tested by the Galápagos Archipelago. Before the *Bahía de Darwin* was looted, there were two hundred of them in aerated tanks of saltwater in the hold.

The waters around Santa Rosalia were surely cold enough for them, but perhaps too deep. There was this about them, at any rate: They were like human beings in that they could eat almost anything, if they had to.

And Captain von Kleist, when he was an old, old man, remembered those lobsters in their tanks. The older he became, the more vivid were his recollections of events of the long ago. And after supper one night, he amused

Akiko, the furry daughter of Hisako Hiroguchi, with a science-fiction fantasy whose premise was that the Maine lobsters had made it to the islands, and that a million years had passed, as they have indeed passed now—and that lobsters had become the dominant species on the planet, and had built cities and theaters and hospitals and public transportation and so on. He had lobsters playing violins and solving murders and performing microsurgery and subscribing to book clubs and so on.

The moral of the story was that the lobsters were doing exactly what human beings had done, which was to make a mess of everything. They all wished that they could just be ordinary lobsters, particularly since there were no longer human beings around who wanted to boil them alive.

That was all they had had to complain about in the first place: being boiled alive. Now, just because they hadn't wanted to be boiled alive anymore, they had to support symphony orchestras, and on and on. The viewpoint character in the Captain's story was the underpaid second chair French horn player in the Lobsterville Symphony Orchestra who had just lost his wife to a professional ice hockey player.

• • •

When he made up that story, he had no idea that humanity elsewhere was on the verge of extinction, and that other life forms were facing less and less opposition, in case they had a tendency to become dominant. The

Captain would never hear about that, and neither would anybody else on Santa Rosalia. And I am speaking only of the dominance of large life forms over other large life forms. Truth be told, the planet's most victorious organisms have always been microscopic. In all the encounters between Davids and Goliaths, was there ever a time when a Goliath won?

On the level of the big creatures, then, the visible strugglers, lobsters were surely poor candidates for becoming as elaborately constructive and destructive as humankind. If the Captain had told his mordant fable about octopi instead of lobsters, though, it might not have been quite so ridiculous. Back then, as now, those squishy creatures had highly developed brains, whose basic function was to control their versatile arms. Their situation, one might think, wasn't all that different from that of human beings, with hands to control. Presumably, their brains could do other things with their arms and brains than catch fish.

But I have yet to see an octopus, or any sort of animal, for that matter, which wasn't entirely content to pass its time on earth as a food gatherer, to shun the experiments with unlimited greed and ambition performed by humankind.

· · ·

As for human beings making a comeback, of starting to use tools and build houses and play musical instruments and so on again: They would have to do it with their beaks this time. Their arms have become flippers in which the hand bones are almost entirely imprisoned and immobilized. Each flipper is studded with five purely ornamental nubbins, attractive to members of the opposite sex at mating time. These are in fact the tips of four suppressed fingers and a thumb. Those parts of people's brains which used to control their hands, moreover, simply don't exist anymore, and human skulls are now much more streamlined on that account. The more streamlined the skull, the more successful the fisher person.

• • •

If people can swim as fast and far as fur seals now, what is to prevent their swimming all the way back to the mainland, whence their ancestors came? Answer: nothing.

Plenty have tried it or will try it during periods of fish shortages or overpopulation. But the bacterium which eats human eggs is always there to greet them.

So much for exploration.

Then again, it is so peaceful here, why would anybody want to live on the mainland? Every island has become an ideal place to raise children, with waving coconut palms and broad white beaches—and limpid blue lagoons.

And all the people are so innocent and relaxed now, all because evolution took their hands away.

Quoth Mandarax:

In works of labour, or of skill,
I would be busy, too;
For Satan finds some mischief still
For idle hands to do.

—ISAAC WATTS (1674–1748)

34

THERE WAS THIS PERUVIAN PILOT a million years
ago, a young lieutenant colonel who had his fighter-
bomber skipping from wisp to wisp of finely divided matter at the very edge of the planet's atmosphere. His name
was Guillermo Reyes, and he was able to survive at such
an altitude because his suit and helmet were inflated with
an artificial atmosphere. People used to be so marvelous,
making impossible dreams they made come true.

Colonel Reyes had had an inconclusive discussion
with a fellow airman one time as to whether anything felt
better than sexual intercourse. He was in contact on his
radio now with that same comrade, who was back at the
air base in Peru, and who was to tell him when Peru was
officially at war with Ecuador.

Colonel Reyes had already activated the brain of the
tremendous self-propelled weapon slung underneath his
airplane. That was its first taste of life, but already it was
madly in love with the radar dish atop the control tower at
Guayaquil International Airport, a legitimate military target, since Ecuador kept ten of its own warplanes there.
This amazing radar lover under the colonel's plane was like

the great land tortoises of the Galápagos Islands to this extent: It had all the nourishment it needed inside its shell.

So the word came that it was all right for him to let the thing go.

So he let the thing go.

His friend on the ground asked him what it felt like to give something like that its freedom. He replied that he had at last found something which was more fun than sexual intercourse.

• • •

The young colonel's feelings at the moment of release had to be transcendental, had to be entirely products of that big brain of his, since the plane did not shudder or yaw or suddenly climb or dive when the rocket departed to consummate its love affair. It continued on exactly as before, with the automatic pilot compensating instantly for the sudden change in the plane's weight and aerodynamics.

As for effects of the release visible to Reyes: The rocket was much too high to leave a vapor trail, and its exhaust was clean, so that, to Reyes, it was a rod which quickly shrank to a dot and then to a speck and then to nothingness. It vanished so quickly that it was hard to believe that it had ever existed.

And that was that.

The only residue of the event in the stratosphere had to be in Reyes's big brain or nowhere. He was happy. He was humble. He was awed. He was drained.

• • •

Reyes wasn't crazy to feel that what he had done was analogous to the performance of a male during sexual intercourse. A computer over which he had no control, once he had turned it on, had determined the exact moment of release, and had delivered detailed instructions to the release machinery without any need of advice from him. He didn't know all that much about how the machinery worked anyway. Such knowledge was for specialists. In war, as in love, he was a fearless, happy-go-lucky adventurer.

The launching of the missile, in fact, was virtually identical with the role of male animals in the reproductive process.

Here was what the colonel could be counted on to do: deliver the goods in an instant.

Yes—and that rod which became a dot and then a speck and then nothingness so quickly was somebody else's responsibility now. All the action from now on would be on the receiving end.

He had done his part. He was sweetly sleepy now—and amused and proud.

• • •

And I worry now about skewing my story, since a few characters in it were genuinely insane, and giving the impression that everybody a million years ago was insane. That was not the case. I repeat: that was not the case.

Almost everybody was sane back then, and I gladly

award Reyes that widespread encomium. The big problem, again, wasn't insanity, but that people's brains were much too big and untruthful to be practical.

• • •

No single human being could claim credit for that rocket, which was going to work so perfectly. It was the collective achievement of all who had ever put their big brains to work on the problem of how to capture and compress the diffuse violence of which nature was capable, and drop it in relatively small packages on their enemies.

I myself had had some highly personal experiences with dreams-come-true of that sort in Vietnam—which is to say, with mortars and hand grenades and artillery. Nature could never have been that predictably destructive in such small spaces without the help of humankind.

I have already told my story about the old woman I shot for throwing a hand grenade. There are plenty of others I could tell, but no explosion I saw or heard about in Vietnam could compare with what happened when that Peruvian rocket put the tip of its nose, that part of its body most richly supplied with exposed nerve endings, into that Ecuadorian radar dish.

• • •

No one is interested in sculpture these days. Who could handle a chisel or a welding torch with their flippers or their mouths?

If there were a monument out here in the islands, though, celebrating a key event in the past, that would be a good one: the moment of mating, right before the explosion, between that rocket and that radar dish.

Into the lava plinth beneath it these words might be incised, expressing the sentiments of all who had had a hand in the design and manufacture and sale and purchase and launch of the rocket, and of all to whom high explosives were a branch of the entertainment industry:

> . . . *'Tis a consummation*
> *Devoutly to be wish'd.*
> —WILLIAM SHAKESPEARE (1564–1616)

35

TWENTY MINUTES before the rocket gave that French kiss to the radar dish, Captain Adolf von Kleist concluded that it was now safe for him to come down from the crow's nest of the *Bahía de Darwin*. The ship had been picked clean, and had fewer amenities and navigational aids, even, than had Her Majesty's Ship *Beagle* when that brave little wooden sailboat began her voyage around the world on December 27, 1831. The *Beagle* had had a compass, at least, and a sextant, and navigators who could imagine with considerable accuracy the position of their ship in the clockwork of the universe because of their knowledge of the stars. And the *Beagle,* moreover, had had oil lanterns and candles for the nighttime, and hammocks for the seamen, and mattresses and pillows for the officers. Anyone determined to spend the night on the *Bahía de Darwin* now would have to rest his or her weary head on nude steel, or perhaps do what Hisako Hiroguchi would do when she couldn't keep her eyes open any longer. Hisako would sit on the lid of the toilet off the main saloon, and lay her head on her arms, which were folded atop the washbasin in there.

• • •

I have likened the mob at the hotel to a tidal wave, whose crest swept past the bus, never to return again. I would say that the mob at the waterfront was more like a tornado. Now that ferocious whirlwind was moving inland in the twilight, and feeding on itself, since its members had themselves become worth robbing—carrying lobsters and wine and electronic gear and drapes and coat hangers and cigarettes and chairs and rolls of carpeting and towels and bedspreads, and on and on.

So the Captain clambered down from the crow's nest. The rungs bruised his bare and tender feet. He had the ship and the entire waterfront all to himself, as far as he could see. He went to his cabin first, since he was wearing only his undershorts. He hoped that the looters had left him a little something to wear. When he turned on the light switch in there, though, nothing happened—because all the light bulbs were gone.

There was electricity, anyway—since the ship still had her banks of storage batteries down in the engine room. The thing was: The light-bulb thieves had blacked out the engine room before the batteries and generators and starter motors could be stolen. So, in a sense, they had unwittingly done humanity a big favor. Thanks to them, the ship would still run. Without her navigational aids, she was as blind as Selena MacIntosh—but she was still the fastest ship in that part of the world, and she could slice water at top speed for twenty days without refueling, if necessary, provided nothing went wrong in the pitch-dark engine room.

As things would turn out, though: After only five days at sea, something would go very much wrong in the pitch-dark engine room.

• • •

The Captain certainly had no plans for putting out to sea as he groped about his cabin for more clothes to hide his nakedness. There wasn't even a handkerchief or a washcloth in there. Thus was he having his first taste of a textile shortage, which at the moment seemed merely inconvenient, but which would be acute during the thirty years of life still ahead of him. Cloth to protect his skin from sunburn in the daytime and from chills at night simply would not be available anymore. How he and the rest of the first colonists would come to envy Hisako's daughter Akiko for her coat of fur!

Everybody but Akiko, until Akiko herself had furry babies, would in the daytime have to wear fragile capes and hats made of feathers tied together with fish guts.

Quoth Mandarax to the contrary:

Man is a biped without feathers.
   —PLATO (427?–347 B.C.)

The Captain remained calm as he searched his cabin. The shower in the head was dripping, and he turned it off tight. That much he could make right, anyway. That was how composed he was. As I have already said, his digestive system still had food to process. Even more important to his peace of mind, though, was that nobody was counting on him for anything. Those who had looted the ship almost all had numerous relatives in dire need, who were starting to roll their eyes and pat their bellies and point down their throats like the Kanka-bono girls.

The Captain was still in possession of his famous sense of humor, and freer than ever to indulge it. For whose sake was he now to pretend that life was a serious matter? There weren't even rats left on the ship. There had never been rats on the *Bahía de Darwin,* which was another lucky break for humankind. If rats had come ashore with the first human settlers on Santa Rosalia, there would have been nothing left for people to eat in six months or so.

And then, after that, the rats, after having eaten what was left of the people and each other, would themselves have died.

Quoth Mandarax:

Rats!
They fought the dogs and killed the cats,
And bit the babies in the cradles,
And ate the cheeses out of the vats,
And licked the soup from the cooks' own ladles,
Split open the kegs of salted sprats,
Made nests inside men's Sunday hats,
And even spoiled the women's chats

By drowning their speaking
With shrieking and squeaking
In fifty different sharps and flats.
—ROBERT BROWNING (1812–1889)

The Captain's clever fingers, working in the blacked-out head, now encountered what would prove to be half a bottle of cognac sitting atop the tank of his toilet. This was the last bottle of any sort still aboard the ship, and its contents were the last substance to be found, from stem to stern and from crow's nest to keel, which a human being could metabolize. In saying that, of course, I exclude the possibility of cannibalism. I ignore the fact that the Captain himself was quite edible.

And just as the Captain's fingers got a firm grip on the bottle's neck in the darkness, something big and strong outside gave the *Bahía de Darwin* an authoritative bump. Also: There were male voices from the boat deck, one deck below. The thing was: The tugboat crew which had delivered fuel and food to the Colombian freighter *San Mateo* was now preparing to haul away the *Bahía de Darwin's* two lifeboats. They had cast off the ship's bowline, and the tug was nosing her bow into the estuary, so that the lifeboat on her starboard side could be lowered into the water.

So that the ship was now married to the South American mainland by a single line at her stern. Poetically speaking, that stern line is the white nylon umbilical cord of all modern humankind.

• • •

The Captain might as well have been my fellow ghost on the *Bahía de Darwin*. The men who took our lifeboats never even suspected that there was another soul aboard.

All alone again, except for me, he proceeded to get drunk. What could that matter now? The tugboat, with the lifeboats following obediently, had disappeared upstream. The *San Mateo,* all lit up like a Christmas tree, and with the radar dish atop her bridge revolving, had disappeared downstream, so that the Captain felt free to shout whatever he pleased from the bridge without attracting unfavorable attention. His hands on the ship's wheel, he called into the starlit evening, "Man overboard!" He was speaking of himself.

Expecting nothing to happen, he pressed the starter button for the port engine. From the bowels of the ship came the muffled, deep-purple rumble of a great diesel engine in perfect health. He pressed the other starter button, giving the gift of life to the engine's identical twin. These dependable, uncomplaining slaves had been born in Columbus, Indiana—not far from Indiana University, where Mary Hepburn had taken her master's degree in zoology.

Small world.

• • •

That the diesels still worked was to the Captain simply one more reason to make himself wild and stupid with cognac. He switched off the engines, and it was a good thing he did. If he had let them run long enough to get really hot, that temperature anomaly might have attracted the electronic attention of a Peruvian fighter-bomber in the stratosphere. In Vietnam, we had heat-sensing instruments so sensitive that could actually detect the presence of people, or at least big mammals of some kind, in the night—because their bodies were just a little bit warmer than their surroundings.

One time I called in an artillery barrage on a water buffalo. Usually it was people out there—trying to sneak up on us and kill us, if they could. What a life! I would have loved to put down all my weapons and become a fisherman instead.

•   •   •

And that was the sort of thing the Captain was thinking up there on the bridge: "What a life!" and so on. It was all very funny, except he didn't feel like laughing. He thought that life had now taken his measure, had found him not worth much of anything, and was now through with him. Little did he know!

He went out on the sun deck, which was aft of the bridge and the officers' cabins, his bare feet on bare steel. Now that the sun deck had been stripped of its carpeting, the plugged holes which were supposed to receive the mounts for weapons were plainly visible, even in starlight. I myself had welded four of the plates on the sun deck.

Most of my work, and my finest work, however, was deep inside.

The Captain looked up at the stars, and his big brain told him that his planet was an insignificant speck of dust in the cosmos, and that he was a germ on that speck, and that nothing could matter less than what became of him. That was what those big brains used to do with their excess capacity: blather on like that. To what purpose? You won't catch anybody thinking thoughts like that today.

So then he saw a shooting star—a meteorite burning up on the edge of the atmosphere, up where Lieutenant Colonel Reyes in his space suit had just received word that Peru was officially at war with Ecuador. The shooting star cued the Captain's big brain to have him marvel yet again about how unprepared people were for meteorites striking the Earth's surface.

And then there was this tremendous explosion out at the airport, as the rocket and the radar dish honeymooned.

• • •

The hotel bus, all painted up outside with the blue-footed boobies and marine iguanas and penguins and flightless cormorants and so on, was at that moment parked in front of a hospital. The Captain's brother *Siegfried was about to go inside to get help for *James Wait, who had lost consciousness. *Wait's heart attack had necessitated this detour on the way to the airport, which had surely saved the lives of all on board.

The great bubble of the shock wave from that explosion was as dense as bricks. To those on the bus, it seemed that hospital itself had exploded. The windows and windshield of the bus were blown inward, but turned out to have been shatterproof. They had not turned to shrapnel. Mary and Hisako and Selena and *Kazakh and poor *Wait and the Kanka-bono girls and the Captain's brother were pelted with seeming kernels of white corn instead.

This would happen on the *Bahía de Darwin* as well. The windows would all be blown in, and white kernels would be underfoot everywhere.

The hospital, so full of light only moments before, was blacked out now, as was the whole city, and there were cries for help coming from inside. The engine of the bus was still running, thank God, and its headlights illuminated a narrow pathway through the debris up ahead. So *Siegfried, becoming more palsied by the second, still managed to drive away from there. What help could he or anybody else on the bus be to the survivors, if any, in the blasted hospital?

And the logic of the maze of rubble directed the creeping bus away from the center of the explosion, the airport, and toward the waterfront. The road across marsh from the edge of the city to the deepwater wharves was in fact almost clear of wreckage, there was so little for the shock wave to knock down out there.

• • •

*Siegfried von Kleist drove to the waterfront because it was the path of least resistance. Only he could see where they were going. The others were still on the floor of the bus. Mary Hepburn had dragged the unconscious *James Wait away from the Kanka-bono girls, so that he was lying flat on his back now, with her lap for a pillow. The big brains of the Kanka-bonos had shut down entirely, for want of even a wisp of a theory as to what was going on. Hisako Hiroguchi and Selena MacIntosh and *Kazakh were similarly immobilized.

And everybody was deaf, since the shock wave had done such violence to the bones in their inner ears, the tiniest bones in their bodies. Nor would any of them recover their sense of hearing entirely. With the exception of the Captain, the first colonists on Santa Rosalia would all be slightly deaf, so that a good deal of their conversations would consist, in one language or another, of "Eh?" and "Speak up" and so on.

This defect, fortunately, was not inheritable.

• • •

Like Andrew MacIntosh and Zenji Hiroguchi, they would never find out what hit them—unless there were answers to questions like that at the far end of the blue tunnel into the Afterlife. They would accept the Captain's theory that the explosion and another explosion still to come had been the impacts of white-hot boulders from outer space—but not wholeheartedly, since the Captain would prove to be laughably mistaken about so many things.

• • •

The Captain's palsied younger brother, his ears ringing, some of his hearing returning, stopped the bus on the wharf near the *Bahía de Darwin*. He had not expected her to be a haven. He was unsurprised to find her dark and apparently deserted, with her windows blown in, her lifeboats missing, and barely secured to the wharf by a single line at her stern. Her freed bow was some distance from the wharf, so that her gangplank dangled over water.

She had of course been looted, like the hotel. The wharf was littered with wrappings and cartons and other trash discarded by the scavengers.

*Siegfried did not expect to see his brother. He had heard that the Captain had left New York, but not that he had actually reached Guayaquil. If the Captain was somewhere in Guayaquil, he was very likely dead or injured, or, in any case, in no position to be of much help to anyone. Nobody in Guayaquil at that point in history was in a position to be of much help to anyone else.

Quoth Mandarax:

Help yourself, and heaven will help you.
　　　　—JEAN DE LA FONTAINE
　　　　(1621–1695)

The most *Siegfried hoped to find was a peaceful stopping place in chaos. This he did. There did not seem to be anybody else around.

So he got out of the bus, to see if he couldn't somehow get the involuntary dancing movements caused by Huntington's chorea under control by doing exercises—jumping jacks and push-ups, and deep-knee bends and so on.

The moon was coming up.

And then he saw a human figure rising to its feet on the sun deck of the *Bahía de Darwin*.

It was his brother, but the Captain's face was in shadow, so *Siegfried did not recognize him.

*Siegfried had heard whispered stories about the ship's being haunted. He believed that he was beholding a ghost. He thought it was me. He thought he was seeing Leon Trout.

36

THE CAPTAIN recognized his brother, though, and he shouted down to him what I might have been tempted to shout, had I been a materialized ghost up there. He shouted this: "Welcome to 'the Nature Cruise of the Century'!"

• • •

The Captain, still holding on to his bottle, although it was empty now, came down to the main deck at the stern, so that he was nearly on a level with his brother, and ★Siegfried, because he was so deaf, came as close as he could without falling into the narrow moat between them. That moat was bridged by the stern line, by that white umbilical cord.

"I'm deaf," said ★Siegfried. "Are you deaf, too?"

"No," said the Captain. He had been much farther away than ★Siegfried from the center of the explosion. He had a nosebleed, though, which he chose to find comical. He had bashed his nose when the shock wave knocked him down on the sun deck. The cognac had exacerbated his sense of humor to the point where everything was screamingly funny.

He thought that the exercises *Siegfried had done on the wharf were a lampoon on the dancing sickness they both might have inherited from their father. "I liked your imitation of Father," he said. The whole conversation was in German—the language of their infancy, the first language they had known.

"Adie!" said *Siegfried. "This isn't funny!"

"Everything is funny," said the Captain.

"Do you have any medicine? Do you have any food? Do you still have beds?" said *Siegfried.

The Captain replied with a quotation well known to Mandarax:

I owe much; I have nothing. I give the rest to the poor.
—FRANÇOIS RABELAIS (1494–1553)

"You're drunk!" said *Siegfried.

"Why not?" the Captain asked. "I'm nothing but a clown." The random damage done to his brain by cognac made him terribly self-centered. He could give no thought to the suffering others must be doing in the dark and blasted city in the distance. "You know what one of my own crewmen said to me when I tried to keep him from stealing the compass, Ziggie?"

"No," said *Siegfried, and he started to dance again.

" 'Out of the way, you clown!' " said the Captain,

and he laughed and laughed. "He dared to say that to an admiral, Ziggie. I would have had him hanged from the yardarm, *hick*—if somebody hadn't stolen the, *hick,* yardarm, *hick*. At dawn, *hick*—if somebody hadn't stolen the dawn."

People still get the hiccups, incidentally. They still have no control over whether they do it or not. I often hear them hiccupping, involuntarily closing their glottises and inhaling spasmodically, as they lie on the broad white beaches or paddle around the blue lagoons. If anything, people hiccup more now than they did a million years ago. This has less to do with evolution, I think, than with the fact that so many of them gulp down raw fish without chewing them up sufficiently.

(PEOPLE)

And people still laugh about as much as they ever did, despite their shrunken brains. If a bunch of them are lying around on a beach, and one of them farts, everybody else laughs and laughs, just as people would have done a million years ago.

37

"HICK," THE CAPTAIN WENT ON, "actually I have been vindicated, *hick,* *Siegfried," the Captain went on. "I have long said that we should expect to be hit by large meteorites from time to time. That has, *hick,* come to, *hick,* pass."

"It was the hospital that blew up," said *Siegfried. So it had seemed to him.

"No hospital ever blew up like that," said the Captain, and, to *Siegfried's dismay, he climbed up on the rail and prepared to jump to the wharf. It wasn't all that much of a jump, really—only about two meters across the moat, but the Captain was very drunk.

The Captain aviated successfully, crashing to his knees on the wharf. This cured his hiccups.

"Is there anybody else on the ship?" said *Siegfried.

"Nobody here but us chickens," said the Captain. He had no idea that he and *Siegfried were responsible for rescuing anybody but each other. Everybody on the bus was still on the floor. *Siegfried, incidentally, had entrusted Mary Hepburn with Mandarax, in case she had to communicate with Hisako Hiroguchi. Mandarax, as

224

I've said, was useless as an interpreter for the Kanka-bonos.

The Captain put his arm across the quaking shoulders of *Siegfried, and said to him, "Don't be scared, little brother. We're from a long line of survivors. What's a little shower of meteorites to a von Kleist?"

"Adie—" said *Siegfried, "is there some way we can get the ship closer to the dock?" He thought the people on the bus might feel a little safer and surely less cramped on shipboard.

"Fuck the ship. Nothing left on her," said the Captain. "I think they even stole old Leon." Again—Leon was me.

"Adie—" said *Siegfried, "there are ten people on that bus, and one of them is having a heart attack."

The Captain squinted at the bus. "What makes them so invisible?" he said. His hiccups were gone again.

"They're all on the floor, and they're scared to death," said *Siegfried. "You've got to sober up. I can't look after them. You're going to have to do whatever you can. I'm not in control of my own actions anymore, Adie. Of all the times for it to happen—I have Father's disease."

Time stopped, as far as the Captain was concerned. This was a familiar illusion for him. He could count on experiencing it several times a year—whenever he received news he could not joke about. He knew how to get time going again, which was to deny the bad news. "It isn't true," he said. "It cannot be."

"You think I dance for the fun of it?" said *Siegfried, and he was involuntarily dancing away from his brother.

He approached the Captain again, just as involuntarily, saying, "My life is over. It probably never should have been lived. At least I never reproduced, so that some poor woman might give birth to yet another monstrosity."

"I feel so helpless," said the Captain, and added wretchedly, "and so goddamn drunk. Jesus—I certainly expected no more responsibilities. I'm so drunk. I can't think. Tell me what to do, Ziggie."

He was too drunk to do much of anything, so he stood by, slack-jawed and goggle-eyed, while Mary Hepburn and Hisako and *Siegfried, whenever poor *Siegfried could stop dancing, hauled the stern of the ship right up to the wharf with the bus, and then parked the bus under the stern, so that it could be used as a ladder up to the lowest deck of the ship, which would have been unreachable otherwise.

And oh, yes, you could say, "Wasn't that ingenious of them?" and, "They could never have done that if they hadn't had great big brains," and, "You can bet nobody today could figure out how to do stuff like that," and so on. Then again, those people wouldn't have had to behave so resourcefully, wouldn't have been in such complicated difficulties, if the planet hadn't been made virtually uninhabitable by the creations and activities of other people's great big brains.

Quoth Mandarax:

*What's lost upon the roundabouts we pulls up on the
swings!*

—PATRICK REGINALD CHALMERS
(1872–1942)

• • •

People expected the most trouble to come from the
unconscious ★James Wait. Actually, the most trouble
would come from the Captain, who was too drunk to be
trusted as a link in the human chain, who could only sit
on the back seat of the bus and rue how drunk he was.

His hiccups had returned.

Here is how they got ★James Wait up on the ship:
There was enough extra stern line on the wharf for Mary
Hepburn to make a harness for him at the free end of the
line. This was all her idea, the harness. She was, after all,
an experienced mountaineer. They laid him beside the
bus with the harness on. Then she and Hisako and ★Sieg-
fried got on the roof and hauled him up as gently as
possible. And then the three of them got him over the rail
and onto the main deck. They would later move him up
to the sun deck, where he would regain consciousness
briefly—long enough for him and Mary Hepburn to become man and wife.

• • •

★Siegfried then came back down to tell the Captain
that it was his turn to get aboard. The Captain, knowing
he was going to make a fool of himself while trying to

reach the roof, played for time. Jumping while drunk was easy. Climbing anything the least bit complicated was something else again. Why so many of us a million years ago purposely knocked out major chunks of our brains with alcohol from time to time remains an interesting mystery. It may be that we were trying to give evolution a shove in the right direction—in the direction of smaller brains.

So the Captain, playing for time, and trying to sound judicious and respectable, although he could scarcely stand up, said to his brother, "I'm not so sure that man was well enough to be moved."

*Siegfried was out of patience with him. He said, "That's too damn bad, isn't it—because we just moved the poor bastard anyway. Maybe we should have called a helicopter instead, and had him flown to the bridal suite at the Waldorf-Astoria."

And those would be the last words the brothers von Kleist would ever exchange, except for "Hup!" and "Allez oop!" and "Whoops!" and so on, as the Captain tried and failed to get up on the roof of the bus again and again.

But he finally did get up, although thoroughly humiliated. He was at least able to go from the roof to the ship without further assistance. And then *Siegfried told Mary to get on the ship with the rest of them, and to do what she could for *Wait, whom they believed to be Willard Flemming. She did as she was told, thinking it was a matter of manly pride for him to climb to the roof without assistance.

• • •

That left *Siegfried all alone on the wharf, looking up at the rest of them. And they expected him to join them, but that was not to be. He sat down in the driver's seat instead. Despite his limbs' jerking this way and that, he started up the engine. His plan was to head back for the city at top speed, and to kill himself by smashing into something.

Before he could put the bus in gear, he was stunned by the shock wave from yet another tremendous explosion. This one wasn't in or near the city. This one was downstream, and out in the virtually uninhabited marsh somewhere.

38

THE SECOND EXPLOSION was like the first one. A rocket had mated with a radar dish. The dish in this instance was atop the little Colombian freighter the *San Mateo*. The Peruvian pilot who gave the rocket the spark of life, Ricardo Cortez, imagined that he had caused it to fall in love with the radar dish of the *Bahía de Darwin,* who no longer had radar and so, as far as that particular sort of rocket was concerned, was without sex appeal.

Major Cortez had made what was called a million years ago "an honest mistake."

And let it be said, too, that Peru would never have ordered an attack on the *Bahía de Darwin* if "the Nature Cruise of the Century" had gone ahead as planned, with a shipload of celebrities. Peru would not have been that insensitive to world opinion. But the cancellation of the cruise made the ship an entirely different kettle of fish, so to speak, a potential troop carrier manned, any reasonable person might assume, by persons who were effectively begging to be blown up or napalmed or machine-gunned or whatever, which is to say "naval personnel."

• • •

So these Colombianos were out there in the marsh in the moonlight, headed for the open ocean and home, eating the first decent meal they had had in a week, and imagining that their radar dish was watching over them like a revolving Virgin Mary. She would never allow any harm to come to them. Little did they know.

What they were eating, incidentally, was an old dairy cow who wasn't able to give all that much milk anymore. That was what had been under the tarpaulin on the lighter which had provisioned the *San Mateo:* that dairy cow, still very much alive. And she had been hoisted aboard on the side away from the waterfront, so that people ashore couldn't see her. There were people ashore desperate enough to kill for her.

She was one hell of a lot of protein to be leaving Ecuador.

• • •

It was interesting how they hoisted her. They didn't use a sling or a cargo net. They made a rope crown for her, wrapped around and around her horns. They embedded the steel hook at the end of the cable of the crane in the tangled crown. And then the crane operator up above reeled in the cable so that the cow was soon dangling in thin air—in an upright position for the first time in her life, with her hind legs splayed, her udder exposed, and with her front legs thrust out horizontally, so that she had the general configuration of a kangaroo.

The evolutionary process which had produced this

huge mammal had never anticipated that she might be in such a position, with the weight of her entire body depending from her neck. Her neck as she dangled was coming to resemble that of a blue-footed booby or swan, or flightless cormorant.

To certain sorts of big brains back in those days, her experience with aviation might have been something to laugh about. She was anything but graceful.

And when she was set down on the deck of the *San Mateo,* she was so severely injured that she could no longer stand. But that was to be expected, and perfectly acceptable. Long experience had shown sailors that cattle so treated could go on living for a week or more, would keep their own meat from rotting until it was time for them to be eaten. What had been done to that dairy cow was a shorter version of what used to be done to great land tortoises back in the days of sailing ships.

In either case, there was no need for refrigeration.

• • •

The happy Colombianos were chewing and swallowing some of that poor cow's meat when they were blown to bits by the latest advance in the evolution of high explosives, which was called "dagonite." Dagonite was the son, so to speak, of a considerably weaker explosive made by the same company, and called "glacco." Glacco begat dagonite, so to speak, and both were descendants of Greek fire and gunpowder and dynamite and cordite and TNT.

So it might be said that the Colombianos had treated the cow abominably, but that retribution had been swift and terrible, thanks largely to the big-brained inventors of dagonite.

• • •

In view of how badly the Colombianos had treated the cow, Major Ricardo Cortez, flying faster than sound, might be seen as a virtuous knight as in days of yore. And he felt that way about himself, too, although he knew nothing about the cow or what his rocket had hit. He radioed back to his superiors that the *Bahía de Darwin* was destroyed. He asked that his best friend, Lieutenant Colonel Reyes, who was back on the ground and who had turned a rocket loose on the airport that afternoon, be given this message in Spanish: *It is true.*

Reyes would understand that he was agreeing that letting the rocket go had been as elating as sexual intercourse. And he would never find out that he had not hit the *Bahía de Darwin,* and the friends and relatives of the Colombianos who were blown to hamburger in the estuary would never learn what became of them.

• • •

The rocket which hit the airport was surely a lot more effective in Darwinian terms than the one that hit the *San Mateo.* It killed thousands of people and birds and dogs and cats and rats and mice and so on, who would otherwise have reproduced their own kind.

The blast in the marsh killed only the fourteen crew-men and about five hundred rats on the ship, and a few hundred birds, and some crabs and fish and so on.

Mainly, though, it was an ineffectual assault on the very bottom of the food chain, the billions upon billions of microorganisms who, along with their own excrement and the corpses of their ancestors, comprised the muck of the marsh. The explosion didn't bother them much, since they weren't all that sensitive to sudden starts and stops. They could never have committed suicide in the manner as *Siegfried von Kleist, at the wheel of the bus, intended to commit suicide, with a sudden stop.

They were simply moved suddenly from one neigh-borhood to another one. They flew through the air, bringing a lot of the old neighborhood with them, and then came splattering down. Many of them even experi-enced great prosperity as a result of the explosion, feasting on what was left of the cow and the rats and the crew, and other higher life forms.

Quoth Mandarax:

> It is wonderful to see with how little nature will be satisfied.
>
> ──MICHEL EYQUEM DE MONTAIGNE
>   (1533–1592)

The detonation of dagonite, son of glacco, direct descendant of noble dynamite, caused a tidal wave in the estuary, which was six meters high when it swept the bus off the wharf at the Guayaquil waterfront and drowned Siegfried von Kleist, who wanted to die anyway.

More importantly: It snapped the white nylon umbilical cord which tied the future of humankind to the mainland.

The wave carried the *Bahía de Darwin* a kilometer upstream, then left her gently aground on a mudbank in the shallows there. She was illuminated not only by moonlight, but by sick, jazzy fires breaking out all over Guayaquil.

The Captain arrived on the bridge. He started the twin diesel engines in the darkness far below. He engaged her twin propellers, and the ship slid off the mudbank. She was free.

The Captain steered downstream, toward the open ocean.

Quoth Mandarax:

> *The ship, a fragment detached from the earth, went on lonely and swift like a small planet.*
> —JOSEPH CONRAD (1857–1924)

And the *Bahía de Darwin* wasn't just any ship. As far as humanity was concerned, she was the new Noah's ark.

BOOK TWO

AND THE
THING BECAME

1

THE THING became a new white motorship at night, without charts or a compass or running lights, but nonetheless slitting the cold, deep ocean at her maximum velocity. In the opinion of humankind, she no longer existed. The *Bahía de Darwin* and not the *San Mateo,* in the opinion of humankind, had been blown to smithereens.

She was a ghost ship, out of sight of land and carrying the genes of her captain and seven of her ten passengers westward on an adventure which has lasted one million years so far.

I was the ghost of a ghost ship. I am the son of a big-brained science fiction writer, whose name was Kilgore Trout.

I was a deserter from the United States Marines.

I was given political asylum and then citizenship in Sweden, where I became a welder in a shipyard in Malmö. I was painlessly decapitated one day by a falling sheet of steel while working inside the hull of the *Bahía de Darwin,* at which time I refused to set foot in the blue tunnel leading into the Afterlife.

It has always been within my power to materialize,

but I have done that only once, very early in the game—for a few wet and blustery moments during the storm my ship encountered in the North Atlantic during her voyage from Malmö to Guayaquil. I appeared in the crow's nest, and one Swedish member of the skeleton crew saw me up there. He had been drinking. My decapitated body was facing the stern, and my arms were upraised. In my hands I was holding my severed head as though it were a basketball.

• • •

So I was invisible as I stood next to Captain Adolf von Kleist on the bridge of the *Bahía de Darwin* as we awaited the end of our first night at sea after our hasty departure from Guayaquil. He had been awake all night, and was sober now, but had a terrible headache, which he had described to Mary Hepburn as ". . . a golden screw between my eyes."

He had other souvenirs of the previous evening's humiliating debauch—contusions and abrasions from the several falls he had taken while trying to get up on the roof of the bus. He would never have gotten that drunk if he had realized that he was going to be saddled with any responsibilities. He had already explained that to Mary, who had been up all night, too—nursing ★James Wait on the sun deck, abaft of the officers' cabins.

★Wait had been put up there, with Mary's rolled-up blouse for a pillow, because the rest of the ship was so dark. At least there was starlight up there after the moon went down. The plan was to move him into a cabin when the sun came up, so he would not fry to death on the bare steel plates.

Everybody else was on the boat deck below. Selena MacIntosh was in the main saloon, using her dog for a pillow, and so were the six Kanka-bono girls. They were using each other for pillows. Hisako was in the head off the main saloon, and had fallen asleep while wedged between the toilet and the washbasin.

· · ·

Mandarax, which Mary had turned over to the Captain, was in a drawer on the bridge. This was the only drawer on the whole ship with anything in it. It was slightly ajar, so that Mandarax had overheard and translated much of what had been said during the night. Thanks to a random setting, it translated everything into Kirghiz, including the Captain's plan of action, which went like this: They would go straight to the Galápagos island of Baltra, where there were docking facilities and an airfield and a small hospital. There was a powerful radio station there, so they would learn for certain what the two explosions had been, and how the rest of the world might be faring, in case a widespread shower of meteorites had taken place, or, as Mary had suggested, World War Three had begun.

Yes, and this plan might as well have been translated into Kirghiz, or some other language that practically nobody understood, because they were on a course which was going to cause them to miss the Galápagos Islands entirely.

His ignorance alone might have been enough to carry the ship far off course. But he compounded his mistakes during the first night, before he was sober, by changing course again and again in order to steer for the probable impact points in the ocean of shooting stars. His big brain, remember, had him believing that a meteorite shower was going on. Every time he saw a shooting star, he expected it to hit the ocean and cause a tidal wave.

So he would steer for it in order to receive the wave on the ship's sharp bow. When the sun came up, he could have been, thanks to his big brain, simply anywhere, and headed for simply anywhere.

• • •

Mary Hepburn, meanwhile, somewhere between sleep and wakefulness, next to *James Wait, was doing something people don't have brains enough to do anymore. She was reliving the past. She was a virgin again. She was in a sleeping bag. She was being awakened in the faintest light of dawn, by the call of a whippoorwill. She was camping in an Indiana state park—a living museum, a patch of what the area used to be before Europeans decreed that no plant or animal would be tolerated which was not tamed and edible by humankind. When young Mary stuck her head out of her cocoon, out of her sleeping bag, she saw rotting logs and an undammed stream. She lay on an aromatic mulch of eons of death and discard. There was plenty to eat if you were a microorganism or could digest leaves, but there was no hearty breakfast there for a human being of a million and thirty years ago.

It was early June. It was balmy.

The bird call was coming from a thicket of briars and sumac fifty paces away. She was glad for this alarm clock, for it had been her intention when she went to sleep to awake this early, and to think of her sleeping bag as a cocoon, and to emerge from it sinuously and voluptuously, as she was now doing, a vivacious adult.

What joy!

What satisfaction!

It was perfect, for the girlfriend she had brought with her slept on and on.

So she stole across the springy woodland floor to the thicket to see this fellow early bird. What she saw instead was a tall, skinny, earnest young man in a sailor suit. And it was he who was whistling the piercing call of a whippoorwill. This was Roy, her future husband.

•   •   •

She was annoyed and disoriented. The sailor suit so far inland was a particularly bizarre detail. She felt intruded upon, and that perhaps she should be frightened as well. But if this very strange person was going to come after her, he would have to get through a tangle of briars first. She had slept in her clothes, so she was fully dressed save for her stocking feet.

He had heard her coming. He had amazingly sharp

ears. So did his father. It was a family trait. And he spoke first. "Hello," he said.

"Hello," she said. She would say later that she thought she was the only person in the garden of Eden, and then she came upon this creature in a sailor suit who was acting as though he already owned everything. And Roy would counter that she was the one, in fact, who acted as though she owned everything.

"What are you doing here?" she said.

"I didn't think people were supposed to sleep in this part of the park," he said. He was right about that, and Mary knew it. She and her friend were in violation of the rules of the living museum. They were in an area where only lower animals were supposed to be at night.

"You're a sailor?" she said.

And he said that, yes, he was—or had been until very recently. He had just been discharged from the Navy, and was hitchhiking around the country before going home, and found people were much more inclined to pick him up if he wore his uniform.

● ● ●

It would make no sense today for somebody to ask, as Mary asked Roy, "What are you doing here?" The reasons for being anywhere today are so invariably simple and obvious. Nobody has a tale as tangled as Roy's to tell: that he took his discharge in San Francisco, and cashed in his ticket, and bought a sleeping bag and hitchhiked to the Grand Canyon and Yellowstone National Park and some other places he had always wanted to see. He was especially fascinated by birds, and could talk to them in their own languages.

So he heard on a car radio that a pair of ivory-billed woodpeckers, a species believed to have been long extinct, had been sighted in this little state park in Indiana. He headed straight for there. The story would turn out to be a hoax. These big, beautiful inhabitants of primeval forests really were extinct, since human beings had destroyed all their natural habitats. No longer was there enough rotten wood and peace and quiet for them.

"They needed lots of peace and quiet," said Roy, "and so do I, and so do you, I guess, and I'm sorry if I disturbed you. I wasn't doing anything a bird wouldn't do."

Some automatic device clicked in her big brain, and her knees felt weak, and there was a chilly feeling in her stomach. She was in love with this man.

They don't make memories like that anymore.

2

*JAMES WAIT interrupted Mary Hepburn's reverie with these words: "I love you so much. Please marry me. I'm so lonesome. I'm so scared."

"You save your strength, Mr. Flemming," she said. He had been proposing marriage intermittently all through the night.

"Give me your hand," he said.

"Every time I do, you won't give it back," she said.

"I promise I'll give it back," he said.

So she gave him her hand, and he gripped it feebly. He wasn't having any visions of the future or the past. He was little more than a fibrillating heart, just as Hisako Hiroguchi, wedged between the vibrating toilet and washbasin below, was little more than a fetus and a womb.

Hisako had nothing to live for but her unborn child, she thought.

• • •

People still hiccup as they always have, and they still find it very funny when somebody farts. And they still try to comfort those who are sick with soothing tones of

246

voice. Mary's tone when she kept *James Wait company on the ship is a tone often heard today. With or without words, that tone conveys what a sick person wants to hear now, and what *Wait wanted to hear a million years ago.

Mary said things like this to *Wait in so many words, but her tone alone would have delivered the same messages: "We love you. You are not alone. Everything is going to be all right," and so on.

* * *

No comforter today, of course, has led a love life as complicated as Mary Hepburn's, and no sufferer today has led a love life as complicated as *James Wait's. Any human love story of today would have for its crisis the simplest of questions: whether the persons involved were in heat or not. Men and women now become helplessly interested in each other and the nubbins on their flippers and so on only twice a year—or, in times of fish shortages, only once a year. So much depends on fish.

Mary Hepburn and *James Wait could have their common sense wrecked by love, given the right set of circumstances, at almost any time.

There on the sun deck, just before the sun came up, *Wait was genuinely in love with Mary and Mary was genuinely in love with him—or, rather, with what he claimed to be. All through the night, she had called him "Mr. Flemming," and he had not asked her to call him by his first name. Why? Because he could not remember what his first name was supposed to be.

"I'll make you very rich," said ★Wait.

"There, there," said Mary. "Now, now."

"Compound interest," he said.

"You save your strength, Mr. Flemming," she said.

"Please marry me," he said.

"We'll talk about that when we get to Baltra," she said. She had given him Baltra as something to live for. She had cooed and murmured to him all through the night about all the good things which were awaiting them on Baltra, as though it were a sort of paradise. There would be saints and angels to greet them on the dock there, with every kind of food and medicine.

He knew he was dying. "You'll be a very rich widow," he said.

"Let's not have any talk like that now," she said.

As for all the wealth she was going to inherit technically, since she really was going to marry him and then become his widow: The biggest-brained detectives in the world couldn't have begun to find a minor fraction of it. In community after community, he had created a prudent citizen who didn't exist, whose wealth was increasing steadily, even though the planet itself was growing ever poorer, and whose safety was guaranteed by the governments of the United States or Canada. His savings account in Guadalajara, Mexico, which was in pesos, had been wiped out by then.

If his wealth had continued to grow at the rate it was growing then, the ★James Wait estate would now encompass the whole universe—galaxies, black holes, comets, clouds of asteroids and meteors and the Captain's meteorites and interstellar matter of every sort—simply everything.

Yes, and if the human population had continued to grow at the rate it was growing then, it would now outweigh the *James Wait estate, which is to say simply everything.

What impossible dreams of increase human beings used to have only yesterday, only a million years ago!

3

*Wait had reproduced, incidentally. Not only had he sent that antiques dealer down the blue tunnel into the Afterlife so long ago, he had also made possible the birth of an heir. By Darwinian standards, as both a murderer and a sire, he had done quite well, one would have to say.

He became a sire when he was only sixteen years old, the sexual prime of a human male a million years ago:

He was still in Midland City, Ohio, and it was a hot July afternoon, and he was mowing the lawn of a fabulously well-to-do automobile dealer and owner of local fast-food restaurants named Dwayne Hoover, who had a wife but no children. So Mr. Hoover was in Cincinnati on business, and Mrs. Hoover, whom *Wait had never seen, although he had mowed the lawn many times, was in the house. She was a recluse because, as *Wait had heard, she had a problem with alcohol and drugs prescribed by her doctor, and her big brain had simply become too erratic to be trusted in public.

*Wait was good-looking back then. His mother and father had also been good-looking. He was from a good-

250

looking family. Despite the fact that it was so hot, ★Wait would not take off his shirt—because he was so ashamed of all the scars he had from punishments inflicted by various foster parents. Later, when he was a prostitute on the island of Manhattan, his clients would find those scars, made by cigarettes and coat hangers and belt buckles and so on, very exciting.

★Wait was not looking for sexual opportunities. He had just about made up his mind to light out for Manhattan, and he did not want to do anything which might give the police an excuse for locking him up. He was well known to the police, who frequently questioned him about this or that burglary or whatever, although he had never committed an actual crime. The police were always watching him anyway. They would say to him things like "Sooner or later, Sonny, you're going to make a big mistake."

So Mrs. Hoover appeared in the front door in a skimpy bathing suit. There was a swimming pool out back. Her face was all raddled and addled, and her teeth were bad, but she still had a very beautiful figure. She asked him if he wouldn't like to come into the house, which was air-conditioned, and cool off with a glass of ice tea or lemonade.

The next thing ★Wait knew, they were having sex in there, and she was saying they were two of a kind, both of them lost, and kissing his scars and so on.

Mrs. Hoover conceived, and gave birth to a son nine months later, which Mr. Hoover believed to be his own.

It was a good-looking boy, who would grow up to be a good dancer and very musical, just like *Wait.

• • •

*Wait heard about the baby after he moved to Manhattan, but he could never consider it a relative. He would go years without thinking about it. And then his big brain would suddenly tell him for no good reason that somewhere in the world there was this young male walking around who wouldn't be in this world, if it weren't for him. It would make him feel creepy. That was much too big a result for such a little accident.

Why would he have wanted a son back then? It was the farthest thing from his mind.

• • •

The sexual prime for human males today, incidentally, comes at the age of six or so. When a six-year-old comes across a female in heat, there is no stopping him from engaging in sexual intercourse.

And I pity him, because I can still remember what I was like when I was sixteen. It was hell to be that excited. Then as now, orgasms gave no relief. Ten minutes after an orgasm, guess what? Nothing would do but that you have another one. And there was homework besides!

4

THESE PEOPLE on the *Bahía de Darwin* weren't uncomfortably hungry yet. Everybody's intestines, including those of *Kazakh, were still wringing the last of the digestible molecules from what they had eaten the previous afternoon. Nobody was consuming parts of his or her own body yet, the survival scheme of the Galápagos tortoises. The Kanka-bonos certainly knew what hunger was already. For the rest it would be a discovery.

And the only two people who had to keep their strength up, and not just sleep all the time, were Mary Hepburn and the Captain. The Kanka-bono girls understood nothing about the ship or the ocean, and could make no sense of anything that was said to them in any language but Kanka-bono. Hisako was catatonic. Selena was blind, and *Wait was dying. That left only two people to steer the ship and care for *Wait.

During the first night, those two would agree that Mary should steer during the daytime, when the sun would tell her unambiguously which way was east, from which they were fleeing, and which way was west, where the supposed peace and plenty of Baltra lay. And the Captain would navigate by the stars at night.

Whoever wasn't steering would have to keep *Wait company, and presumably would catch some sleep while doing so. These were certainly long watches to stand. Then again, this was to be a very brief ordeal, since, according to the Captain's calculations, Baltra was only about forty hours from Guayaquil.

If they had ever reached Baltra, which they never did, they would have found it devastated and depopulated by yet another airmailed package of dagonite.

• • •

Human beings were so prolific back then that conventional explosions like that had few if any long-term biological consequences. Even at the end of protracted wars, there still seemed to be plenty of people around. Babies were always so plentiful that serious efforts to reduce the population by means of violence were doomed to failure. They no more left permanent injuries, except for the nuclear attacks on Hiroshima and Nagasaki, than did the *Bahía de Darwin* as it slit and roiled the trackless sea.

It was humanity's ability to heal so quickly, by means of babies, which encouraged so many people to think of explosions as show business, as highly theatrical forms of self-expression, and little more.

What humanity was about to lose, though, except for one tiny colony on Santa Rosalia, was what the trackless sea could never lose, so long as it was made of water: the ability to heal itself.

As far as humanity was concerned, all wounds were about to become very permanent. And high explosives weren't going to be a branch of show business anymore.

●   ✔   ●

Yes, and if humanity had continued to heal its self-inflicted wounds by means of copulation, then the tale I have to tell about the Santa Rosalia Colony would be a tragicomedy starring the vain and incompetent Captain Adolf von Kleist. It would have spanned months rather than a million years, since the colonists would never have become colonists. They would have been marooned persons who were noticed and rescued in a little while.

Among them would have been a shamefaced Captain, solely responsible for their travail.

After only one night at sea, though, the Captain was still able to believe that all was well. It would soon be time for Mary Hepburn to relieve him at the wheel, at which time he would give her these instructions: "Keep the sun over the stern all morning, and over the bow all afternoon." And the Captain saw as his most pressing task the earning of his passengers' respect. They had seen him at his very worst. By the time they docked at Baltra, he hoped, they would have forgotten his drunkenness, and would be telling one and all that he had saved their lives.

That was another thing people used to be able to do, which they can't do anymore: enjoy in their heads events which hadn't happened yet and which might never occur. My mother was good at that. Someday my father would stop writing science fiction, and write something a whole lot of people wanted to read instead. And we would get a new house in a beautiful city, and nice clothes, and so on. She used to make me wonder why God had ever gone to all the trouble of creating reality.

Quoth Mandarax:

> Imagination is as good as many voyages—and how much cheaper!
> —GEORGE WILLIAM CURTIS (1824–1892)

So there the Captain was, half naked on the bridge of the *Bahía de Darwin,* but in his head he was on the island of Manhattan, where most of his money and so many of his friends were anyway. He was going to get there somehow from Baltra, and buy himself a nice apartment on Park Avenue, and the hell with Ecuador.

• • •

Reality intruded now. A very real sun was coming up. There was one small trouble with the sun. The Captain had imagined all night that he was sailing due west, which meant that the sun would be rising squarely astern. This particular sun, however, was astern, all right, but also very much to starboard. So he turned the ship to port until the sun was where it was supposed to be. His big brain, which was responsible for the error he corrected, assured his soul that its mistake was minor and very recent, and had happened because the stars were dimmed by dawn. His big brain wanted the respect of his soul as much as he wanted the respect of his passengers. His brain had a life of its own, and the time would come when he would actually try to fire it for having misled him.

But that time was still five days away.

He still trusted it when he went aft to learn how "Willard Flemming" was, and to help Mary, according to plan, move him into the shade of the gangway between the officers' cabins. I do not put a star before the name of Willard Flemming, since there wasn't really such an individual—so he couldn't die.

And the Captain was so uninterested in Mary Hepburn as a person that he did not even know her last name. He thought it was Kaplan, the name over the pocket of her war-surplus fatigue blouse, which *Wait was using for a pillow now.

*Wait believed her last name to be Kaplan, too, no matter how often she corrected him. During the night he had said to her, "You Jews sure are survivors."

She had replied, "You're a survivor, too, Willard."

"Well," he had said, "I used to think I was one, Mrs. Kaplan. Now I'm not so sure. I guess everybody who isn't dead yet is a survivor."

"Now, now," she had said, "let's talk about something pleasant. Let's talk about Baltra."

But the blood supply to his brain must have been momentarily dependable then, because *Wait had continued to follow this line of reasoning. He'd even given a dry little laugh. He'd said, "There are all these people bragging about how they're survivors, as though that's something very special. But the only kind of person who can't say that is a corpse."

"There, there," she'd said.

• • •

When the Captain appeared before Mary and *Wait after sunrise, Mary had just consented to marry *Wait. He had worn her down. It was as though he had been begging for water all night, so that finally she was going to give him some. If he wanted betrothal so badly, and betrothal was all she had to give him, then she would give him some.

She did not expect, however, to have to honor that pledge almost immediately, or perhaps ever. She certainly liked all he had told her about himself. During the night, he had discovered that she was a cross-country skiing enthusiast. He had responded warmly that he was never happier than when he was on skis, with the clean snow all around, and the silence of the frozen lakes and forests. He had never been on skis in his life, but had once married and ruined the widow of the owner of a ski lodge in the White Mountains in New Hampshire. He courted her in the springtime, and left her a pauper before the green leaves turned orange and yellow and red and brown.

This wasn't a human being Mary was engaged to. She had a pastiche for a fiancé.

Not that it mattered much what she was engaged to, her big brain told her, since they certainly couldn't get married before they got to Baltra, and "Willard Flemming," if he was still alive, would have to go into intensive care immediately. There was plenty of time, she thought, for her to back out of the engagement.

So it did not seem a particularly serious matter when *Wait said to the Captain, "I have the most wonderful news. Mrs. Kaplan is going to marry me. I am the luckiest man in the world."

Fate now played a trick on Mary almost as quick and logical as my decapitation in the shipyard at Malmö. "You are in luck," said the Captain. "As captain of this ship in international waters, I am legally entitled to marry you. Dearly beloved, we are gathered here in the sight of God—" he began, and, two minutes later, he had made "Mary Kaplan" and "Willard Flemming" man and wife.

5

UOTH MANDARAX:

Oaths are but words, and words but wind.
—SAMUEL BUTLER (1612–1680)

And Mary Hepburn on Santa Rosalia would memorize that quotation from Mandarax, and hundreds of others. But as the years went by, she took her marriage to "Willard Flemming" more and more seriously, even though this second husband had died with a smile on his face about two minutes after the Captain pronounced them man and wife. She would say to furry Akiko when she was an old, old lady, bent over and toothless, "I thank God for sending me two good men." She meant Roy and "Willard Flemming." It was her way of saying, too, that she did not think much of the Captain, who was then an old, old man, and the father or grandfather of all the island's young people, save for Akiko.

• • •

Akiko was the only young person in the colony eager to hear stories, and particularly love stories, about life on the mainland. So that Mary would apologize to her for having so few first-person love stories to tell. Her parents had certainly been very much in love, she said, and Akiko enjoyed hearing about how they were still kissing and hugging each other right up to the end.

Mary could make Akiko laugh about the ridiculous love affair, if you could call it that, she had had with a widower named Robert Wojciehowitz, who was head of the English Department at Ilium High School before the school closed down. He was the only person besides Roy and "Willard Flemming" who had ever proposed marriage to her.

The story went like this:

Robert Wojciehowitz started calling her up and asking her for dates only two weeks after Roy was buried. She turned him down, and let him know that it was certainly too early for her to start dating again.

She did everything she could to discourage him, but he came to see her one afternoon anyway, even though she had said she very much wished to be alone. He drove up to her house while she was mowing the lawn. He made her shut off the mower, and then he blurted out a marriage proposal.

Mary would describe his car to Akiko, and make Akiko laugh about it, even though Akiko had never seen and never would see any sort of automobile. Robert Wojciehowitz drove a Jaguar which used to be very beautiful, but which was now all scored and dented on the driver's side. The car was a gift from his wife while she was dying. Her name was *Doris, a name Akiko would give to one of her furry daughters, simply because of Mary's story.

*Doris Wojciehowitz had inherited a little money, and she bought the Jaguar for her husband as a way of thanking him for having been such a good husband. They had a grown son named Joseph, and he was a lout, and he wrecked the beautiful Jaguar while his mother was still alive. Joseph was sent to jail for a year—as a punishment for operating a motor vehicle while under the influence of alcohol.

There is our brain-shrinking old friend alcohol again.

Robert's marriage proposal took place on the only freshly mowed lawn in the neighborhood. All the other yards were being recaptured by wilderness, since everybody else had moved away. And the whole time Wojciehowitz was proposing, a big golden retriever was barking at them and pretending to be dangerous. This was Donald, the dog who had been such a comfort to Roy during the last months of his life. Even dogs had names back then. Donald was the dog. Robert was the man. And Donald was harmless. He had never bitten anybody. All he wanted was for someone to throw a stick for him, so he could bring it back, so somebody could throw a stick for him, so he could bring it back, and so on. Donald wasn't very smart, to say the least. He certainly wasn't going to write Beethoven's Ninth Symphony. When Donald slept, he would often whimper and his hind legs would shiver. He was dreaming of chasing sticks.

Robert was frightened of dogs—because he and his mother had been attacked by a Doberman pinscher when Robert was only five years old. Robert was all right with dogs as long as there was somebody around who knew how to control them. But whenever he was alone with one, no matter what size it was, he sweated and he trembled, and his hair stood on end. So he was extremely careful to avoid such situations.

But his marriage proposal so surprised Mary Hepburn that she burst into tears, something nobody does anymore. She was so embarrassed and confused that she apologized to him brokenly, and she ran into the house. She didn't want to be married to anybody but Roy. Even if Roy was dead, she still didn't want to be married to anybody but Roy.

So that left Robert all alone on the front lawn with Donald.

If Robert's big brain had been any good, it would have had him walk deliberately to his car, while telling Donald scornfully to shut up and go home, and so on. But it had him turn and run instead. His brain was so defective that it had him run right past his car, with Donald loping right behind him—and he crossed the street and climbed an apple tree in the front yard of an empty house belonging to a family which had moved to Alaska.

So Donald sat under the tree and barked up at him.

Robert was up there for an hour, afraid to come down, until Mary, wondering why Donald had been barking so monotonously for so long, came out of her house and rescued him.

When Robert came down, he was nauseated by fear and self-loathing. He actually threw up. After that, and he had spattered his own shoes and pants cuffs, he said snarlingly, "I am not a man. I am simply not a man. I will of course never bother you again. I will never bother any woman ever again."

And I retell this story of Mary's at this point because Captain Adolf von Kleist would hold the same low opinion of his worth after churning the ocean to a lather for five nights and days, and failing to find an island of any kind.

He was too far north—much too far north. So *we* were all too far north—much too far north. I wasn't hungry, of course, and neither was James Wait, who was frozen solid in the meat locker in the galley below. The galley, although stripped of light bulbs and without portholes, could still be illuminated, albeit hellishly, by the heating elements of its electric ovens and stoves.

Yes, and the plumbing was still working, too. There was plenty of water on tap everywhere, both hot and cold.

So nobody was thirsty, but everybody was surely ravenous. Kazakh, Selena's dog, was missing, and I put no star before her name, for Kazakh was dead. The Kankabono girls had stolen her while Selena slept, and choked her with their bare hands, and skinned and gutted her with no other tools than their teeth and fingernails. They had roasted her in an oven. Nobody else knew that they had done that yet.

She had been consuming her own substance anyway. By the time they killed her, she was skin and bones.

If she had made it to Santa Rosalia, she wouldn't have had much of a future—even in the unlikely event that there had been a male dog there. She had been neutered, after all. All she could have accomplished which might have outlasted her own lifetime would have been to give the furry Akiko, soon to be born, infantile memories of a dog. Under the best of circumstances, Kazakh would not have lived long enough for the other children born on the island to pet her, and to see her wag her tail and so on. They wouldn't have had her bark to remember, since Kazakh never barked.

6

I SAY NOW of Kazakh's untimely death, lest anyone should be moved to tears, "Oh, well—she wasn't going to write Beethoven's Ninth Symphony anyway."

I say the same thing about the death of James Wait: "Oh, well—he wasn't going to write Beethoven's Ninth Symphony anyway."

This wry comment on how little most of us were likely to accomplish in life, no matter how long we lived, isn't my own invention. I first heard it spoken in Swedish at a funeral while I was still alive. The corpse at that particular rite of passage was an obtuse and unpopular shipyard foreman named Per Olaf Rosenquist. He had died young, or what was thought to be young in those days, because he, like James Wait, had inherited a defective heart. I went to the funeral with a fellow welder named Hjalmar Arvid Boström, not that it can matter much what anybody's name was a million years ago. As we left the church, Boström said to me: "Oh, well—he wasn't going to write Beethoven's Ninth Symphony anyway."

I asked him if this black joke was original, and he

266

said no, that he had heard it from his German grandfather, who had been an officer in charge of burying the dead on the Western Front during World War One. It was common for soldiers new to that sort of work to wax philosophical over this corpse or that one, into whose face he was about to shovel dirt, speculating about what he might have done if he hadn't died so young. There were many cynical things a veteran might say to such a thoughtful recruit, and one of those was: "Don't worry about it. He wasn't going to write Beethoven's Ninth Symphony anyway."

• • •

After I myself was buried young in Malmö, only six meters from Per Olaf Rosenquist, Hjalmar Arvid Boström said that about me, as he left the cemetery: "Oh, well— Leon wasn't going to write Beethoven's Ninth Symphony anyway."

Yes, and I was reminded of that comment when Captain von Kleist chided Mary for weeping about the death of the man they believed to be Willard Flemming. They had been out to sea for only twelve hours then, and the Captain still felt easily superior to her, and, for that matter, to practically everyone.

He said to her, while he told her how to hold the ship on its western course, "What a waste of time to cry about a total stranger. From what you tell me, he had no relatives and was no longer engaged in any useful work, so what is there to cry about?"

That might have been a good time for me to say as a disembodied voice, "He certainly wasn't going to write Beethoven's Ninth Symphony."

He made a sort of a joke now, but it didn't really sound like much of a joke. "As captain of this ship," he said, "I order you to cry only when there is something to cry about. There's nothing to cry about now."

"He was my husband," she said. "I choose to take that ceremony you performed very seriously. You can laugh if you want." Wait was right out back on the subject still. He hadn't been put in the freezer yet. "He gave a lot to this world, and he had a lot still to give, if only we could have saved him."

"What did this man give the world that was so wonderful?" asked the Captain.

"He knew more about windmills than anybody alive," she said. "He said we could close down the coal mines and the uranium mines—that windmills alone could make the coldest parts of the world as warm as Miami, Florida. He was also a composer."

"Really?" said the Captain.

"Yes," she said, "he wrote two symphonies." I found that piquant, in view of what I have just been saying, that Wait during his last night on earth should have claimed to have written two symphonies. Mary went on to say that when she got back home, she was going to go to Moose Jaw and find those symphonies, which had never been performed, and try to get an orchestra to give them a premiere.

"Willard was such a modest man," she said.

"So it would seem," said the Captain.

• • •

One hundred and eight hours later, the Captain would find himself in direct competition with the reputation of this modest paragon. "If only Willard were still alive," she said, "he would know exactly what to do."

The Captain had wholly lost his self-respect, and, although he had thirty more years to live, he would never get it back again. How is that for a real tragedy? He was abject in the face of Mary's mockery. "I am certainly open to suggestions," he said. "You have only to tell me what the wonderful Willard would have done, and that is what I will most gladly do."

He had by then fired his brain, and was navigating on the advice of his soul alone, turning the ship this way and then that way. An island the size of a handkerchief would have inspired the Captain to sob in gratitude. And, yes, yet again the sun, now dead ahead, now to port, now astern, now to starboard, was going down.

On the deck below, Selena MacIntosh was calling for her dog: "Kaaaaaaaa-zakh. Kaaaaaaaa-zakh. Has anybody seen my dog?"

Mary yelled back, "She's not up here." And then, trying to imagine what Willard would have done, she came up with the idea that Mandarax, along with being a clock and translator and so on, might also be a radio. She told the Captain to try to call for help with it.

The Captain didn't know the instrument was a Mandarax. He thought it was a Gokubi, and he had a Gokubi in his handkerchief drawer, along with some cuff links and shirt studs and watches, in his house back in Quito. His brother had given it to him the previous Christmas, but he hadn't found it useful. To him, it was just another toy, and he knew this much about it: that it was certainly not a radio.

Now he weighed what he thought was a Gokubi in his hand, and he said to Mary, "I would give my right arm to have this piece of junk be a radio. I promise you, though, not even the saintly Willard Flemming could send or receive a message with a Gokubi."

"Maybe it's time you stopped being so absolutely certain about so much!" said Mary.

"That thought has occurred to me," he said.

"Then send an SOS," said Mary. "What harm can it do?"

"No harm, surely," said the Captain: "Mrs. Flemming, you are absolutely right. It can surely do no harm." He spoke into the tiny microphone of Mandarax, saying the international word for a ship in distress a million years ago: "Mayday, Mayday, Mayday," he intoned.

He then held the screen of Mandarax so that he and Mary might both read any reply which might appear there. As it happened, they had tapped into that part of the instrument's intellect, lacking in Gokubi, which knew so many quotations on every conceivable subject, includ-

ing the month of May. On the little screen these utterly
mystifying words appeared:

> *In depraved May, dogwood and chestnut, flowering Judas,*
> *To be eaten, to be divided, to be drunk*
> *Among whispers . . .*
> —T. S. ELIOT (1888–1965)

7

THE CAPTAIN AND MARY were able to believe for a moment that they had made contact with the outside world, although no response to an SOS could have come that fast and been so literary.

So the Captain called again, "Mayday! Mayday! This is the *Bahía de Darwin* calling, position unknown. Do you read me?"

To which Mandarax replied:

> *May will be fine next year as like as not:*
> *Oh ay, but then we shall be twenty-four.*
> —A. E. HOUSMAN (1859–1936)

So then it was evident that the word *May* was triggering quotations from the instrument itself. The Captain puzzled over this. He still believed he had a Gokubi, but that it might be slightly more sophisticated than the one he had at home. Little did he know! He caught on that he was getting responses to the word "May." So then he tried "June."

And Mandarax replied:

June is bustin' out all over.

—OSCAR HAMMERSTEIN II
(1895–1960)

"October! October!" cried the Captain.
And Mandarax replied:

The skies they were ashen and sober;
The leaves they were crispèd and sere—
The leaves they were withering and sere;
It was night in the lonesome October
Of my most immemorial year.

—EDGAR ALLAN POE (1809–1849)

So that was that for Mandarax, which the Captain
still believed to be a Gokubi. And Mary said that she
might as well go back up into the crow's nest, to see what
she could see.

Before she went up there, though, she had one more
barb for the Captain. She asked him to name the island
she might expect to see very soon. This was something he
had done all through the third day at sea, naming islands
which were just below the horizon and dead ahead, supposedly. "Keep your eyes peeled for San Cristóbal, or
maybe Genovesa—depending on how far south we are,"
he had said, or, later in the day, "Ah! I know where we
are now. At any moment we will be seeing Hood Island—
the only nesting place in the world for the waved alba-
tross, the largest bird in the archipelago." And so on.

Those albatrosses, incidentally, are still around today and still nesting on Hood. They have wingspreads as great as two meters, and remain as committed as ever to the future of aviation. They still think it's the coming thing.

As the fifth day drew to a close, though, the Captain remained silent when Mary asked him to name any island he believed to be nearby.

So she asked him again, and he told her this: "Mount Ararat."

• • •

When she got up into the crow's nest, though, I was surprised that she did not cry out in wonderment at what I mistook for a very queer weather phenomenon taking place right over the stern of the ship, and then trailing aft—over the wake. It seemed electrical in nature, although very silent, a close relative of ball lightning, maybe, or Saint Elmo's fire.

That former high school teacher looked right at it, but gave no sign that she found it at all out of the ordinary. And then I understood that only I could see it, and so knew it for what it was: the blue tunnel into the Afterlife. It had come after me again.

I had seen it three times before: at the moment of my decapitation, and then at the cemetery in Malmö, when Swedish clay was thumping wetly on the lid of my coffin and Hjalmar Arvid Boström, who certainly was never going to write Beethoven's Ninth Symphony, said of me, "Oh, well—he wasn't going to write Beethoven's

Ninth Symphony anyway." Its third appearance was when I myself was up in the crow's nest—during a storm in the North Atlantic, in the sleet and spray, holding my severed head on high as though it were a basketball.

The question the blue tunnel implies by appearing is one only I can answer: Have I at last exhausted my curiosity as to what life is all about? If so, I need only step inside what I liken to a vacuum cleaner. If there is indeed suction within the blue tunnel, which is filled with a light much like that cast off by the electric stoves and ovens of the *Bahía de Darwin,* it does not seem to trouble my late father, the science fiction writer Kilgore Trout, who can stand right in the nozzle and chat with me.

• • •

The first thing Father said to me from above the stern of the *Bahía de Darwin* was this: "Had enough of the ship of fools, my boy? You come to Papa right now. Turn me down this time, and you won't see me again for a million years."

A million years! My God—a million years! He wasn't fooling. As bad a father as he had been, he had always kept his promises, and he had never knowingly lied to me.

So I took one step in his direction, but not a second one. I was like a female blue-footed booby at the start of a courtship dance. As in a courtship dance, that uncertain first step was the first tick of a clock, which would become irresistible. Already I was changed, although I was still a long way from the nozzle. The throbbing of the *Bahía de Darwin*'s engines became fainter and the steel sun deck became transparent, so that I could see into the main saloon below, where the Kanka-bono girls were gnawing the bones of their innocent sister Kazakh.

That first step toward my father made me think this about the Indian girls and Mary up in the crow's nest to my back, and Hisako Hiroguchi and her fetus in the lavatory and the demoralized Captain and the blind Selena on the bridge, and the corpse in the walk-in freezer: "Why should I ever have cared about these strangers, these slaves of fear and hunger? What do they have to do with me?"

• • •

When I failed to take a second step in his direction, my father said, "Keep moving, Leon. No time to be coy."

"But I haven't completed my research," I protested. I had chosen to be a ghost because the job carried with it, as a fringe benefit, license to read minds, to learn the truth of people's pasts, to see through walls, to be many places all at once, to learn in depth how this or that situation had come to be structured as it was, and to have access to all human knowledge. "Father—" I said, "give me five more years."

"Five years!" he exclaimed. He mocked me with the three previous bargains I had made with him: " 'Just one more day, Dad.' 'Just one more month, Daddy.' 'Just six more months, Pop.' "

"But I'm learning so much about what life is really like, how it really works, what it's really all about!" I said.

"Don't lie to me," he said. "Did I ever lie to you?"

"No, sir," I said.

"Then don't lie to me," he said.

"Are you a god now?" I said.

"No," he said. "I am still nothing but your father, Leon—but don't lie to me. For all your eavesdropping, you've accumulated nothing but information. You might as well be a collector of baseball cards or bottlecaps. For the sense you can make of all the information you have now, you might as well be Mandarax."

"Just five more years, Daddy, Dad, Father, Pa," I said.

"Not nearly enough time for you to learn what you hope to learn," he said. "And that, my boy, is why I give you my word of honor: If you send me away now, I won't be back for a million years.

"Leon! Leon! Leon!" he implored. "The more you learn about people, the more disgusted you'll become. I would have thought that your being sent by the wisest men in your country, supposedly, to fight a nearly endless, thankless, horrifying, and, finally, pointless war, would have given you sufficient insight into the nature of humanity to last you throughout all eternity!

"Need I tell you that these same wonderful animals, of which you apparently still want to learn more and more, are at this very moment proud as Punch to have weapons in place, all set to go at a moment's notice, guaranteed to kill everything?

"Need I tell you that this once beautiful and nourishing planet when viewed from the air now resembles the diseased organs of poor Roy Hepburn when exposed at his autopsy, and that the apparent cancers, growing for the sake of growth alone, and consuming all and poisoning all, are the cities of your beloved human beings?

"Need I tell you that these animals have made such a botch of things that they can no longer imagine decent lives for their own grandchildren, even, and will consider it a miracle if there is anything left to eat or enjoy by the year two thousand, now only fourteen years away?

"Like the people on this accursed ship, my boy, they are led by captains who have no charts or compasses, and who deal from minute to minute with no problem more substantial than how to protect their self-esteem."

· · ·

As in life, he still needed a shave. As in life, he was still pale and haggard. As in life, he was still smoking a cigarette. And one reason, surely, that I found it hard to take another step in his direction was that I did not like him.

I had run away from home when I was sixteen because I was so ashamed of him.

If there had been an angel in the mouth of the blue tunnel, instead of my father, I might have skipped right in.

• • •

James Wait ran away from home because people were inflicting physical pain on him all the time. He might as well have gone straight from the delivery room to the Spanish Inquisition, so ingenious were some of the tortures the big brains of foster parents had devised for him. I ran away from a real parent who had never once in anger laid a hand on me.

But when I was too young to know any better, my father had made me his co-conspirator in driving my mother away forever. He had me jeering along with him at Mother for wanting to take a trip somewhere, to make some friends and have them over to dinner, to go to a movie or a restaurant sometime. I agreed with my father. I then believed that he was the greatest writer in the world, since that was all I could think to be proud of. We had no friends, and ours was the shabbiest house in the neighborhood, and we didn't even own a television set or an automobile. So why wouldn't I have defended him against my mother? To his credit, anyway, he never suggested that he might have greatness. When I was green in judgment, though, I found greatness implied in his insistence on doing nothing but writing and smoking all the time—and I mean all the time.

Oh, yes, and there was one other thing I could be proud of, and this really counted for something in Cohoes: My father had been a United States Marine.

When I got to be sixteen, though, I myself had arrived at the conclusion my mother and the neighbors had reached so long ago: that my father was a repellent failure, his work appearing only in the most disreputable publications, which paid him almost nothing. He was an insult to life itself, I thought, when he went on doing nothing with it but writing and smoking all the time—and I mean all the time.

I was then flunking every course but art at school. Nobody flunked art at Cohoes High School. That was simply impossible. And I ran away to find my mother, which I never did.

• • •

Father had published more than a hundred books and a thousand short stories, but in all my travels I met only one person who had ever heard of him. Encountering such a person after so long a search was so confusing to me emotionally, that I think I actually went crazy for a little while.

I never telephoned Father or dropped him so much as a postcard. I did not know he had died until I myself had died, and he appeared to me for the first time at the mouth of the blue tunnel into the Afterlife.

Yet I had honored him for the one thing I thought he had to be proud of still: I, too, had been a United States Marine. It was a family tradition.

And by golly if I haven't now become a writer, too, scribbling away like Father, without the slightest hint that there might actually be a reader somewhere. There isn't one. There can't be one.

• • •

So now we have both been like courting blue-footed boobies, doing what we had to do, whether there was anybody to notice—or, far more likely, not.

• • •

Now Father said to me from the nozzle, "You're just like your mother."

"In what way?" I said.

"You know what her favorite quotation was?" he said.

I certainly did, and so did Mandarax. It is the epigraph of this book.

• • •

"You believe that human beings are good animals, who will eventually solve all their problems and make earth into a Garden of Eden again."

"Could I see her, please?" I said. I knew she was somewhere at the other end of the tunnel, that she was dead. That was the first thing I had asked Father after I myself was dead: "Do you know what became of Mother?" I had searched everywhere for her, before joining the United States Marines.

"Is that Mother right behind you?" I said. The blue tunnel was in a restless state of peristalsis. Its squirms often afforded me glimpses deep into its interior. I saw this woman in there, that third time father appeared, and I thought it might be Mother—but no such luck.

"It's Naomi Tharp, Leon," the woman called out to me. She was the neighbor woman who, after my real mother left, did her best to be my mother for a little while. "It's Mrs. Tharp," she called. "You remember me, don't you, Leon? You come in here just like you used to come in through my kitchen door. Be a good boy now. You don't want to be left out there for another million years."

I took another step toward the nozzle. The *Bahía de Darwin* became a fantasia of cobwebs. The blue tunnel became as substantial and sensible a means of transportation as the Malmö streetcar which used to take me to and from the shipyard every day.

But then, behind me, from up in the *Bahía de Darwin*'s gossamer crow's nest, I heard the dim spook which Mary had become shouting something over and over again. She was in agony of some sort, I thought. I could not make out her words, but her tone would have been appropriate if she had been shot in the stomach.

I had to know what she was saying, and so I took two steps backwards, and then turned and looked up at her. She was sobbing, she was laughing. She was bent over the rim of the steel bucket, so that her head was upside down as she shouted to the Captain on the bridge: "Land ho! Land ho! Praise God! Dear God! Land ho! Land ho!"

8

It was Santa Rosalia which Mary Hepburn saw. The Captain would of course steer for it at once, hoping to find it inhabited by people—or at least populated by animals he and the others could cook and eat.

What remained in question was whether I would be along to see what happened next. The price I would have to pay for satisfying my curiosity about the destinies of the people on the ship was unambiguous: to continue to haunt the earth, without a chance of parole, for a million years.

The decision was made for me by Mary Hepburn, by "Mrs. Flemming," whose joy in the crow's nest held my attention so long that when I looked back at the tunnel, the tunnel was gone.

• • •

I have now completed that sentence of one thousand millennia. I have paid in full my debt to society or whatever. I can expect to see the blue tunnel again at any time. I will of course skip into its mouth most gladly. Nothing ever happens around here anymore that I haven't seen or heard so many times before. Nobody, surely, is going to write Beethoven's Ninth Symphony—or tell a lie, or start a Third World War.

Mother was right: Even in the darkest times, there really was still hope for humankind.

• • •

On the afternoon of Monday, December 1, 1986, Captain Adolf von Kleist, whose ship was without a utile anchor, intentionally ran the *Bahía de Darwin* aground on a lava shoal which was close to shore. He believed that she could drag herself free, as she had done in Guayaquil, when it was time to sail again.

When did he plan to sail again? As soon as the larders were stocked with eggs and boobies and iguanas and penguins and cormorants and crabs, and anything else that was edible and easy to catch. When he had a food supply to match his stores of fuel and water, he could return at leisure to the mainland, and seek a peaceful port which would take them in. He would rediscover the South American continent.

He switched off his faithful engines. That would be the end of their faithfulness. For reasons he was never able to determine, they would never start again.

This meant that the stoves and ovens and refrigerators would soon be out of business, too—as soon as the batteries ran down.

• • •

There were still ten meters of stern line, of white nylon umbilical cord, coiled by a cleat on the main deck. The Captain tied knots in this, and then he and Mary climbed down it to the shoal, and waded ashore to gather eggs and kill lower animals who had no fear of them. They would use Mary's blouse and James Wait's new shirt, which still had the price tag on it, for grocery bags.

They wrung the necks of boobies. They caught land iguanas by their tails, and beat them to death on black boulders. And it was during this carnage that Mary would scratch herself, and a fearless vampire finch would take its first sip of human blood.

• • •

The killers left the marine iguanas alone, believing them to be inedible. Two years would pass before their discovery that partially digested seaweed in the bellies of these creatures was not only a tasty hot meal, ready cooked, but a cure for vitamin and mineral deficiencies which had troubled them up to then. That would complete their diet. Some people, moreover, could digest this purée better than others, so that they were healthier and nicer looking—more desirable as sexual partners. So the Law of Natural Selection went to work, with the result, a million years later, that human beings can now digest seaweed for themselves, without the intervention of marine iguanas, which they leave alone.

That is such a much nicer arrangement for everyone.

People still kill fish, though, and, in times of fish shortages, they will still eat boobies, who still aren't afraid of them.

I could stay here another million years, and that still wouldn't be time enough, I'm sure, for the boobies to realize that people are dangerous. Yes, and as I've already said, they still dance and dance at mating time.

• • •

The people had quite a feast on the *Bahía de Darwin* that night. They ate on the sun deck, and the deck itself was the serving platter, and the Captain was the chef. There were roasted land iguanas stuffed with crabmeat and minced finches. There were roasted boobies stuffed with their own eggs and basted with melted penguin fat. It was perfectly delicious. Everybody was happy again.

And at first light the next morning, the Captain and Mary went ashore again, and took the Kanka-bono girls along. The girls could finally understand something which was going on. They all killed and killed, and hauled corpses and hauled corpses, until the ship's freezer contained, in addition to James Wait, enough birds and iguanas and eggs to last for a month, if necessary. Now they had not only plenty of fuel and water, but no end of food, and good food, too, as well.

Next the Captain would start the engines. He would head the ship due east at maximum velocity. There was no way he could miss South America or Central America or North America, the Captain told Mary, his sense of

286

humor returning, ". . . unless we are unlucky enough to pass through the Panama Canal. But if we do go through the canal, I can virtually guarantee you that we will be in Europe or Africa by and by."

So he laughed, and she laughed. Everything was going to be all right after all. But then the engines wouldn't start.

9

By the time the *Bahía de Darwin* slid beneath the dead calm ocean, which was in September of 1996, everybody but the Captain was calling her by a nickname given to her by Mary, which was "the *Walloping Window Blind*."

This disparaging title was taken from a song Mary learned from Mandarax, which went like this:

> *A capital ship for an ocean trip*
> *Was the* Walloping Window Blind.
> *No gale that blew dismayed her crew*
> *Or troubled the captain's mind.*
> *The man at the wheel was taught to feel*
> *Contempt for the wildest blow,*
> *And it often appeared, when the weather had cleared*
> *That he'd been in his bunk below.*
> —CHARLES CARRYL (1842–1920)

Hisako Hiroguchi and her furry daughter Akiko and Selena MacIntosh all called her "the *Walloping Window Blind*," and so did the Kanka-bono women, who loved the sound of the words without understanding them. And when the Kanka-bono women bore children, which they hadn't done yet, they would teach their young that they themselves had come from the mainland on a magic ship, since vanished, called "the *Walloping Window Blind*."

Akiko, who was fluent in Kanka-bono as well as English and Japanese, and who was the only non-Kanka-bono who could converse with the Kanka-bonos, would never find a satisfactory way to translate this into Kanka-bono: "the *Walloping Window Blind*."

The Kanka-bonos could no more understand it and its comical intent than could a modern person, if I were to whisper in his or her ear as he or she basked on a white sandy beach by a blue lagoon: "the *Walloping Window Blind*."

• • •

It was soon after the *Walloping Window Blind* went to the bottom that Mary began her artificial insemination program. She was then sixty-one. She was the sole sexual partner of the Captain, who was sixty-six, and whose sexual drive was no longer all that compelling. And he was determined not to reproduce, since he felt that there was still a good chance that he could pass on Huntington's chorea. Also, he was a racist, and so not at all drawn to Hisako or her furry daughter, and least of all to the Indian women who would ultimately bear his children.

Remember: These people were expecting to be rescued at any time, and had no way of knowing that they were the last hope for the human race. So that they engaged in sexual activities simply to pass some of the time pleasantly, to relieve an itch, or to make themselves sleepy, or what you will. So far as anybody knew, reproducing would actually be irresponsible, since Santa Rosalia was no place to raise children, and children would also place strains on the food supply.

Mary felt this as strongly as anyone before the *Walloping Window Blind* joined the Ecuadorian fleet of submarines: that it would be a tragedy if a child were born.

Her soul continued to feel that, but her big brain began to wonder, idly, so as not to spook her, if the sperm which the Captain squirted into her about twice a month could be transferred to a fertile woman somehow—with, hey presto, a resulting pregnancy. Akiko, who was only ten then, wasn't yet ovulating. But the Kanka-bono women, who ranged in age from fifteen to nineteen, surely were.

• • •

Mary's big brain told her what she had so often told her students: that there was no harm, and possibly a lot of good, in people's playing with all sorts of ideas in their heads, no matter how supposedly impossible or impractical or downright crazy they seemed to be. She reassured herself there on Santa Rosalia, as she had reassured the adolescents of Ilium, that mental games played with even the trashiest ideas had led to many of the most significant scientific insights of what she, a million years ago, called "modern times."

She consulted Mandarax about curiosity.
Quoth Mandarax:

Curiosity is one of the permanent and certain charac-
teristics of a vigorous mind.
　　—SAMUEL JOHNSON (1709–1784)

What Mandarax didn't tell her, and what her big brain certainly wasn't going to tell her, was that, if she came up with an idea for a novel experiment which had a chance of working, her big brain would make her life a hell until she had actually performed that experiment.

That, in my opinion, was the most diabolical aspect of those old-time big brains: They would tell their owners, in effect, "Here is a crazy thing we could actually do, probably, but we would never do it, of course. It's just fun to think about."

And then, as though in trances, the people would really do it—have slaves fight each other to the death in the Colosseum, or burn people alive in the public square for holding opinions which were locally unpopular, or build factories whose only purpose was to kill people in industrial quantities, or to blow up whole cities, and on and on.

● ● ●

Somewhere in Mandarax there should have been, but was not, a warning to this effect: "In this era of big brains, anything which can be done will be done—so hunker down."

The closest Mandarax came to saying anything like that was a quotation from Thomas Carlyle (1795–1881):

> *Doubt, of whatever kind, can be ended in Action alone.*

• • •

Mary's doubts about whether a woman could be impregnated by another one on a desert island without any technical assistance led to her taking action. In a trancelike state, she found herself visiting the camp of the Kankabono women on the other side of the crater, having brought Akiko along as an interpreter.

And now I catch myself remembering my father when he was still alive, when he was still an ink-stained wretch in Cohoes. He was always hoping to sell something to the movies, so that he wouldn't have to take odd jobs, and we could get a cook and cleaning lady.

But no matter how much he might yearn for a movie sale, the crucial scenes in every one of his stories and books were events which nobody in his right mind would ever want to put into a movie—not if he wanted the movie to be popular.

So now I myself am telling a story whose crucial scene could never have been included in a popular movie of a million years ago. In it Mary Hepburn, as though hypnotized, dips her right index finger into herself and then into an eighteen-year-old Kanka-bono woman, making her pregnant.

Mary would later think of a joke she might make about the rash, inexplicable, irresponsible, plain crazy liberties she had taken with the bodies of not just one but all of the Kanka-bono teenagers. She was no longer on speaking terms, though, with the colonist who would have understood the joke, who was the Captain, so she had to keep it to herself. The joke, if articulated, would have gone like this:

"If only I had thought of doing this when I was still teaching at Ilium High School, I would be in a cozy New York State prison for women instead of on godforsaken Santa Rosalia now."

10

WHEN THE SHIP WENT DOWN, it took the bones of James Wait with it, all mixed up on the floor of the meat locker with the bones of reptiles and birds of a sort which are still around today. Only bones like Wait's are unclothed with flesh today.

He was some kind of male ape, evidently—who walked upright, and had an extraordinarily big brain whose purpose, one can guess, was to control his hands, which were cunningly articulated. He may have domesticated fire. He may have used tools.

He may have had a vocabulary of a dozen words or more.

● ● ●

When the ship went down, the Captain had the only beard on the island. One year after that, his son Kamikaze would be born. Thirteen years after that, the island would have its second beard, the beard of Kamikaze.

Quoth Mandarax:

> *There was an Old Man with a beard,*
> *Who said: "It is just as I feared!*

Two owls and a hen,
Four larks and a wren
Have all built their nests in my beard."
—EDWARD LEAR (1812–1888)

By the time the ship went down, when the colony was ten years old, the Captain had become a very boring person, without enough to think about, without enough to do. He spent much of his time in the neighborhood of the island's only water supply, which was a spring at the base of the crater. When people came to get water, he would receive them as though he were the kindly and knowledgeable master of the spring, its assistant and conservator. He would tell even the Kanka-bonos, who never understood a word he said, how the spring was that day—characterizing its dribbling from a crack in a rock as being ". . . very nervous today," or ". . . very cheerful today," or ". . . very lazy today," or whatever.

The dribbling was in fact quite steady, and had been for thousands of years before the colonists got there, and remains so, although people no longer have to depend on it, to the present day. Here was how it worked, and it didn't take a graduate of the United States Naval Academy to understand its mysteries: The crater was an enormous bowl which caught rainwater, which it hid from the sunshine beneath a very thick layer of volcanic debris. There was a slow leak in the bowl, which was the spring.

There was no way in which the Captain, with so much time on his hands, might have improved the spring.

The water already dribbled most satisfactorily from a crack in a lava boulder, and was already caught in a natural basin ten centimeters below. That basin was and still is about the size of the washbasin in the lavatory off the main saloon of the *Walloping Window Blind*. If emptied, that basin, with or without encouragement from the Captain, would in twenty-three minutes and eleven seconds, as timed by Mandarax, be brimming full again.

How would I describe the declining years of the Captain? I would have to say that he felt quietly desperate. But he surely needn't have been marooned on Santa Rosalia in order to feel that way.

Quoth Mandarax:

The mass of men lead lives of quiet desperation.
—HENRY DAVID THOREAU (1817–1862)

And why was quiet desperation such a widespread malady back then, and especially among men? Yet again I trot onstage the only real villain in my story: the oversize human brain.

• • •

Nobody leads a life of quiet desperation nowadays. The mass of men was quietly desperate a million years ago because the infernal computers inside their skulls were incapable of restraint or idleness; were forever demanding more challenging problems which life could not provide.

• • •

I have now described almost all of the events and circumstances crucial, in my opinion, to the miraculous survival of humankind to the present day. I remember them as though they were queerly shaped keys to many locked doors, the final door opening on perfect happiness.

One of those keys, surely, was the absence of tools on Santa Rosalia, save for feeble combinations of bones and twigs and rocks and fish guts—and bird guts.

If the Captain had had any decent tools, crowbars and picks and shovels and so on, he surely would have found a way, in the name of science and progress, to clog the spring, or to cause it to vomit the entire contents of the crater in only a week or two.

• • •

As for the balance the colonists established between themselves and their food supply: I have to say that that, too, was based on luck rather than intelligence.

Nature chose to be generous, so there was enough to eat. The birds on the other islands were having good years, and so sent emigrants from overpopulated rookeries to Santa Rosalia to take over the nests of those eaten by the people. There was no such natural replacement scheme for the marine iguanas, who were not long-distance swimmers. But the repulsiveness of those scrofulous reptiles and the contents of their intestines inspired people to use them for nourishment only during dire shortages of almost any other sort of food.

The most satisfactory food, everybody agreed, was an egg cooked for hours on a nice flat rock in the sunshine. There was no fire on Santa Rosalia. After that came a fish stolen from a bird. After that came a bird itself. After that came the green pulp from inside a marine iguana.

Nature, in fact, was so bountiful that there was a reserve supply of food, of which the colonists were aware, but to which they never had to turn. There were seals and sea lions of all ages, none of them suspicious or ferocious, save for the males at mating time, lolling everywhere, making goo-goo eyes at passing human beings. They were edible as hell.

• • •

It just might have been fatal that the colonists killed off all the land iguanas almost immediately—but it turned out not to have been a disaster. It could have mattered a lot. It just happened that it didn't matter much at all. There have never been great land tortoises on Santa Rosalia, or the colonists probably would have exterminated them as well. But that wouldn't have mattered either.

Meanwhile, in other parts of the world, particularly in Africa, people were dying by the millions because they were unlucky. It hadn't rained for years and years. It used to rain a lot there, but now it looked as though it might never rain again.

At least the Africans had stopped reproducing. That much was good. That was some help. That meant that there was that much more of nothing to be spread around.

• • •

The Captain did not realize that any of the Kanka-
bono women were pregnant until a month before the first
one of them gave birth—gave birth, as it happened, to the
first human male native to the island, who came to be
known by the nickname the furry Akiko gave him, expressing her delight in his maleness, which was "Kamikaze," Japanese for "sacred wind."

• • •

The original colonists never became a family which
included everyone. Subsequent generations, though, after
the last of the old people died, would become a family
which included everyone. It had a common language and
a common religion and some common jokes and songs
and dances and so on, almost everything Kanka-bono.
And Kamikaze, when it was his turn to be an old, old
man, became something the Captain had never been,
which was a venerated patriarch. And Akiko became a
venerated matriarch.

It went very fast—that formation from such random
genetic materials of a perfectly cohesive human family.
That was so nice to see. It almost made me love people
just as they were back then, big brains and all.

11

T HE C APTAIN found out that a Kanka-bono woman was pregnant only very late in the game because nobody was about to tell him, certainly, but also because the Kanka-bono women hated him so much, mainly on racist grounds, that he hardly ever saw one. They came to his side of the crater for water only late at night, when he was usually sound asleep, just so they could avoid him. They would go on hating him that much right up to the end of his life, even though he was the father of all the children they loved so much.

But a month before Kamikaze was born, the Captain could not sleep on his and Mary's feather bed. His big brain made him itch and squirm with a scheme for digging down to the water supply from the top of the crater, and locating the leak, and thus gaining control of what nobody had any reason to complain about: the rate of flow of the spring.

This was an engineering project, incidentally, about as modest as the construction of the Great Pyramid of Khufu or the Panama Canal.

So the Captain got out of bed and went for a walk in the middle of the night. The moon was full and directly overhead. When he came to the spring, there were the six Kanka-bonos, patting the top of the water in the brimming basin as though it were a friendly animal, and sprinkling each other and so on. They were having so much fun, and they were especially happy because they were all going to have babies soon.

They stopped having fun as soon as they saw the Captain. They thought he was evil. But the Captain was also dismayed—because he was naked. He hadn't expected to run into anybody. He had not bothered to put on his iguana-skin breechclout. So now, after ten years on Santa Rosalia, the Kanka-bonos were getting their first look at his genitalia. They had to laugh, and then they couldn't stop laughing.

• • •

The Captain retreated to his dwelling, where Mary was fast asleep. He dismissed the laughter as simpleminded. He thought, too, that one of the women had a tumor or a parasite or an infection in her belly, and that, despite her merriment, she would probably die quite soon.

He mentioned this swelling to Mary the next morning, and she gave him a very strange smile.

"That's something to smile about?" he said.

"Was I smiling?" she said. "My goodness—it's certainly nothing to smile about."

"A swelling that big—" he said, "it can't be anything minor."

"I couldn't agree with you more," she said. "We will just have to watch and wait. What else can we do?"

"She was so cheerful," he marveled. "She didn't seem to mind at all—that awful swelling."

"As you've said so often," said Mary, "they aren't like us. They're very primitive in their thinking. They try to make the best of whatever happens. They figure they can't do much of anything about anything anyway, so they take life as it comes."

She had Mandarax there in bed with her. She and the furry Akiko, who was then only ten years old, were the only colonists who still found the instrument at all amusing. If it weren't for them, the Captain or Selena or Hisako, feeling mocked by its useless advice or inane wisdom or ponderous efforts to be humorous, would have pitched it into the ocean long ago.

The Captain, in fact, had felt personally insulted by Mandarax since it had come up with the poem about the ridiculous captain of the *Walloping Window Blind*.

So Mary was able to come up now with a comment concerning the supposed ignorance of the Kanka-bono woman, who was so happy despite the growth in her belly, to wit:

> *The happiest life consists in ignorance,*
> *Before you learn to grieve and to rejoice.*
> —SOPHOCLES (496–406 B.C.)

Mary was toying with him in a way which I, as a former fellow male of the Captain, was bound to think smug and mean-spirited. If I had been a woman in life, I might have felt differently. If I had been a woman, perhaps I would have been jubilant over Mary Hepburn's secret jeering at the limited role males played in reproduction back then, and which they still play today. That has not changed. There are still these big lunks who can be counted upon to squirt lively sperm in season.

Mary's secret jeering was about to become overt and nasty, too. After Kamikaze was born, and the Captain learned that this was his own son, he would stammer that he surely should have been consulted.

And Mary would reply: "You didn't have to carry that child for nine months, and then have it fight its way out from between your legs. You can't breast-feed it, even if you'd like to, which I somehow doubt. And nobody expects you to help raise it. The hope is, in fact, that you will have absolutely nothing to do with it!"

"Even so—" he protested.

"Oh, my God—" she said, "if we could have made a baby out of marine-iguana spit, don't you think we would have done that, and not even disturbed Your Majesty?"

12

AFTER SHE SAID THAT to the Captain, there was no way that their relationship could continue as before. A million years ago, there was a great deal of big-brained theorizing about how to keep human couples from breaking up, and there was at least one way Mary could have gone on living with the Captain for a little while longer anyway, if she had really wanted to. She could have told him that the Kanka-bono women had engaged in sexual intercourse with sea lions and fur seals. He would have believed it, not only because he held a low opinion of the women's morals, but because he could never even have suspected that artificial insemination had taken place. He would not have considered it possible, although the procedure, in fact, turned out to be child's play, as easy as pie.

Quoth Mandarax:

> *Something there is that doesn't love a wall.*
> —ROBERT FROST (1874–1963)

To which I add:

Yes, but something there is which adores a mucous membrane.

—LEON TROTSKY TROUT
(1946–1,001,986)

So Mary might have saved the relationship with a lie, although there would still have been Kamikaze's blue eyes to explain. One person in twelve today, incidentally, has the Captain's blue eyes and his curly golden hair. Sometimes I will joke with such a specimen, saying, "*Guten morgen,* Herr von Kleist," or, "*Wie geht's es Ihnen,* Fräulein von Kleist?" That's about all the German I have.

It is more than enough today.

• • •

Should Mary Hepburn have saved her relationship with a lie? The question remains moot after all this time. They were never an ideal couple. They had been stuck with each other after Selena and Hisako paired off and raised Akiko, and the Kanka-bono women moved to the far side of the crater, preserving the purity of their Kanka-bono beliefs and attitudes and ways.

One of the Kanka-bonos' customs, incidentally, was to keep their names a secret from anyone who wasn't a Kanka-bono. I was privy to their secrets, though, just as I was privy to everybody else's secrets, and there seems no harm in my now revealing that the first to have a baby by the Captain was Sinka, and the

305

second to have a baby was Lor, and the third to have a baby was Lira, and the fourth to have a baby was Dirno, and the fifth to have a baby was Nanno, and the sixth to have a baby was Keel.

• • •

After Mary moved out on the Captain, and made a canopy and a feather bed of her own, she would say to Akiko that she was no lonelier then than she had been when she lived with the Captain. She had several specific complaints about the Captain, faults he might easily have remedied, if he himself had been at all interested in making their relationship viable.

"Both people have to work at a relationship," she advised Akiko. "If just one works on it, you might as well forget about it. It's just no good, and whichever one does all the work winds up the way I did, feeling like some kind of fool all the time. I was really happily married one time, Akiko, and would have been really happily married twice, if Willard hadn't died—so I know how it's supposed to work."

She enumerated the four most serious faults which the Captain might have remedied easily, but wouldn't, as follows:

1. When he spoke of what he would do after they were rescued, he never included her in his plans.
2. He made fun of Willard Flemming, although he

knew how much this hurt her, doubting very much
that he had written two symphonies or knew
anything about windmills, or that he could even ski.

3. He complained constantly about the beeping sounds
Mandarax made when she pressed the different
buttons, although they could hardly be heard, and
although he knew how rewarding it was for her to
improve her mind, to memorize famous quotations
and to learn new languages and so on.

4. He would rather choke to death than ever say, "I
love you."

"And those are just the four big ones," she said. So
there was a great deal of pent-up resentment coming out
when Mary spoke to the Captain as she did about marine-
iguana spit.

• • •

I can't see that the breakup was tragic, since there
were no dependent children involved, and neither party
found living alone absolutely unendurable. Both were visited regularly by Akiko, and then, after Kamikaze
sprouted a beard, Akiko had furry children of her own to
bring along.

• • •

Mary was accorded no special status by the Kanka-
bono women, although she had made it possible for them
to have babies. They and then their children feared her as

much as they feared the Captain, believing her capable of doing great evil as well as good.

And twenty years went by. Hisako and Selena had committed suicide by drowning eight years before. Akiko was now a matronly thirty-nine years old, the mother of seven furry children by Kamikaze—two boys and five girls. She was fluent in three languages without the help of Mandarax: English, Japanese, and Kanka-bono. Her children spoke only Kanka-bono, except for two English words: *Grandpa* and *Grandma*. That was what she had them call the Captain and Mary Hepburn. That was what she herself called them.

• • •

One morning, at seven-thirty A.M. on May 9, 2016, according to *Mandarax, Akiko woke *Mary, and told her that she should go make her peace with the *Captain, who was so sick that he would probably not last out the day. Akiko had visited him the previous evening, and had sent her children home and stayed and nursed him through the night, although there was very little she could do for him.

So *Mary went, although she was no longer any spring chicken herself. She was eighty—and toothless. Her spine was shaped like a question mark, thanks, according to *Mandarax, to the ravages of osteoporosis. She didn't need *Mandarax to tell her it was osteoporosis. Her mother and grandmother's bones were made as weak as reeds by osteoporosis before they died. There is another hereditary defect unknown in the present day.

As for what was wrong with the *Captain, Mandarax made the educated guess that he had Alzheimer's disease. The old poop couldn't look after himself anymore, and hardly knew where he was. He would have starved to death if Akiko hadn't brought him food every day and, one way or another, made sure he swallowed at least some of it. He was eight-six.

Quoth *Mandarax:

> *Last scene of all,*
> *That ends this strange eventful history,*
> *Is second childishness and mere oblivion,*
> *Sans teeth, sans eyes, sans taste, sans everything.*
> —WILLIAM SHAKESPEARE (1564–1616)

So *Mary, all stooped over, shuffled under the *Captain's feather canopy, which used to be her own as well. She had not been there for twenty years. The canopy had been renewed many times since her departure, and so, of course, had been the mangrove poles and stakes which held it up, and the feather bed. But the architecture was the same, with a view cut through living mangroves right down to the water, and framing the shoal on which the *Walloping Window Blind* had been run aground so long ago.

What had finally dragged that ship off the shoal, by

the way, was an accumulation of rainwater and seawater in her stern. The seawater leaked in around the drive shaft of one of her mighty screws. She slid under during the night. Nobody actually saw her begin that last leg of "the Nature Cruise of the Century," three kilometers straight down to the locker of Davy Jones.

13

THAT WAS SURE some lugubriously historic shoal outside the *Captain's home! I was surprised that he wanted to look at it every day. It was down that same half-drowned hump that *Hisako Hiroguchi and the blind *Selena MacIntosh had waded hand in hand, seeking and finding together the blue tunnel into the Afterlife. *Selena was then forty-eight and still fertile. *Hisako was fifty-six, and had not ovulated for quite some time.

Akiko was still upset every time she saw the shoal. She couldn't help feeling responsible for the suicides of the two women who had raised her—even though *Mandarax had said it surely *Hisako's intractable, monopolar, and probably inherited depression which had killed them both.

But there was the fact, inescapable for Akiko, that *Hisako and *Selena had killed themselves soon after Akiko set up housekeeping on her own.

She was then twenty-two. Kamikaze hadn't reached puberty yet, so he had nothing to do with it. She was simply living alone, and enjoying it quite a bit. She was well past the age when most people flew the nest, and I was all for her doing it. I had seen how much pain it caused her when *Hisako and *Selena continued to speak to her in baby talk long after she had become such a robust and capable woman. And yet she had put up with it for an awfully long time—because she was so grateful for all they had done for her when she was genuinely helpless.

On the day she left, they were still cutting up her booby meat for her, if you can believe it.

For a month after that, they still set a place for her at every meal, with the meat already all cut up, and they cooed at her and teased her gently even though she wasn't there anymore.

And then, one day, life just wasn't worth living anymore.

• • •

*Mary Hepburn, for all her ailments, was still self-sufficient when she went to see the *Captain on his deathbed. She still gathered and prepared her own food, and kept her home as neat as a pin. She was proud of this, and should have been. The *Captain was a burden on the community, which was to say a burden on Akiko. *Mary was surely not. She had often said that, if ever she felt that she was about to become a burden to anybody, she would follow Hisako and Selena down the shoal, and join her second husband on the ocean floor.

The contrast between her feet and those of the pampered *Captain were striking. Their feet certainly had very different stories to tell. His were white and soft. Hers were tough and brown as the rock-climbing boots she had brought with her to Guayaquil so long ago.

So she said to this man to whom she hadn't spoken for twenty years, "They tell me you're very sick."

Actually, he was still quite handsome and well fleshed out. He was nice and clean, since Akiko bathed him every day, and shampooed and combed his beard and hair. The soap she used, which was made by the Kanka-bono women, was composed of ground-up bones and penguin fat.

One of the exasperating things about the *Captain's disease was that his body was still perfectly capable of taking care of itself. It was a lot stronger than *Mary's. It was his deteriorating big brain which was having him spend so much time in bed, and allowing him to soil himself and refuse to eat and so on.

Again: His condition wasn't peculiar to Santa Rosalia. Back on the mainland, millions of old people were as helpless as babies, and compassionate young adults like Akiko had to look after them. Thanks to sharks and killer whales, problems connected with aging are unimaginable in the present day.

• • •

"Who is this hag?" the *Captain asked Akiko. "I hate ugly women. This is the ugliest woman I ever saw."

"It's *Mary Hepburn—it's Mrs. Flemming, Grandpa," said Akiko. A tear skittered down her furry cheek. "It's Grandma," she said.

"Never saw her before in my life," he said. "Please get her out of here. I will close my eyes. When I open them again, I want her gone." He closed his eyes, and began counting out loud under his breath.

Akiko came over to *Mary and gripped her frail right arm. "Oh, Grandma—" she said, "I had no idea he would be like this."

And *Mary said to her loudly, "He's no worse than he ever was."

The *Captain went on counting.

From the neighborhood of the spring, half a kilometer distant, came a male cry of triumph and peals of female laughter. The male cry was a familiar one on the island. It was Kamikaze's customary announcement to one and all that he had caught a female of some sort, and that they were about to copulate. He was nineteen then, barely past his sexual prime, and, as the only virile male then on the island, was likely to copulate with anybody or anything at any time. This was another sorrow Akiko had to bear— the blatant infidelities of her mate. This was a truly saintly woman.

The female Kamikaze had caught by the spring was his own aunt Dirno, who was then beyond childbearing age. He didn't care. They were going to copulate anyway. He had even copulated with sea lions and fur seals when he was younger, until Akiko had persuaded him that, for her sake, if not his own, he could at least stop doing that.

No sea lion or fur seal got pregnant by Kamikaze, which in a way is a pity. If he had succeeded in impregnating one, the evolution of modern humankind might have taken a good deal less than a million years.

Then again: What was the hurry, after all?

• • •

The *Captain opened his eyes, and he said to *Mary, "Why aren't you gone?"

She said, "Oh, don't mind me. I'm just a woman you lived with for ten years."

At that moment, Lira, another of the Kanka-bono women, called to Akiko in Kanka-bono that Orlon, Akiko's four-year-old son, had broken his arm, and that Akiko was needed at home immediately. Lira wouldn't come any closer than that to the *Captain's home, which she believed to be infected with very bad magic.

So Akiko asked *Mary to keep watch over the *Captain while she went home. She promised to come back as soon as possible. "You be a good boy now," she said to the *Captain. "You promise?"

He promised grumpily.

• • •

*Mary had brought along *Mandarax at the request of Akiko, in the hopes of using it to diagnose what had caused the *Captain to lapse into several deathlike comas during the past day and night.

But when she showed him the instrument, and before she could ask him the first question, he did a perfectly astonishing thing: He snatched it away from her, and he

315

stood up as though there were nothing wrong with him. "I hate this little son of a bitch more than anything in the whole world," he said, and then he went tottering down to the shore and lurching out onto the shoal, up to his knees in water.

Poor *Mary pursued him, but she was certainly in no condition to restrain a man that big. She watched helplessly as he threw *Mandarax into what turned out to be about three meters of water on the slope of the shoal. The shoal sloped steeply, like the back of a marine iguana.

She could see where it was. There it was—the priceless heirloom she had promised to leave to Akiko when she died. So that game old lady went right in after it. She got one hand on it, too, but then a great white shark ate both her and Mandarax.

• • •

The *Captain had a lapse of memory, and so did not know what to make of the bloody water. He didn't even know what part of the world he was in. The most alarming thing to him was that he was being attacked by birds. These were harmless vampire finches going after his bedsores, some of the commonest birds on the island. But to him they were new and terrifying.

He slapped at them, and cried out for help. More and more finches kept coming, and he was so convinced that they meant to kill him that he jumped into the water, where he was eaten by a hammerhead shark. This animal had its eyes on the ends of stalks, a design perfected by the

Law of Natural Selection many, many millions of years ago. It was a flawless part in the clockwork of the universe. There was no defect in it which might yet be modified. One thing it surely did not need was a bigger brain.

What was it going to do with a bigger brain? Compose Beethoven's Ninth Symphony?

Or perhaps write these lines:

> *All the world's a stage,*
> *And all the men and women merely players.*
> *They have their exits and their entrances;*
> *And one man in his time plays many parts . . . ?*
> —WILLIAM SHAKESPEARE (1564–1616)

14

I HAVE WRITTEN THESE WORDS in air—with the tip of the index finger of my left hand, which is also air. My mother was left-handed, and so am I. There are no left-handed human beings anymore. People exercise their flippers with perfect symmetry. Mother was a redhead, and so was Andrew MacIntosh, although their respective children, I and Selena, did not inherit their rusty tresses—nor has any humankind, nor could humankind. There aren't any redheads anymore. I never knew an albino personally, but there aren't albinos anymore, either. Among the fur seals, albinos do still turn up from time to time. Their pelts would have been much prized for ladies' fur coats a million years ago, to be worn to the opera and charity balls.

Would the pelts of modern people have made nice fur coats for their ancestors in olden times? I don't see why not.

• • •

Does it trouble me to write so insubstantially, with air on air? Well—my words will be as enduring as anything my father wrote, or Shakespeare wrote, or Beethoven wrote, or Darwin wrote. It turns out that they all wrote with air on air, and I now pluck this thought of Darwin's from the balmy atmosphere:

Progress has been much more general than retrogression.

'Tis true, 'tis true.

• • •

When my tale began, it appeared that the earthling part of the clockwork of the universe was in terrible danger, since many of its parts, which is to say people, no longer fit in anywhere, and were damaging all the parts around them as well as themselves. I would have said back then that the damage was beyond repair.

Not so!

Thanks to certain modifications in the design of human beings, I see no reason why the earthling part of the clockwork can't go on ticking forever the way it is ticking now.

• • •

If some sort of supernatural beings, or flying-saucer people, those darlings of my father, brought humanity into harmony with itself and the rest of Nature, I did not catch them doing it. I am prepared to swear under oath that the Law of Natural Selection did the repair job without outside assistance of any kind.

It was the best fisherfolk who survived in the greatest numbers in the watery environment of the Galápagos Archipelago. Those with hands and feet most like flippers were the best swimmers. Prognathous jaws were better at catching and holding fish than hands could ever be. And any fisherperson, spending more and more time underwater, could surely catch more fish if he or she were more streamlined, more bulletlike—had a smaller skull.

• • •

So my story is told, except for the tacking on of a few not very important details I failed to cover elsewhere. I tack them on in no particular order, since I now must write in haste. Father and the blue tunnel will be coming for me at any time.

• • •

Do people still know that they are going to die sooner or later? No. Fortunately, in my humble opinion, they have forgotten that.

• • •

Did I myself reproduce when I was still alive? I got a high school girl pregnant by accident in Santa Fe shortly before I joined the United States Marines. Her father was the principal of her high school, and she and I didn't even like each other very much. We were just fooling around, as young people were bound to do. She had an abortion, for which her father paid. We never even found out if it would have been a daughter or a son.

That certainly taught me a lesson. After that, I always made sure that I or my partner was employing a birth-control device. I never married.

And I have to laugh now, thinking of what a loss of dignity and beauty it would be if a modern person were, before making love, to equip himself or herself with a typical birth-control device of a million years ago. Imagine, moreover, their having to do that with flippers instead of hands!

•   •   •

Have natural rafts of vegetable matter from anywhere here in my time, with or without passengers? No. Have mainland species of any sort reached these islands since the *Bahía de Darwin* was run aground? No.

Then again, I've only been here for a million years—no time at all, really.

•   •   •

How did I get from Vietnam to Sweden?

After I shot the old woman who had killed my best friend and worst enemy with a hand grenade, and what was left of our platoon burned her village to the ground, I was hospitalized for what was called "nervous exhaustion." I was given tender, loving care. I was also visited by officers who impressed on me how important it was that I not tell anyone what had happened in the village. Only then did I learn that our platoon had killed fifty-nine villagers of all ages. Somebody had counted them afterwards.

While on a pass from the hospital, I contracted syphilis from a Saigon prostitute while drunk and also high on marijuana. But the first lesion of that disease, another one unknown in the present day, did not appear until I reached Bangkok, Thailand, where I was sent with many others for so-called "Rest and Recreation." This was a euphemism understood by one and all to mean more whores and drugs and alcohol. Prostitution was then a major earner of foreign currency in Thailand, second only to rice.

After that came rubber.

After that came teak.

After that came tin.

I did not want the Marine Corps to know that I had syphilis. If they found out about it, they would dock my pay during the time I was under treatment. The treatment period, moreover, would be tacked on to the year I was supposed to serve in Vietnam.

So I sought the services of a private physician in Bangkok. A fellow Marine there recommended a young Swedish doctor who treated cases like mine, who was doing research at the University of Medical Sciences there.

During my first visit, he questioned me about the war. I found myself telling him about what our platoon had done to the village and villagers. He wanted to know what I had felt, and I replied that the most terrible part of the experience to me was that I hadn't felt much of anything.

• • •

"Did you cry afterwards, or have trouble sleeping?" he said.

"No, sir," I said. "In fact, I was hospitalized because all I wanted to do was sleep."

I hadn't come close to crying. Whatever else I was, I wasn't a weeping Willy, a bleeding heart. And I wasn't much for crying even before the Marine Corps made a man out of me. I hadn't even cried when my redheaded, left-handed mother had walked out on Father and me.

But then that Swede found something to say which made me cry like a baby—at last, at last. He was as surprised as I was when I cried and cried.

Here is what he said: "I notice your name is Trout. Is there any chance that you are related to the wonderful science-fiction writer Kilgore Trout?"

This doctor was the only person I ever met outside of Cohoes, New York, who had heard of my father.

I had to come all the way to Bangkok, Thailand, to learn that in the eyes of one person, anyway, my desperately scribbling father had not lived in vain.

• • •

The doctor made me cry so much that I had to be sedated. When I woke up on a cot in his office an hour later, he was watching me. We were all alone.

"Feel better now?" he said.

"No," I said. "Or maybe. It's hard to tell."

"I've been thinking about your case while you slept," he said. "There is one very strong medicine I could prescribe, but I leave it up to you whether or not you want to try it. You should be fully aware of its side effects."

I thought he was talking about how resistant syphilis organisms had become to antibiotics, thanks to the Law of Natural Selection. My big brain was wrong again.

He said he had friends who could arrange to get me from Bangkok to Sweden, if I wanted to seek political asylum there.

"But I can't speak Swedish," I said.

"You'll learn," he said. "You'll learn, you'll learn."